MW01121049

TIME HAS A WAY

The continuing story of the LaRosa family and friends.

TIME HAS A WAY

❀

Another Work of Fiction

by K Spirito

To Jean,
May the portrait of life
you paint inspire
future generations
K Spirito

Writer's Showcase
San Jose New York Lincoln Shanghai

Time Has A Way
Another Work of Fiction

All Rights Reserved © 2002 by K Spirito

No part of this book may be reproduced or transmitted in any form or by any means, graphic, electronic, or mechanical, including photocopying, recording, taping, or by any information storage retrieval system, without the permission in writing from the publisher.

Writer's Showcase
an imprint of iUniverse, Inc.

For information address:
iUniverse, Inc.
5220 S. 16th St., Suite 200
Lincoln, NE 68512
www.iuniverse.com

Front Cover by Sal Spirito Jr.

Excerpts from Listen Copyright © 1972
The Benedictine Foundation of the State of Vermont.
Composer: Gregory Norbert

ISBN: 0-595-21244-1

Printed in the United States of America

for Nellie…

"…to leave the world a bit better, whether by a healthy child, a garden patch, or a redeemed social condition; to have played and laughed with enthusiasm and sung with exultation; to know that even one life has breathed easier because you have lived—this is to have succeeded."

—Ralph Waldo Emerson

Contents

CHAPTER 1

With a start Julie Spencer awoke from a fitful night of sleep reigned by images of brutality. Swollen, cracked lips mutilated her confusion, "Where am I?" Horror-struck eyes shot to the bedroom door where beyond came muffled sounds of activity. She couldn't breathe. *Who's out there? How'd I end up here?*

Memory refused answer.

Shoving honey-blond strands off her face, Julie winced as broken fingernails raked across a clotted gash. She glared at her fingers. "Blood!" her insides screamed. As the day before blasted into her brain, ice raced throughout her being. Trying to deny it all, she squeezed her eyes shut. Heartbeats hammered. Burrowing into the pillow failed to put down the sensations of Jim Martin mounted on her back, flogging the daylights out of her. Her eyes shot open. She clutched the blankets. Knuckles drained of color. Slowly, she lifted her head, her eyes scouring every inch of the unfamiliar room. Where is that monster? He's here…Julie just knew it. He's lurking in the shadows, ready to pounce on her for refusing him…for leaving him. Wait…that old lady… Julie squinted at the door. Her grip on the blankets loosened. "Who's that old lady?" A name echoed cryptically across her brain. "What is it?" She just couldn't bring it forth. "Humph," came a frustrated breath. "Mmm?" *What's that?* Julie raised her nose. *That smell.* She breathed in the aroma flooding her surroundings. *Fresh-brewed coffee. Sweet cinnamon...toast... and...and bacon!* Her stomach growled. When was the last time she had eaten? Her eyes bore into the door. *But who's out there...beyond that door? How safe is it to go out there? Is food all that important?*

She turned her head towards the window where November sunlight sifted through sheer, snowy Priscillas and speckles of dust cavorted, seeming to mock her circumstance. Her eyes turned away and tracked the white chair rail bisecting the walls horizontally. Delicate blue cornflowers danced across the top half then weaved in and out of golden-hued vertical bands that lined the lower half. *How nice.* The post of the four-poster bed she was lying in interrupted her gaze. It was made of cherry wood and though it was of an old vintage, it was incredibly beautiful. The end table and bureau with roses etched into its mirror matched the bed. Spotting her pocketbook lying on the bureau, she wondered why she had even bothered to take it. The only things of any value in it were her driver's license and a picture of herself and her mother. Julie didn't have a car and Jim Martin barred all broads (as he indignantly labeled the opposite sex) from ever driving his precious automobile. And Mom—Mom's out there—somewhere. Tears pooled in Julie's eyes. *If only Mom was here to talk to.*

Julie picked up a corner of the comforter and caressed her cheek with the soft, blue flannel backing. Her fingers drifted across the top, which was richly endowed with the same blue cornflowers that cheered the walls. She had never owned such things and figured that at this point it was doubtful that she ever would. Visions of her bedroom in that shabby first floor flat that she rented in Brighton Massachusetts came to mind. The nondescript metal bed frame and mattress were covered with a washed-out plaid bedspread that she had brought from home when she moved. Working in a restaurant didn't leave much extra for comforts after the rent was paid. Oh well, at least she was able to get a free meal out of it.

Julie reached for the extra pillow next to her and stuffed it behind her shoulders. As she propped herself up against the carved headboard, her teeth gnashed, partly from the pain, but mostly from the looming image of Jim pursuing her, his hand clutching her hair and yanking her head backwards, his rabid voice howling, "You ain't goin' nowhere!"

She had broken away and tried to run. Still, at this very moment, she could feel his fingers digging into her ankle, dragging her back and his hands around her neck, strangling her. Her chest heaved. His breath reeking of hot stale beer continued to taunt her senses. In the shadowy darkness his hair whipped across his bestial eyes as he invaded her body, her mind, her life. "No," Julie shrieked, but her horror was lost within the thickness of the bedroom. Her cocoa eyes took on the appearance of those of a cornered animal, darting about, scrutinizing every indistinct crevice. Surely Jim Martin was still out to get her. Oh God, what should she do? Move back with Mom? "No," Julie gasped. "He knows where Mom lives." What would that monster do to her mother? Julie bit her bottom lip. Swollen tissues railed. She winced. Her tongue soothed them. *Perhaps, it might be best to leave Massachusetts entirely.* She fingered a strand of hair. *Maybe even chop off this mop, get it permed, dye it black.* "Oh, God." *How hard it had been to move away from Mom and into that flat.* She didn't know a soul there. Only a few miles away from where she had lived all her life, but it felt like the other side of the world. And these days, making friends was just about impossible. People don't even utter a fleeting hello any more much less get involved in more serious matters like... Her body twitched trying to shake off the perversion intent on zapping her back in time.

Julie Spencer was nineteen, petite and slender, her skin fair and her eyes an expressive cocoa with tawny lashes that picked up golden hues of a sunny day. Her engaging smile deliberately outlined cheekbones blessed with the blush of ripe peaches.

On several occasions she had walked past the bulldozed building lot where a full-color poster announced to the world the coming of a high-rise complex. It was five blocks from where Julie waitressed and three from her flat. One particular day, a surveying crew was staked out there, taking a break as she returned home from an early morning shift. Jim Martin, crew leader, stood tall and solidly built. His face was flawless and baby smooth. Propping one leg up on a construction horse, he took a long drag on a cigarette as his striking blue eyes cast fleeting sideways glances at the female passerby. Three other surveyors whistled and howled.

Self-conscious and wanting to get out of there real quick, Julie hurried on her way. By the next day, her mind had blanked out the episode so she unwittingly took the same route home. She kicked herself when once again the hecklers accosted her. "Hey, how's it going lil' lady?" taunted one pulpy surveyor who sported a grown-out buzz cut and a grimy, faded khaki uniform. Needing a shave real bad, he gnawed on some unknown substance and looked like mangy buffalo.

The other barrel-chested guerrilla-type was wearing the same type of attire plus a navy watch cap that was pulled down over his ears. As his face contorted, his eyebrows twitched. "Why don'cha stop an' chitchat for a while? We ain't gonna bite."

Noticing Jim, so quiet and polite, standing off in the distance, Julie laughed and pointed, "I'll only talk to him."

"Oooh, Jimbo's got hisself a admirer," snickered buzz-cut.

Fingers with nails outlined with filth beckoned as guerilla snorted, "Hey man, get yer butt ovah he-ah an' talk ta dis he-ah lil' gal."

Jim crushed his spent cigarette into the dirt as his left eye cast the female passerby a sideways once-over. He fished a cigarette pack out of his breast pocket. Tapping it on the back of his hand until one white spike jutted forth, he gripped it between his teeth. He dragged a wooden match across the construction horse and cupping his hands over the flame, lit up. His eyes slit as gray fumes rolled out and up into his face. He shook out the match and took a deep drag. His face betrayed no emotion nor did a single word part his lips. Jim Martin made no moves on Julie Spencer.

Julie bit her bottom lip. Maybe those ignoramuses were embarrassing him or something. Wait a minute. Did his head gesture ever so slightly just then? Was he sending her some kind of signal? What should she do? As Julie pondered her options, one hand twisted the fingers of the other. She was not going out with anyone at the moment. And shoot, that flat of hers felt like a vacuous cave when she was all by herself—and she was always all by herself. Sometimes it was more than she could bear. From the kitchen table she could look into the living room, bathroom, and bedroom, which was just big enough for a double bed and nothing else. She had been incredibly lonely since moving out of Mom's. This was a golden opportunity to finally get to know another human being. Her tongue dampened her bottom lip. What the heck. She had nothing to lose. Taking a deep breath, Julie trekked over to the blue-eyed hunk and said, "Hi. I'm Julie Spencer."

His lips twitched into an impotent smile. "Jim Martin," he uttered with a hitch of his chin then squinted off into the distance. Cigarette smoke billowed back into his face.

Awkward silence caught Julie groping for words. *Geez, this guy certainly isn't very assertive.* She cleared her throat and asked, "How long are you guys going to be working here?"

Jim sucked on the cigarette. Gray smudge erupted with every word. "A week or so."

Silence…again. Julie scraped her foot across a tuft of crabgrass. *What's the matter with this guy? What a pillar of stone. Am I boring him or what?* The feeling ate at her that there was something very strange about Jim Martin. Unraveled, Julie turned and hurriedly withdrew. "Well, see ya."

All the way home Julie ruminated on the enigma. Jim Martin was extremely neat and clean, considering his job. His blond hair was stylishly cut, though as she thought it over, it was a bit Elvis-like. How strange that his eyes never seemed to focus on anything, least of all her. Julie scratched her head. His expressionless demeanor did lend an air of mystery to the rugged hunk.

That night Julie tossed and turned. Why was Jim Martin so distant? So remote? Then it came to her, *"He's just shy, that's all.* By morning she had come up with the excuse that shyness was not necessarily a bad thing and decided that if there was ever going to be anything between this hunk and her, she would have to be the one to take the initiative. *Yup, I'm taking the first step…today.* The gullible young woman should have known better than to even consider wandering down such a murky path, yet on her way home from work, she ignored the warnings rumbling in her gut and the hecklers and strutted right up to Jim Martin. "How about coffee…at my place…tonight?"

"Sure," he breezed. Lumbering away, he failed to ask where she lived.

Julie rushed after him, spouting her address. She was positive that he had heard her, though he totally ignored her. Confused, she stuttered, "At seven?"

"Shur," he grunted.

The other guys whooped and hollered. Julie was at a loss as to why they shot thumb's-up signals to the seemingly disinterested Jim Martin.

Seven o'clock came and went. No Jim. Seven-thirty, and still no Jim. Heaviness crept over Julie. "Shoot. That guy stood me up. God," she agonized as she shut off the coffeemaker. "Oh. I could just die." Slouching against the kitchen counter, she crossed her arms tight across her chest. "Now what am I supposed to do?" Her eyes wandered the ceiling. She heaved a sigh. "Well. That's it then, I'm not gonna walk by there any more. Imagine how those jerks will razz me after this." She bit her bottom lip. Suddenly her arms uncrossed.

"Jim's just like the rest of them!" Her hands jammed into her hips. "Shy. Yeah, right. What a bunch of bull."

Time passed. Julie brooded on the couch in front of a dark television screen. Ten minutes till nine, a single thump rattled the door. Julie squinted at it. Why didn't whoever it was ring the doorbell? She got to her feet and listened. Nothing. She crossed the room and cracked open the door. Jim Martin…gazing off into the universe as if absolutely nothing was wrong. Should she let him in or what? She chewed the inside of her cheek while studying him. He was freshly showered and his hair was combed just so. His tan pants bore freshly ironed creases and his blue golf shirt brought out the blue of his indolent eyes. Excitement mixed with displeasure. Julie slid the chain off the door and stepped back.

Jim strolled in, his eyes scanning the apartment. There wasn't much to see. Julie didn't have much. Without so much as asking he plopped down upon the green couch that she had picked up at the Goodwill Store for ten bucks. She wrung her hands, bewildered by his brazen demeanor. "Coffee?" she asked.

"Shur," he spat without so much as a glance her way.

Julie took off for the kitchen where she reheated the pot of coffee. Anticipation caused her to drop a spoon. Picking it up, she rinsed it under the tap then swiped it across a hand towel. Placing it on a tray along with another spoon, she noticed a droplet of water cradled in its bowl. She picked up the spoon and buffed it against the belly of her blouse all the while wondering what the heck was up with this Jim Martin guy. She placed it on the tray again then arranged napkins, packets of sugar, and single serving size creamers that patrons had left behind on the table at the restaurant. Geez, he didn't even look at her. Maybe she wasn't pretty enough. Julie ducked into the bathroom. Squinting at the medicine cabinet mirror, she scanned the right side of her face and then the left. Gee, she didn't look all that bad. She straightened her blouse and slacks, flounced up her hair, and puckered her lips to make sure her lipstick was still okay.

She smoothed out the color with her pinkie finger and feigned a quick smile before scurrying back to the kitchen. Checking to make sure everything was perfect with the tray, Julie returned to the living room.

Jim had turned on the TV and was watching a sitcom that she didn't recognize. TV did not interest her much. Most times, the programs were mindless and bored her to no end. Why she had even bought a TV in the first place was beyond her. She preferred reading—romance novels. "I made a fresh pot," she fibbed. "It'll be ready in a minute."

Jim gave a scant nod while crossing one leg over the other on top of the coffee table. Moments passed. Her presence didn't faze him in the least and although his eyes remained glued to the screen, Julie found it odd that he remained impassive to all the humor. She fidgeted, feeling insignificant, minuscule. She slipped off to the kitchen. While one hand poured two cups of coffee, the fingers of the other hand toyed with her bottom lip. Staring into the steam wafting off the coffee, she was lost in an uncertain fog. She took a deep breath. "Oh, well." Picking up the tray, she headed back to the living room. As she set it down on the coffee table, Julie said good-naturedly, "Here we are."

Without the slightest acknowledgment, Jim tore off creamer lids, one after another, dumping the contents of each container into one of the cups, filling it to the brim. He tossed the empties onto the table as he went, then ripped open half a dozen sugar packets at one time and tipped the contents into the coffee. When he flipped the empty packets at the table, they ricocheted off the empty creamer containers and landed on the floor. Unruffled, Jim picked up a spoon and stirred, sloshing the mixture all over the coffee table. He bent over and delicately slurped up enough so that it would not overflow when he lifted it. He dried the bottom of the cup with a napkin and was careful not to drip any on his pants as he leaned back. His eyes never left the TV as he downed the coffee.

Julie gawked at the coffee table. What a mess. She blotted up the moisture with a napkin then glanced at Jim. She wanted to ask, well, do you like my coffee or not, but wondering why he wouldn't open up kept her from doing so. She picked at a fingernail. Gee, sure would be nice to get to know this guy. Finally she ventured, "Do you like to dance?"

Without taking his eyes off the TV, Jim gave a slight nod.

Julie twisted her hands together. "There's a great band playing at the Blue Moon Lounge in Saugus tomorrow night. Wanna go?"

His voice was barely audible when he said, "Sure." He put down his empty coffee cup and got to his feet. "Be ready at seven." And just like that, Jim Martin was out the door.

Julie stood there, stunned, staring at the door that remained ajar. Moments passed. Finally she got up off the sofa and plodded across the room. After closing the door and securing both locks, she turned and leaned against it. Dull eyes fell upon the mess that Jim had left behind. Without letting her mind quibble about it, Julie cleaned it up. After all, she had to count herself lucky to have any company at all.

The next day, Julie Spencer was still unsure of what to make of Jim Martin. That inner voice told her once again not to stop by the construction site on her way home from work. But like before, she cast it aside just as easily as the wave of her hand that dismissed the hecklers as she stepped up to Jim and muttered, "Hi."

"Hey," Jim snorted while going about his business.

Julie felt as if she was standing naked in the middle of an unforgiving desert. The other guys taunted, circling like hyenas around their next meal. "What's the matter? Jimbo's kinda on his quiet side today, missy?"

Disgusted by their rudeness and Jim's ambivalence, Julie blasted, "Remember, Blue Moon Lounge tonight. Seven. That's what you said." She spun around and started for home. Laughter reverberated in her head long after she got out of range. What the heck was wrong with that Jim Martin anyway? That moron had made absolutely no effort to put off those jackals.

It was after eight-thirty when Jim finally showed up at her flat. Again, he offered no excuses for his tardiness nor did his face show any sign of emotion when he mumbled, "Let's go."

Anger or relief? Julie weighed her emotions. She wasn't at all sure that she wanted to go any more. But when Jim disappeared out the door, she grabbed her coat and rushed after him. On the way to the Blue Moon Lounge, she sat sideways in the front seat of his car and jabbered on and on. Hey, if he didn't want to talk, she would. As they walked through the parking lot, she grabbed his hand. A look of disdain sheeted his face that was unmistakable even beneath the dim streetlight. He shook her off, saying, "I hate public displays of affection."

Jim Martin sure could dance, slow songs, fast songs, didn't matter. Hey, that was great, Julie thought. Most guys didn't dance half that much, that is, if they danced at all. But Jim never looked at her while they were dancing and that bothered Julie. He didn't have much to say either. His eyes were always off in the distance, unfocused, as if he was grooving along to the music without a partner.

Several hours later, Julie and Jim were sitting in his car outside her flat. She gazed at him. The streetlight shrouded his dark, silent profile. His hands gripped the steering wheel. She wanted to be kissed, but he made no moves, so she placed a hand on top of his. He glanced at her as if not at all surprised. She curled up next to him and looked up, begging to be kissed. He got the message loud and clear. His lips fell upon hers, cold, passionless, hard. An overwhelming sense of fear and exhilaration shot through her. "Wanna come in?" she whispered.

Though the lighting wasn't all that good, it seemed as if a slight smirk accompanied his nod. Well, Julie soughed it off. She's usually wrong about stuff like that. Out of the corner of her eye, she noticed him reaching under the seat for a brown paper bag. She disregarded that, too. Nothing mattered. Nothing at all. No, he was following her into the apartment. That's all Julie cared about.

Jim plunked down on the couch as Julie went to the kitchen. After pouring two glasses of Coke, she returned to the living room. Her heart sank. Jim had turned on the TV and was leaning back on the sofa with his feet wedged against the coffee table—so much for that romantic interlude. Julie sat down and offered a glass to him. Her eyebrows arched when he took a bottle of rum out of the brown paper bag and without asking, dumped a lavish portion into both glasses. He took one and slugged it down. When he looked at her as if to say, well? Julie took a sip. It tasted acrid. She swallowed it quickly. Repugnance raked over her all the way to her toes. There was no way that she could even nurse the rest of that nasty concoction. When Jim wasn't looking, Julie set it on the coffee table.

Jim went straight to pouring himself half a glass of straight rum. Holding most of that in his mouth briefly, he swallowed loud and slammed the glass onto the coffee table. What was left jumped out of the glass. The back of his hand swiped across his lips as one eye lobbed a sideways glance at Julie. A chill shot through her. Suddenly he was in her face, kissing her hard, so hard that her head snapped backwards. She grabbed his wrist and gave a muffled, "No."

As his hand groped under her skirt, he barked, "Shut up!"

Her world turned topsy-turvy. The coffee table screeched sideways. One of the glasses upended and rolled onto the floor, shattering on impact. Tiny shards impaled her cheek as Jim climbed on top of her and forced her hands over her head. Julie screeched while twisting her hips, struggling to keep his knees from spreading her thighs. His size and weight crushed her against the floor. She heard the tenants upstairs stomping. A hand clamped her wrists together, holding them above her head while his open mouth covered her lips, muffling her cries. She felt his teeth and blood foul her mouth. She struggled to break loose. "Cut the crap," he growled as his other hand feigned a backhanded swipe.

Suffocating terror turned her muscles to stone. When was this nightmare going to end? And then just like that, it was over and Jim Martin crawled off to the bathroom. Julie collected herself and managed to somehow pull herself up onto the couch. How could that have possibly satisfied him? Propping herself up into one corner, she heard grunts and groans coming from the bathroom. What was he doing in there? Something was crawling down her cheek. She swiped at it. Whatever it was was thick and wet. She inspected her fingers—blood! Dabbing the pads of her fingers against the wound, she tried to check the flow.

Jim came back from the bathroom, zipping up his pants. He collapsed, spread-eagled, in the opposite corner of the couch. Julie gawked at him as he snagged the neck of the rum bottle and took short quick gulps. When he tossed the empty rum bottle on the couch between them, she flinched. He snickered. Making no eye contact with her, he lit up a cigarette. The tip glowed red and smoke billowed into the beam of the TV casting his silhouette into a grotesque, ominous form. Moments passed. A vintage comedy program seemed to aggravate him and he let out a grunt. Snuffing out his cigarette butt on the floor, he got to his feet and as the front door slammed behind him, Jim Martin snarled, "Tomorrow. Same time same station."

Looking back on the whole ugly affair, Julie still could not comprehend how she had ever let that freak back in her house. But there she was, without a brain in her head, opening the door the next night when the hour got late and letting Jim Martin in. He plunked down on the sofa and took over the TV. This time he did not leave. He took up residency as if the tiny flat belonged to him, never stirring outside the house except for work. He had a fondness for rum and beer. Every night, he made excuses that he was tired and all he wanted to do was sit in front of the TV to catch a few Zs. After which he demanded sex, if that's what one might call it, regardless of how Julie felt about it. Foreplay never entered into the picture and caressing of any sort was out of the question. Jim demanded that Julie lay there, not moving, not making a peep, as he continued on and on, never achieving satisfaction. Yet when he got pissed off at her he would accuse her of being a dead log. He never told her he loved her and never wanted anything to do with her afterward. He avoided any form of casual touch.

Julie convinced herself that there must be something wrong with her. Jim was too well built and handsome—there couldn't possibly be anything wrong with him. Well, she would find a way to make him love her. Yes, she was going to have to change herself and become what he wanted. Maybe this was the way things really were between men and women. After all, they say the romance one reads in books or sees in the movies and on the tube is not a true reflection of the way things really are. Just look at Mom. She had never had a man around and showed no interest in the opposite sex at all. *Maybe Mom had put up with this stuff too. And when Dad died, she wanted no more part of men.*

Julie didn't know what to do. It was not right that Jim had moved in so early in their relationship, but if she asked him to leave, he might never come back and she would have nobody. Loneliness was so hard to take. And stifling. She craved attention—no matter what kind. So Julie shoved all fear aside and functioned around it. She had learned early in life that some things were just the way they were, no sense in fighting it.

Weeks dragged by. One night, Julie came home from work and there Jim was on the couch surrounded by a cloud of cigarette smoke, eyes glued to the TV, and beer bottles at his feet. She had enough. "Come on. Shut off the TV and let's go for a walk."

"Nah," he grumbled unfazed.

"Aw, come on. Just a little walk? Please?" She should have known she was skating on thin ice when she shut off the TV.

His eyes narrowed then leveled on her. A tick throbbed under his left eye as his fingers drummed the arm of the sofa. Sullen and silent, he chugged on the bottle of rum then glared at her again. He leaned his head against the back of the sofa. His chest heaved and he let out an audible breath. His head butted the back of the sofa. Slowly he got to his feet. Taking wide, deliberate steps, he came at Julie. She slid him a wary look and backed out of his way. He turned the TV back on and stomped back to the sofa. But before he got there, she shut off the TV again and gave a shrill whine, "Come on. I'm so tired of hanging around all the time. Let's do something."

In the deadly silence, the iceman spun around. The color had vanished from his eyes. Black, sinister pupils dilated. His hulk sent a chill racing through Julie. The hair on the back of her neck bristled all the way up into her scalp when he growled, "You really piss me off."

Julie could tell she was in for a pummeling as Jim tromped over to her. She swung a fist. Missed. There was no time for retreat as his full hand arced into the air like a gargantuan hammer and bashed against the side of her head. The muscle in her neck coiled and she spun across the room like a top. Hitting the wall, she slithered to the floor. Jim hovered above her. His fists threatened, keeping time with his words. "What do I have to do to get through to you? Leave the fucking TV alone."

Suddenly, all that was left was the sickening silence. That frightened her more than his rage. He crouched down and pulled her by the ankles away from the wall. "No," she screeched and twisted to get away. Her elbow caught his nose and he howled. Wrenching herself free, Julie scrambled on her hands and knees for the door. Her hand was on the knob when he grabbed her arm and yanked her back. Julie turned over and kicked with both legs. "Get away from me," she bellowed and the tenants upstairs stomped on their floor. One foot got him—not hard enough, not low enough.

Jim leapt back at her. His fist cracked her cheekbone and she saw nothing but white pain. "I'll kill you if you move one single muscle," he seethed.

While the monster had his way, Julie lay there. The ceiling seemed to mock her. If only the people up there would call the cops.

Finally Jim slithered off her. Bare-butt, he staggered into the bedroom and sprawled upon the covers. Satisfying himself, he then passed out.

After that episode Julie retreated into submissive silence. Her eyes lost their sparkle and her mouth rarely turned up to accent her apple cheeks. The neighbors upstairs didn't care. Nobody cared. So she resigned herself to the fact that she had asked for this relationship and somehow it would all play itself out. Still, she knew surprisingly little about Jim, only that he had lived with his parents before he moved uninvited into her place. He never suggested that Julie should meet them, intimating that his father was a boozer and his mother was a lousy housekeeper. The mere mention of them rankled him so Julie avoided the subject. Meaningful conversation became nonexistent and offensive sexual encounters went beyond disgusting. One night when she said no, Jim nailed her against the wall.

"I'm not up to it tonight," Julie begged. "Please."

"Too God damned bad," Jim snarled.

"Come on, I've been good," she whined.

Her whining only made matters worse. "Not good enough," he howled and grabbed a fistful of her hair. Yanking her to the floor, he sat on her stomach while his fists clobbered her again and again. "Don't play dumb-ass games with me, whore."

"No," she screamed and wriggled away. As he came at her, she raised her arm to fend him off. He grabbed it. She dug the fingernails of her other hand into his face.

"Yeeoww." he bellowed. The neighbors upstairs stomped. Pain riddled his face as he let go and took a step backwards. His fingertips dabbed the wound. He looked at them then at Julie. The vein in the middle of his forehead began to pulsate. "Don't you ever do that to me again," he hollered and lunged at her. His powerful fist imbedded in her stomach.

Writhing in pain, Julie was unable to catch her breath. Blood dripped on her face as he ripped off her clothes and drove into her. The room spun like some kind of absurd merry-go-round. Suddenly, he bayed like a wolf as a flood of pent up frustrations let loose and moments later his full weight came down upon her. Ceiling plaster sprinkled on the floor beside her. Afraid to move, she looked up, cursing those do-nothings up there.

Moments later, Jim rolled off Julie and got to his feet. Naked from the waist down, he staggered to the bedroom. She grabbed her blouse and covered herself. When she thought he was asleep, she limped to the bathroom. Seeing herself in the mirror, she gasped. Her lips were cracked, bleeding, and swelling with every passing second. The skin on her right temple was torn and a bruise was ripening on her cheekbone. Blood oozed from somewhere in her scalp. She picked through slimy strands to find the source but it was too painful, so she gave up. Her eyes closed as she leaned her forehead against the mirror. Her head moved side to side in disbelief. When she opened her eyes and saw her blouse, she backed away from the mirror. It was stained and torn. "Well, you said you hate my clothes," she hissed and flung it at the mirror as if the mirror was Jim. She spun around and crossed her arms. Her fingers dug into her upper arms, squeezing. The stink of his sweat and semen was all over her. If only she could wash it off, but showering might wake him. She was so frightened. Collapsing on the toilet, she cried hot, salty tears that stung her bruised face. How was she ever going to get this monster out of her home?

The next morning while Jim rustled about the kitchen, Julie feigned sleep. As he was leaving for work, she felt him hovering over her. Her stomach knotted. What was he going to do, hit her? Make her do it again? Eternal moments passed. Tremors became impossible to contain as she heard him step toward the door. It closed. She lay there motionless, barely breathing. One eye slit open. He's gone? Both eyes shifted towards the door. She expected it to open at any moment and he would come back. She would feel his fists again, his perversion. Silence. No footsteps on the front porch. When she was sure it was safe, she tried to get up. Her body was like petrified wood. She concentrated and finally was able to nudge the covers aside. Staggering to her feet, her body reeled. She grappled for the arm of the couch. Steadying herself, she tiptoed to the phone. Dialing the restaurant, her boss answered. He was not happy when she made the excuse that she had the flu so bad that returning to work would be impossible for several days. As she set the handset down on its cradle, she figured she no longer had a job. How in the world she was going to pay the rent if she didn't work? Oh God, now what was she going to do?

In the bathroom her eyes avoided the mirror as she stepped into the shower. Dried blood spiraled down the drain. "How could he do this to me?" she brooded. Tears flooded down her face, burning like acid. "I was faithful. I cooked and cleaned. And did all the shopping." With a small sense of satisfaction, she thought how he had to buy his own alcohol because she was too young to do that. But yet he always had one of those brown bags clutched in the crook of his arm when he got home from work. He'd carry them as if they contained trophies of some sort.

Later, thoughts were still muddled as Julie straightened up the apartment. In all this time Jim had never once spoken her name. "Why doesn't he love me?" She paused to ponder that question and concluded that love was not in his vocabulary. "Well, too bad. He doesn't have to love me, 'cause I certainly don't love him. I don't even like him!" She jammed her hands into her hips. Her stomach turned. "Look at this place." She picked up a couple empty beer bottles and an almost empty bag of chips and dropped them into the trash. Cigarette butts and ashes were everywhere. "He's got no business here. I'm calling the cops. I want him out. After all, this is my place. I should have a voice about who comes and goes." She reached for the phone but then shrank against the doorjamb and drew a deep breath. Raising that voice was not going to be easy. She detested her weakness. Suddenly, she heard a key in the front door. Jim! Terror sliced the length of her. Her eyes fled to the clock. It wasn't even noon. She should have changed the locks or... She dropped the receiver and froze. Jim swaggered in and came straight towards her. Trying not to look at him, she cowered backwards into the kitchen. Without so much of a glimpse, he passed her, but the stink of his beer breath and body odor caught her just right. He went directly to the refrigerator for a beer and swigging down half the can, belched. He eyed her. "You look like shit," he said.

"Well, what do you expect?" Julie muttered glaring sideways at Jim.

"Humph," he snickered and swilled down the rest of the beer.

Her chin jutted forth as she glared directly into his expressionless face. "What did I do to deserve this?"

He belched again as his fist crushed the beer can.

"How could you do this to me?" she cried.

His voice was slushy when he shouted, "I ain't done nothing to you, bitch!"

"What's wrong with you?" she fired back.

Jim flung the mangled beer can at her. "If you don't shuddup, I'll give you some more!"

Julie ducked. As she straightened, she spotted his fists clenching. Her stomach somersaulted as he took a step towards her. Desperately searching for a weapon, she screeched, "Don't come near me or..."

His head tilted back as he sneered, "Or what?" His pupils narrowed to pinpoints, boring right through her. "You'll run to dear ol' Mom? You know damned well that maggot can't stand the sight of you."

That remark slammed Julie worse than any fist could. Pursing her lips, she shook her head as hate seared him. The only thing she ever told him was that her mother had few friends and preferred to be left alone. That was why Julie had left. "You don't even know Mom."

Jim took another step. Fear rippled through her. He was playing games with her. He took another step and she retreated backwards, shrieking, "Stay away from me!"

His laughter was rich with contempt as he kept coming at her. "You can't get away from me."

She banged into the corner. Her heart thundered. Her eyes darted about. She was a sitting duck. "No!"

Jim howled with laughter. "You're nuttin' but a piece of scum." He grabbed her hair and spun her into the center of the kitchen. "There's a million of ya out there."

Her arms flailed as she tried to catch her balance. Striking the edge of the table, Julie pulled it down on top of her. The wound on her scalp ruptured, sending blood gushing down the side of her face. She started to cry.

He grabbed her blouse and yanked her out from under the table. "Stop your fuckin' cryin'. I hate fuckin' cryin'," Jim bellowed. He smacked her face, propelling her against the kitchen wall where she collapsed face down.

Blood and fear egged him on. He pounced upon her and straddling her, yanked her arm behind her head and twisted her wrist. At first one fist punched the back of her head, then the other. Right fist, left fist. Over and over again. Her brain thundered with white agony. Her fingernails clawed into the cracks between the floor planks trying to keep him from turning her over. His hands constricted her neck. Broken fingernails clawed at his wrists. Choking for air, her own vomit filled her airways. And then blackness washed over her.

When Julie came to her senses, the apartment was still. For a moment nothing registered. She shook the disorder out of her head and listened. Not even the steady tick of the alarm clock filled the silence. It had not been wound up. She let out a breathless shriek, "Jim!" She coughed. Her hand hooded her mouth, but her muffled terror seemed to echo like gongs throughout the shadows. A beam of streetlight sliced the darkness, highlighting shards of broken glass that littered the floor next to the unrolled and torn window shade. The kitchen table was jammed against the sink and chairs were upended. A rum bottle, lying on its side, teetered on the edge of the shelf. Its contents had spilled, smelling up the place like a barroom.

Adjusting her torn bra that dangled off one shoulder, she glanced at herself. She was naked. At first she was confused, but then her insides revolted. She stumbled to her feet. Her legs were wobbly. The walls, cabinets, everything began to spin. She propped herself into a corner and fumbled to cover her nakedness with the torn bra. "Oh God, oh God, oh God," she whimpered. She spied her panties and glanced around to see if Jim Martin was lurking anywhere. No, he was nowhere in sight. She squatted and snatched up the panties, wincing from the pain that doing this caused. She pulled them up over her thighs. The material grated her skin like steel wool, so she slipped them off and wriggled into her jeans. Zipping them up was too painful so she left them unzipped and grabbed her blouse. It was ripped, but she didn't notice. Hooking it over her shoulders, she fastened the middle button. She spotted her pocketbook and grabbed for anything close at hand, stuffing all of it into the pocketbook. She heard something. Her eyes skewed around the half-open bedroom door. Feet, naked legs, and bare butt were splayed across the top of the washed-out plaid bedspread. She swallowed hard. Fear and panic raced through her body and she leaned against the wall. *Get out of here*, her insides hissed like an electric serpent. *Get out. Get out. GET OUT!*

Hastily she tiptoed through the living room and noiselessly slipped out the front door, leaving it ajar. Half naked, she fled down the front steps. Hitting the sidewalk in an irregular gait, she broke into a dead run. As fast as her wounded legs could carry her, she put that place far behind her. She had made a colossal mistake and now she would be lucky to get out of it with her life. But Julie vowed to God Almighty above that she would never go back there again.

Shaking off the nightmare, Julie slipped out of the vintage four-poster bed with the blue cornflower comforter. As her bare feet hit the hardwood floor, its chill raced up her spine. She straightened. Her limbs were heavy and stiff. She paused to gather strength. The thought that her life was over at nineteen weighed her down. Scrutinizing the bedroom so exceptionally neat and smelling of lemon oil, Julie caught her face reflecting back at her in the bureau mirror. The pupils of her eyes were as enormous as those of a caged animal. Her fingertips skimmed the bruises on her face and her swollen lips. How had she ever come to this? She had given up her interests for him and what few acquaintances she had. And her job. And her body. Her fun-loving, outgoing ways had now been replaced by fear and distrust that only a broken dog could fathom.

Julie picked up the pink robe at the foot of the bed and noticed the blood stains on the beautiful blue linen. Embarrassed and ashamed, she quickly turned away and hobbled to the window. Inching the sheer white fabric to one side, she held her breath while dissecting the yard. She half-expected to see Jim lurking down there. No sign of that ogre. Only a belligerent blue jay perched on the grape arbor, screeching displeasure at a vagabond squirrel that was robbing birdseed from the feeder that hung off one of several red maple trees. Julie let down her guard and pushed the Priscilla off to the side. Leaning her bruised forehead against the windowpane, she closed her eyes against the pain and let the morning sun warm her face and soul.

Somewhere wind chimes tinkled. Her eyelids fluttered open. She sought out the source. From the cornice of the white gazebo that centered on the lawn area, teardrop prisms cavorted around one another on the November breeze, sparkling with music. And as if spirits of past sweethearts lingered there, a wooden glider swung back and forth from chains attached to inside beams. Planters, mounted on the railings, contained frostbitten flowers colored in shades of autumn. Leaves had mounded up around the base of the birdbath; some were floating upon the tainted water overflowing the basin. It must have rained during the night, for everything sparkled with moisture. The pristine view filled her with an unusual sense of serenity.

Unexpectedly a bevy of sparrows buzzed past the window. Julie jumped back. She shuddered then peeked out the window again. Several of the birds had landed on the birdbath. Their heads bobbed while their eyes cocked at one another and then at the others that had settled in the bushes beneath the window. They seemed to be second-guessing their decision about landing on the birdbath. Had they made a terrible mistake? Their shrill twittering overpowered the melody of the wind chimes. Her heart lightened as once again the sound of humming reached her ears. She glanced at the bedroom door. It was the old lady. Someone had actually cared.

Julie took a steadying breath. Somehow, she would survive. Sliding her arms into the pink robe, she felt safe for the first time in a very, very long time.

CHAPTER 2

*H*umming a favorite tune, Emma LaRosa palmed the ripples out of a white damask tablecloth with corners of cross-stitched pink rosebuds and emerald leaves. She placed a small pot of yellow mums bedecked in green foil in the center of the table then set out breakfast choices she had prepared for her unexpected guest. Emma could not get over how strange it felt to have another person in this old house overnight. After all the years of constant activity this house had seen? She bit her lip. The days that had followed Seth's passing left only emptiness and utter stillness everywhere, stillness that continually echoed from every corner of her being.

Emma recalled that first night after Seth died as if it was only yesterday. She had pressed her weathered fingertips against the paint-laden door that had given way with a resistive groan. She stood there, gazing into the bedroom that she had shared with her beloved husband for over fifty-two years. How was she ever going to go on living without Seth? She would only be in the way, a burden on the children, a burden on society, a burden on life itself. It was at that moment that Emma had caught the scent of roses, the only flowers she had saved from the funeral. Seth had always loved roses. She breathed in and closed her eyes. And it seemed as if her forever love was there with her once again, transforming her grief into bridal bloom, making a night fifty-two years ago live again.

Roses from the garden below had sweetened summer's breath that night as transparent Priscillas fluttered and moonbeams waltzed across freshly-papered walls of pastel. The nuptials were over and the cacophonous guests had withdrawn from the house. Now…now was Seth and Emma's secret time in their timeless haven away from an intrusive world.

Perched upon the edge of the bed, Emma had waited expectantly, her fingertips gliding across tufts of chenille, the color of lemon gelato. Did two people really need such a big bed? Her ebony eyes drifted to the door that seemed so intent on remaining closed. She sighed and looked away. The mahogany dresser. Emma smiled remembering how Seth's indecision had nearly driven a poor salesman mad, though all along she and Seth had known full well that this furniture was exactly what they had in mind. Scarlet tea roses and daisies, arranged in the jade vase that her Mama had given her, reflected in the etched mirror. Emma contemplated the ecru doilies. How determined she had been to crochet them herself. And sugar-starch them herself, too. And iron those edges into stiff rolling ridges. She nodded. Indeed, the right choices had gone into this, their special room.

Emma got to her feet. Was she going to make a good wife? As far as housekeeping and child rearing were concerned, she was quite confident. But those were things she had seen and experienced through years of caring for her younger sisters. Those things people talked about openly. But what went on behind the bedroom door of marriage? Well, none of that had ever reached her ears. Her pulse quickened. Cold palms patted her flushed cheeks as Emma brushed off such thoughts and stepped over to the dresser. She slid out the top drawer and selected the eyelet nightgown that she had put away for this occasion. Placing it on the dresser, she looked at herself reflecting in the mirror behind the red tea roses. What a shame to remove all that lovely ceremonial splendor. If only she could wear this gown just a little longer. Her lips puckered. Well, sooner or later, it had to be done.

As Emma draped each elegant piece over the bedroom chair, a satin munchkin took form wearing a feathery veil, bespeckled with rhinestones. Her slender fingers drifted across it stirring the memory of the laughter, song, and wine that had filled the day. She felt light-headed once again. She was dancing with her handsome groom, so tall, his midnight eyes sparkling with infatuation.

The cotton nightgown slid down her five-foot frame. Her naked-ness beneath felt vulnerable, fragile. Emma shivered. What did time have in store for her and her new husband? At seventeen she had never known a man. As her fingers struggled with the last stubborn button, the door closed with barely a sound. Her eyes met his. Lost in awkward silence, they gazed at one another. Innermost thoughts connected. Seth took a step. Emma backed away. But his eyes soothed away her anxiety and she faltered. His hand enveloped her fingers, warming them. His lips kissed her open palm. As he brushed her fingertips across his freshly-shaven cheek, his voice was soft and velvety. "I have waited a lifetime for you, my sweet Emma, and now that you are here in my life, I will love and cherish you for all of God's lifetime." He drew her to him. The gentle strength of his arms surrounded her. "You will always find me here, my love. I will never leave you."

Like dew upon a rose at dawn, concern dissipated and her arms encircled his slender waist. Emma snuggled against his chest. His smooth youthful skin soothed hers that seemed to burn like wildfire. Her entire being drank up his essence. As she gazed up into his long-ing eyes, it seemed as though at that moment only the two of them existed in the vast universe. Seth was patient and gentle, and as they melted in radiant embrace, the passion that soared within Emma pleased her. She was he. He was she.

By and by, Seth had drifted off into a lover's deep repose. Emma propped herself up on her right elbow to study his tranquil face.

How handsome he was, and so caring and intelligent. Her fingers toyed with his indigo hair tousled about the pillow. His low, even breathing deepened her contentment. She sighed, adrift in newborn serenity, one that she had never before experienced. Oh, to stop these sacred moments from passing.

Sleep did not come for Emma. Nor did she wish for it. Lifting the blanket, Emma noiselessly slipped out of bed. She picked up her disheveled nightgown on the floor and slid it over her head. A smile wrinkled her lips. The last stubborn button was still undone.

She leaned over Seth and kissed his brow then tiptoed to the open window where she knelt in the blessed stillness. Below the ledge, bushes rustled, urging rosebuds to release their essence. The breeze cooled her blush. Grasping chestnut tresses that fluttered about, she glanced up into the starry night where cotton clouds cavorted across the radiant moon. Thoughts of their first passion overflowed and parted her lips. As the night train saluted the brilliant star that was Margaret Bascuino, Emma whispered, "I promise to make Seth happy."

Emma did not remember falling asleep that night, but Seth had roamed her dreams. She did not wake when his hand caressed her shoulder or when he scooped her into his arms and brought her back to the bed. Her body sank into it as though it were a luxuriant bath. As he drew up the covers, she clutched them against her cheek.

The next morning, the sun blazed in through the open window as Emma blinked away slumber. For a moment her surroundings were unfamiliar. Then her new life took over her thoughts and she smiled. Resolving that she and her new husband would have the best that life could offer, she reached out for him. But Seth was not there. Somewhere within distant dreams, he had kissed her good-bye, murmuring, "I love you, my sweet Emma."

During the next short year, Emma discovered the man, his triumphs, and his losses, especially that of his beloved Margaret Bascuino, stolen away as a mere child by the malignant hand of the

Spanish Influenza. Devotion grew, forging a love that was uniquely theirs, one that knew no earthly bounds. The tender base that Emma and Seth molded provided the unwavering strength and unexpressed understanding needed for the busy years to come. Their first child came along, changing tender moments. Rituals of everyday life took over. Never again would they share the blossoming intimacy and bliss that they had known that first year. Never enough time or privacy, they found unspoken connection most often within each other's eyes.

The years passed swiftly. Good times and bad came and went. Emma, a natural homemaker and mother, could not have asked for a better husband. A strong father figure, Seth conscientiously provided for their growing family in the two-story Dutch colonial home that he had built in Brighton, Massachusetts before their marriage. There had been a time when the white clapboard house with green shutters was the only building on the dead end street and at nighttime with its lights on, it had taken on the appearance of a ship in full sail. As the years passed, maples had overshadowed the street that had become crowded with other homes.

Seth and Emma had raised four children, one girl—Margi, named after his childhood sweetheart, Margaret Bascuino—and three boys—Adam, Timothy, and Samuel. All had grown and were married now, spawning rambunctious grandchildren who picked the roses from the potted bush below the windowsill. The pot had been Seth's attempt to make up for the flower garden that the macadam driveway had replaced. Each spring, Emma made it a point to be hanging out the window, poking fun at Seth when he placed a rose bush there, trellis and all. "You should have left the flower garden right where it was," she teased. "You're still going to hit that pot when you drive in, if you're not careful. Isn't that the reason for getting rid of the garden in the first place?" Seth had always shrugged it off with a wide flourish of an Italian hand.

Emma smiled. She had never dreamed that two very ordinary people could be so blessed. Her childish schoolgirl dreams had been fulfilled beyond all imagination. She and Seth had become the cornerstones of future generations. But now…

She hated for him to go…no…Seth must not leave…not yet. It was much too soon. There was still so much left undone…still so many words left unsaid. He was her nourishment. His life-giving body must give warmth to hers just one more time. Emma was not ready to be left behind, but here she was alone…alone in a room filled with the scent of roses and mahogany furniture that was as outdated as she…alone in the desolate, unforgiving vacuity that she and Seth had shared for so many fruitful years.

Emma knelt at the window. The summer breeze from long ago seemed to be teasing her cheeks with her chestnut tresses…but the window was closed…and her salt-and-pepper hair remained undisturbed within the November night. The bushes below the ledge rustled, enticing rosebuds to release their guarded freshness…but the window was closed and the blossoms had withered with summer's fading light, leaving behind only sterile black macadam. Vacant eyes gazed into the night where no moon waxed nor stars twinkled. The night train howled at the solid cloud mass above, ordering that the star named for Margaret Bascuino be revealed. In Emma's soul the night was clear and the brightness of the star taunted her. Her eyes narrowed and her chin jutted forward. Her teeth clenched and her jaw flexed. Resentfully she breathed, "Seth has come to you…"

Grief choked Emma. She detested the infernal beating of her heart. She would have given her life to save his. She would have traded places with him. Oh, if only not to be the one left behind…alone. Her head dropped onto her arms that were crossed upon the windowsill. Oh, if only to be that bride of long ago, dancing with her handsome young groom.

A white-crowned sparrow lit upon the narrow, cracked ledge and peered in through the unyielding windowpane. Emma struggled to focus. The bird turned away. Unsure wings twitched. Ordained destiny beckoned. He must go. He gazed again at her—deep into her lost, forlorn eyes. Moments passed. Within each second only the woman and the bird existed. He lingered, though they both knew it was time for him to go.

Tears brimmed her eyes. "No," she lightly sobbed, "Stay..."

Abruptly the untrammeled bird unfolded his wings, up and away. The sill was deserted, empty, worn.

Dark dreamless sleep enshrouded Emma. Seth was there, placing his hand upon her shoulder...yet Seth was gone.

Emma heard noises upstairs. She shook off the reverie. Was Julie finally stirring about? Peeking around the corner to the stairway, the old woman listened. Silence. She stepped back into the kitchen and turned on the thirteen-inch television that set on the counter. The news was on. Nothing good as usual. She switched it off.

The girl's name was Julie Spencer. That's all Emma knew, other than that some very unkind individual or individuals had used the poor girl worse than a doormat. The old woman shuddered as the memory of those horrible cigarette burns came flooding back. Rejecting the mere thought that anyone could do a thing like that to another person, she shook her head. "Such barbarity. Tsk, tsk, tsk. Something should be done about this."

Emma took a deep breath. But what? She settled herself on a chair at the kitchen table and waited. Thoughts of Seth took over her mind. Had he actually been there that night? When she had awoken the next morning, she had found herself lying on her back in bed. Automatically her head had turned to check the pillow beside her, but Seth was not there.

Glancing at the closed window, she squinted. Dust particles glimmered like miniature diamonds within the sun beaming to the hardwood floor. For heaven sake, how did she get from that window to the bed? Her mind searched the night of fleeting dreams. A shadow. Seth? Try as she might the old woman just could not piece together the night, so she groped about the night table for the alarm clock that had failed to raise her. Holding it close to her eyes, Emma had mumbled, "Ten fifteen." Her eyes widened. She glared at it. "Ten fifteen? That cannot be." She had never slept this late in her entire life. Emma dropped the clock onto the edge of the night table and it had fallen to the floor. "What is wrong with you, old woman?"

Tossing off the covers, her arm halted in midair. Roses. She smelled roses. There, on the bureau, several bouquets of drooping roses and baby's breath… "Oh, my…" The reality of recent days struck. The flowers had come from Seth's funeral.

Her arm dropped as grief stole over her like a dark cloud. Every ray of hope vanished from her hapless world. No longer did she need to get up to make Seth his breakfast. Wait a minute. That bird…Her eyes zoomed back to the window. Why had that bird landed on the sill like that? Could it have been…? Was it just her imagination? Had there even been a bird at all?

Emma fell back upon the pillow and rubbed her forehead. Why did Seth leave her here so all alone? She simply could not go on without him. How could he expect her to? What did life mean if he was not here with her, giving her his strength through unflinching love? Having no desire to get up, the old woman willed herself to return to that profound sleep that kept melancholy at bay. But it was no use.

Her eyes scanned the bedroom where everything embodied her beloved Seth. Her eyes fixed upon the family portrait propped upon the mahogany bureau—a sacred testament to better times. Better times. How could there ever be better times again without Seth? But there he was, seated in the center of the picture with their youngest son Samuel perched upon his lap, grinning that wide toothy grin of his. In a proper motherly manner, Emma posed behind Seth, slightly to the right, with one hand resting upon his shoulder. She looked so much younger then…and happier. Their oldest son Adam was standing off Seth's left shoulder. Timothy and Margi hovered on opposite sides of their father. Margi bore dark Italian features, as did Adam. Timothy was fairer and Samuel even more so. Both had Grandpa LaRosa and Uncle Rom's penetrating hazel eyes. All four children had inherited their father's expression.

How swiftly time had passed. The house that once pulsated with life now languished in silence. Emma focused on Margi's cherubic face. The girl had resisted putting on that frilly dress and was driven to tears by that satin ribbon belt that was too tight no matter how loose Ma had tied it. And those patent leather Mary Janes. Oh, how the girl hated them! She wanted to take the picture without wearing them, but her Papa had convinced her that the athlete's foot germs that roamed stuffy photography studios were not of the ordinary kind and could eat right through those lacy socks of hers lickety-split. Those germs would eat her feet like gypsy moths eat leaves on a hot August day. So there Margi was, standing with her weight solidly placed upon the side of her right foot, revealing the sole of the shoe.

Emma puffed with amusement. The girl had blossomed into a beautiful, caring woman and mother. Emma bit her lip thinking how hard Margi had taken her father's death, even though he had suffered with ill health for quite some time. Emma gasped as electric charges bolted through her. "Margi! She'll be dropping by any moment now. Get yourself up, old woman, this instant!"

Once again Emma tossed off the covers. But the black outfit she had worn the day before had twisted around her body so bad that she had to wriggle into a standing position before she was able to free her legs. She trudged to the bathroom and after filling the claw-footed cast-iron tub halfway, measured out capfuls of oil, the essence of honeysuckle.

Taking off her wrinkled blouse, she was about to stuff it into the hamper when she hesitated. She held it up at eye level, then her eyes dropped to her underwear and the black skirt that she was still wearing. She had never slept in her clothes before. The blouse rumpled to the tile floor. The rest of what she was wearing ended up heaped on top.

Emma stepped into the scented tub. The water was not as warm as she liked it, so she rotated the hot water spigot. Settling back, she took a deep cleansing breath, allowing the water to dissolve her weathered bones. Her eyes closed and the scent of honeysuckle wafted up into her nostrils, rekindling life with Seth. She smiled. He always went nuts when she wore honeysuckle perfume. He always made sure she had an abundant supply of it. As she turned off the hot water, her senses tugged her back to a day so long ago when she had worn honeysuckle perfume. That was one of the happiest days of her life, the wedding day of Seth's niece, Avita Maria. He had given the bride away since the girl's father had passed on several years before. Seth was handsome beyond words, standing tall and straight in his black tuxedo with a red rosebud and a sprig of baby's breath pinned to his lapel. At the wedding reception that followed in a sprawling hotel across the street from the Boston Common, nobody dared to cut in on Emma and Seth as they danced away the day and half the night. The giddy pair felt so devilish, because they had not told a soul about their first child being in the oven. Emma fell in love with Seth over and over again that wonderful day. He was her only thought. And every time he smiled down at her, her receptive heart swelled into a sea of emotion that drowned all reason.

Later as they drove home, Emma had snuggled as close as possible while holding his hand that draped across her shoulder. Arm in arm, they cuddled their way to the back door where Seth fumbled with the keys. As he tried to get the correct one into the lock, she insistently plastered him with kisses. It was a good thing that at the time they had no neighbors who could see this outrageous display of lust.

Emma and Seth stumbled inside. As he kicked the door shut, his arms wrapped about her. He kissed her, long and passionately. She found herself against the wall, clutching him as the world revolved around her. Ecstasy smothered her senses as they groped their way through the house and almost gave up in the kitchen, because they could not wait until they got to the bedchamber that seemed to be a God-awful distance away.

Clothing littered the trail. By the time they reached their destination, they could no longer contain the overwhelming desire to possess one another. His cool flesh thrilled hers that burned with wild desire. He kissed her forehead, her cheeks, her chin, her mouth. Endless waves of passion surged and should have gone on as long as there was time itself. But exhaustion overtook them and they fell apart.

Still, they could not stop touching one another. Seth kissed her fingertips. Emma kissed the palms of his hands. They loved each other endlessly in a honeysuckle rapture that did not dissipate until the night gave way to day.

"Ma? Are you in there?" A fist pounded on the bathroom door. "Ma! You all right? Ma?"

Blissful reverie shattered. Emma struggled to bring herself back from a place she never wanted to leave, a place she felt safe, warm, and complete. But the banging persisted and so did her daughter's voice. "Ma! You need help or somethin'?"

With all the strength the old woman could muster, she muttered, "No, sweetheart. I will be out in one moment."

Emma sat there, listening to Margi's footsteps fade down the stairs. Resenting the intrusion, she willed visions of Seth to return, but that was not meant to be.

Reluctantly, Emma raised herself. Water sheeted off her body as one unsteady foot stepped out of the tub. Stretching for the pink chenille robe draped over the commode, Emma wrapped it around her body and cinched the belt. Suddenly, she realized that she had not dried herself with a towel.

Confusion befuddled her. She brushed aside her forgetfulness with a wisp of her hand and reached into the tub to pull the plug. The water's chill startled her. She had soaked in the tub much longer than she had intended. As oil and soap scum spiraled away with the cold water, Emma got the feeling that it was also taking away Seth. Her stomach knotted.

Heaving a sigh, she opened the bathroom door, half-expecting to see that her anxious daughter had returned. Disappointment crept over the old lady when she realized that was not the case. She looked towards the bedroom, so empty without Seth. Brooding all the way down the stairs and into the kitchen, Emma went to kiss Margi but instead found herself wrapped in a bear hug. "Ma! You're freezing." Margi jumped back with a horrified look plastered across her face. Her hands clamped onto Emma's shoulders and rocked her back and forth. "You all right, Ma? Go get some clothes on, and I'll make you a coffee." All this without a single breath.

Amused at the boisterous concern that jarred her out of her funk, Emma said, "Thank you, sweetheart. I will be right back." Plodding back up the stairs, Emma noted how much Margi was like Seth. He had never put up with Emma stewing over troubles either. He always prodded her with kindness and humor until she came out of her mood. Sometimes he even made her a fluffernutter. That usually did the trick, though she was not at all partial to that kind of sand-wich—"sangwich" as Seth used to say. He had really made it for him-self. Still, the sight those two pieces of bread oozing white goo into his hand as he offered it to her always made her laugh. At his insis-tence she inevitably ended up taking at least one nibble. It was either that or have the entire sangwich plastered all over her face.

Emma had been chuckling when she got up to the bedroom, but gloom quickly overtook her. The sanctuary that the room had pos-sessed earlier no longer existed. Barren and dark, it smelled like a funeral parlor. It became incredibly painful to be there and seemed to be sucking every last bit of strength she possessed. "I have to get out of here."

Grabbing underwear, a navy blue frock with white collar and cuffs, and one-inch heels, she hastily retreated to the bathroom where she leaned against the basin and gasped for air. She glanced into the medicine cabinet where the mirror reflected her withered face riddled with anxiety. She turned away to dress and spotted yesterdays clothing on the floor. She hesitated then picked them up. She wanted to throw them away—throw away all those last dreadful days. She glanced at the trash container and then the hamper. She stuffed the clothing into the hamper and quickly got dressed. Without benefit of the mirror, she ran a comb through her hair and clipped on silver earrings.

In the kitchen a fresh cup of coffee awaited Emma when she returned. Margi was placing a jar of strawberry preserves on the table next to two pieces of toast on a saucer. As Emma sat down at the ancient Formica table devoid of a tablecloth, she was at a loss as to when she had taken off the dirty one. It wasn't like her to not replace it with a clean one. The cup warmed her hands, still chilled from the bath. Sipping the coffee, she ignored the toast, fearing that she might not keep it down.

"We're s'posed to meet Adam and Janice at Julio's at one thirty," said Margi while busily wiping up around the stove and sink. "Sam and Carol will be there, too. They're goin' back to Connecticut this afternoon, you know. Too bad Tim had to go 'n fly back to Atlanta last night," she said sarcastically. Jamming her hands into her hips, she rolled her eyes. "He should've stayed longer. Humph. Well, anyways. You're outta dish soap, ya know. How 'bout stoppin' at the grocery on the way home? I don't see your list."

Emma was lost in a fog.

Margi gave her mother a pained look. "Aw, don't worry about it. We'll wing it," she spouted with a wave of the dishcloth and continued to rave on and on. "It's so nice outside. A person wouldn't have a clue that it's November in New England if they didn't know better. Maybe we won't get much snow this winter." She rolled her eyes again then said dryly, "We can only hope."

Emma glanced languidly out the window. Sure enough, the sun was shining bright. Odd, the bedroom had seemed so dark and dreary a moment ago. Margi's chatter battered the old woman's thoughts. The companionship forced her back to the living. Likewise, the prospect of dining at Julio's Ristorante gave a lift to her spirits. For many a year it had been a LaRosa family favorite—Seth's favorite. They knew the owners quite well and also most of the waiters who were always delighted to see the LaRosas. The cuisine was traditional Sicilian, much like Emma's Mama used to cook. Emma smiled, remembering how Daddy Benedetto had loved Mama's zabaglione laced with Marsala wine. Oh, my heavens, that man could eat, just like Seth...

The Black Forest cuckoo squawked in the living room. Emma glanced at the kitchen clock. "My goodness, Margi," she lamented and raised her torpid body, "the day is half gone."

"Where'd it go?" Margi huffed as she picked up her mother's empty coffee cup and hurriedly rinsed it under the faucet. She placed it in the rack to air dry and spouted, "Well then. Let's get a move on, Ma."

❦   ❦   ❦

Anthony, the short, portly maitre d', had been anxiously waiting outside Julio's Ristorante and opened the car door before the engine quit. "Ah. There you are, my dear Emma. I have missed you these past days," he said with great flourish as he gave his hand to her.

Emma smiled although she could see the sadness in his eyes that he tried so hard to hide. Even though Anthony had retired several years before, he still worked part time at Julio's where he and Seth had played cards together many an afternoon while smoking smelly stogies and drinking Anthony's homemade port. Poor Anthony. He longed so for his departed friend as much as she did. "I have missed you, too, dear," Emma said.

Graciously, Anthony kissed her hand then wrapped it around his forearm. "Come, my dear Emma. I have prepared a table special for you and your family." He helped her to take off her coat at the cloakroom then once again linked her arm around his to steer her through the old world restaurant. Margi trailed close behind. A few patrons still lingered over the remains of their lunch, listening to mandolins playing Italian arias. A jade vase of roses and daisies brightened the table where Adam and Janice were seated with Samuel and Carol. Anthony knew that Seth had always made sure Emma had lots of flowers in her life.

"Here you are, my dear Emma," Anthony said while pulling out a chair. "This young man here—his name is Paulie—he will take good care of you. If he doesn't, I'll…" His hand gestured as if giving the pinhead waiter a decisive backhand off the back of his head.

Emma smiled reassuringly at the embarrassed young man. "I am quite sure Paulie will do a splendid job."

After their initial greeting, her children settled back and became unusually quiet. Emma could not help thinking how hard their father's passing had been on them. Gazing at his menu, Adam finally spoke up. "What are you going to have, Mother?"

"Oh," Emma said lightly as she folded her menu and placed it on the table. "Perhaps the stuffed manicotti. It is always delicious." She took a sip of water. She did not feel much like eating, but she had to be strong—at least in front of the children.

Samuel dropped his menu on his plate and said, "I want all of you to come to Connecticut for Christmas. None of you have seen my new house."

After Paulie skillfully poured steaming coffee into her coffee cup, Emma picked up a teaspoon. Though she never used cream or sugar, she stirred the coffee just to cool it a bit. She studied Samuel who was built like Seth and had mannerisms much like him. Her youngest son was fairer though, and his light brown hair was finer in nature. He wore it long, in a ponytail, which flabbergasted Seth to no end. Emma fidgeted trying to follow Samuel's words, but it was becoming more difficult by the moment since two elderly biddies seated at the table behind her were carrying on quite boisterously. They must be hard of hearing, thought Emma while continuing to stir her coffee. She had no choice than to eavesdrop.

"I haven't seen Alice and Gianni around lately," commented one of the old women.

The other one cackled, "Well, my dear. Gianni went the way of all good husbands—before his wife, I mean. He has been dead for almost a year now."

Emma dropped her spoon. It bounced off the saucer and rattled across the table. She had all she could do to restrain herself from turning around and giving those two old hens a piece of her mind. How in the world could anyone utter such words, so insensitive, so heartless? Seth was a good husband. That certainly did not mean he was required to die before she. She scanned her children's faces. All eyes were upon her. She smiled weakly and nervously went to stir her coffee. She gaped at her hand. Where was the spoon she had been holding? Then she noticed it, halfway across the table. How on earth did it get way over there? She picked up her coffee cup. Her hands trembled. She could barely hold the cup.

Once again, Samuel and his siblings became engrossed in a big Christmas scheme. Relief sheeted over Emma. Nobody else had heard that rude remark—thank goodness. Yet she still wanted to turn around and scream at those insensitive crones that Seth had always provided for the children and had given of himself with every breath in his body. Even in the last months while suffering so much from heart problems, he had always been there for her and the children.

Glancing up at the ceiling, Emma held back welling moisture. How many mornings had she opened her eyes and caught Seth gazing at her? And when she had smiled at him, his withered carpenter hand reached for hers and clasped it to his breast. She snuggled into his arms and with her head on his shoulder, felt the warmth of his body and listened to his heartbeat while birds outside the window incessantly nagged for the sun to hasten its appearance. Seth spoke soft words of love that consumed her and they both thanked God for granting them one more day to spend together.

Emma gave a weak smile. Making love was more than just a sexual act. As she took a sip of coffee, that dreadful moment last week flooded over her. Sickening waves of nausea smothered her with the same helplessness that she had felt when she had awoken to that dark house. She could not deny the voice that rumbled deep within her, *something is wrong*. Groping for the lamp on the nightstand, she turned it on and discovered Seth in great distress. His shallow breaths had haunted her every hour of the day since. As the flat black of night slowly grayed into an overcast morning, she had run downstairs and telephoned for an ambulance. Details were lost to a whirl of red lights and screech of sirens. At the hospital, monitors beeped as the archbishop gave his lifelong parishioner and friend the Last Rites of the Church.

Emma had stood over her dear Seth. His skin looked so awfully pale, his face so drawn. His eyelids flickered, and his lips quivered into a weak smile. Her hands enfolded his face as she kissed his forehead. His trembling hand lifted off the bed. She grasped it and held it to her heart. A hush of the voice she had come to know so well whispered, "I am sorry…I didn't make love to you this morning…my lovely Emma."

Fighting back tears, she smiled at Seth, knowing all the while that she must let him go. Tenderly she kissed his lips that felt clammy and unresponsive. She backed away, but only enough so that she might gaze upon his face. Oh Lord, if only she had the power to cure him. A tremor passed through his body. He took an abysmal breath…and he was gone.

"I am so sorry too, my dear Seth…" Her throat tightened as she gazed into his sightless eyes that had settled upon hers. Tears overflowed. Cradling his face in her palms, she could not breathe. Her lips grazed his forehead where beads of moisture lingered, and her heart cried out, "…we did not make love this morning."

CHAPTER 3

$\mathcal{T}$he guest room door opened. Emma was sure she heard it this time. She rushed to the stairway. Julie was coming down, cautiously, cinching the pink terry cloth robe that the old woman had given her last night. They caught each other's gaze. The girl faltered. Eyes sullen and remote, her countenance bore a heavy burden for someone so young. Feeling a tug inside, Emma pretended not to notice the bruises that were quite apparent in the light of day. "Good morning, dear," she beamed and led the way back to the kitchen.

Taking uncertain steps down the rest of the stairs, Julie stood in the doorway of the sunlit kitchen and warily considered the small round woman with pink rollers in her salt and pepper hair flutter about the kitchen. Dressed in a blue gingham housedress, the old woman was humming an unfamiliar melody that was so even and flowing that somehow it felt quite comforting to Julie.

"Come and sit down," Emma spouted. "You must be hungry. My goodness, you slept for a quite a long time. Coffee?"

When Julie gave a timid nod, the old lady went to the stove and shut off the low flame beneath the coffee pot. Fishing a potholder out of her apron pocket, she then picked up the pot and brought it to the table. As she poured fresh brew into a flowered china cup, she commanded, "Here now. Come on. Sit."

Watching the old woman returning the pot to the stove, Julie sensed that it would be useless to argue, so she made her way to the table and carefully lowered herself onto a chair. She scanned the yellow flowers wrapped in green foil, a pitcher filled with orange juice, the four-ounce juice glasses with oranges painted on them, the old-fashioned dishes, and breakfast choices. Julie could not believe all the breakfast choices! Hunger knotted her stomach. Her hands encircled the cup and wicked up the heat. As she picked it up, succulent steam filled her nostrils and cleared her brain. She took a sip. It felt good going down.

"Help yourself to the cream and sugar," Emma offered. "And take some cereal. There's fruit there, too!"

Julie made no attempt to eat. She was afraid that her stomach would not keep anything down.

The old woman stood with her hands on the back of a chair. The girl looked like something the cat dragged in. Perhaps she was more injured than first thought. "Want me to fix you an egg?" Emma asked.

Julie shook her head no.

"An English muffin?"

Another wave of the head.

"But you must eat," Emma prodded.

The girl shrugged. Her voice was soft, childlike. "I don't do breakfast."

Emma felt helpless. She spied a bunch of bananas centering the huge bowl of fruit and plucked one off. "Here," she said, "Take a bite of this while I fix some strawberries. You've got to have something on your stomach."

Giving a weak smile, Julie watched the old woman clean strawberries. Toying with the banana, she had no motivation to peel it.

Emma placed the bowl of cleaned strawberries in front of her guest then poured herself a cup of coffee and sat down. The dejected young soul looked so frail and vulnerable sitting there all hunched over. Instinct spurred Emma into trying to ease the suffering, but all she could think of was to pat the back of the girl's hand.

Julie wanted to dig a hole and climb into it, hoping that a boulder would roll over the opening and seal her away from this dreadful world. Physical and mental pain wracked her entire being. "I…I'm sorry," she choked as she glanced sideways at the old woman. Tears welled. "I can't remember your name."

"Oh, well, my goodness, sweetheart, don't you worry one particle bit about it." The old woman reached around the girl's shoulders and gave a squeeze. "I am Emma LaRosa."

"Thanks…" Julie heaved, "for helping me out last night…Mrs. LaRosa. You're very kind."

"Call me Emma. And I am sure anyone would have helped you out. I'm just the one who happened to be there."

Julie's eyes went wide as she spouted, "No. Nobody ever helped. People just looked the other way." A tremor raked her body as she remembered the stomping that came from upstairs every time Jim started his garbage. She dug what was left of her fingernails into the palms of her hands. "But that monster will never come near me again."

"Your boyfriend?" Emma guessed.

"Not any more." Julie's lips pursed remembering how desperately she had wanted to call someone boyfriend. And now she had no one. And now she had to move on. How in the world was she supposed to do that? Without a job? Without a place to live?

Emma watched as Julie picked up a fork and nudged a strawberry. Worrying if there was going to be more trouble from that brute, she probed, "What is his name?"

Julie hesitated. Her fork dangled in midair. The mere mention of that ogre's name would surely cause him to appear. She drew in a deep breath. "Uhm, Jim…" Shivers ran through her body. She glanced at Emma then spat out his name as if cobra's venom laced it. "Jim Martin."

"Where is your family?" Emma asked.

"My father died before I was born," Julie muttered. "Mom lives in Boston." She hesitated. Picking up a strawberry, she whispered, "But I can't ask her for help. She's got problems of her own."

"No brothers or sisters?"

Julie shook her head as she fingered the strawberry. "I have a grandmother and an uncle who live in Arizona. I never met them."

"So where will you go?"

"Not back to that apartment, that's for sure. He's there." Julie dropped the strawberry on her dish.

"What about all your things?"

Julie fell sobbing on her arms. "I'm not going back! I'm not!"

"It's all right," Emma said while gently rubbing the girl's back. "Nobody's going to make you do anything that you don't want to do." Lifting the girl's chin, the old woman looked into panicky eyes and waved her head side to side. "Nobody." Emma smiled reassuringly then picked up another strawberry and handed it to Julie.

The girl squinted at the strawberry then peered at the old woman who gave a decisive nod. Gingerly, Julie took the strawberry and popped it into her mouth. "Ooo," she winced as her fingers pressed against her lips. "It stings."

It shocked Emma to see the girl's pain, yet at the same time it pleased her to see the young woman eating. "Does you mother know what that man did?" Emma asked.

"I haven't talked to her since last winter," mumbled Julie.

Emma's eyebrows arched. "Last winter?"

Julie shrugged.

Emma could not fathom a mother and an only daughter not communicating more than that. Something had to be terribly wrong, but if Julie wanted her to know about it, Julie was going to have to volunteer it. "So your mother doesn't know about Jim?"

Julie shook her head. "He didn't like meeting people." She coughed then blotted her lips with a napkin. "And he had no use for his parents either."

"Well, sweetheart, you are more than welcome to use my telephone anytime you wish to call your mother." Emma looked up at the wall clock shaped like a black and white cat. Its tail kept cadence with the second hand. "Oh, my, look at the time! It's almost eleven. Margi will be here any minute now. We better find you some clothes!"

"Oh, don't bother," Julie said as she waddled to the sink with the empty strawberry dish. "I'll put on the clothes I had on last night and get out of your hair."

"Nonsense. I won't hear a word of it," Emma insisted. "Besides, I put all your dirty things in the laundry, so I guess we have no other choice but to find you something else to wear." She bit the corner of her mouth, knowing full well that she had already stuffed the torn and bloodied garments into a plastic bag and hid it behind the vacuum cleaner in the utility closet. Emma intended to throw it out the first chance she got. "You're about Margi's size, well, before she got married...although you're a little bit shorter than she is. But all that is fixable."

Julie gave a half smile. Somehow she was drawn to this diminutive old lady with salt and pepper hair wrapped around pink rollers, but she didn't know why, only that Emma seemed to be a magnet from which the young woman drew strength like never before. Following Emma upstairs, Julie thought how all her life she had lived a murky existence. Perhaps this gentle, energetic senior who hummed all the time might lead her into daylight. Feeling as though being here was somehow meant to be, she decided to let events take their own course.

When Emma opened the closet door in the guest room and started to sort through a vast array of dresses, blouses, pants, and sweaters kept there for unplanned visits by her grandchildren or their parents, Julie's mouth fell open. In all her short life, she had never seen so many clothes packed into one small space. Emma held up a hanger draped with a pair of black jeans and another with a red plaid turtleneck. "Here," she happily announced. "These look like they will fit you. And here is a navy button-down if you get chilly. I like navy, don't you?" Without waiting for an answer, she dropped the clothes into Julie's arms and continued. "And there's underwear in the drawer. Help yourself." Emma tapped her chin with one finger and studied Julie's bare feet. "Hmm...the only problem is shoes. What size do you wear?"

"Seven and a half," Julie replied while searching the room for her shoes. She felt embarrassed knowing how crummy they were. "But don't worry about it. I can wear my old shoes."

"You can't." Emma stopped short.

Julie squinted at the old person.

Emma immediately looked away, saying, "You had on only one shoe last night, and it was soaked clear through and through. It was awfully mangled." Julie's face reddened, but the old woman did not see, for by then Emma was rustling around the closet floor. Holding up a pair of black tennis shoes that were in pretty good shape, she beamed, "Here, try these on. I will let you get dressed now, but if you need anything else, just give a holler."

As the bedroom door closed, Julie dropped onto the edge of the bed. She could hear the old lady humming all the way down the stairs and into the kitchen. Where did that woman get all her energy? This was all too incredible. Yesterday, a cruel monster had beaten her young body to a pulp, yet today, a guardian angel was offering sanctuary. An aura of security surrounded Julie—an aura of which she was not in any hurry to rid herself. She got to her feet and dressed. Without realizing it she began to hum the same infectious melody as Emma. For a change Julie was not looking over her shoulder. But while fishing around in her pocketbook for a brush and comb, she made the mistake of glancing at the mirror. She gasped. Her own mutilated face stared back at her. Grabbing the brush and comb, Julie rushed to the kitchen.

Emma, minus pink hair rollers, was pouring a cup of coffee for Margi. "My goodness, those clothes fit you to a T. How about the shoes?" Leaning close to inspect, she looked up into the girl's eyes and asked. "Comfortable enough? I could find you another pair if you wish."

Julie felt her face flush. Avoiding the old lady's eyes, she choked back a tear. "No, no. These are perfect. You've been too kind to me already. I'll never be able to repay you."

With a wave of a hand, Emma sputtered, "We don't pay for kindness around here. Here, give me that brush and sit down."

"You mean to tell me Ma didn't make you wear my old red, three-inch spikes?" Margi teased as the side of her face scrunched up and one eye squeezed shut. The fingers of her left hand formed the perfect sign.

"Oh, hush you," Emma scolded while threatening with the brush. She turned to Julie. "This is my daughter Margi. I've been telling her how I ran onto you yesterday."

"Nice meetin' ya," Margi grabbed Julie's hand and shook it heartily. She was an in-your-face sort, a victim of emotion who smiled on a whim and seconds later frowned with thick, puckered lips. Vast, jet-black eyes sparkled with love one moment and the next fired off heated animosity. Her usual attire consisted of stonewashed jeans and faded, oversized sweatshirts—today's was gray and flaunted Cape Cod in burgundy block letters. She had a thing for $3 sneakers. When they got dirty, she had no qualms about trashing them. Most days, lipstick and other makeup were a bother. Her raven hair, not yet streaked with strands of silver, was cut into a bob, but was in a constant state of disarray and was most often chucked beneath a hastily chosen bandanna. "Feeling better? Terrible thing that idiot did. I say we should get the cops to haul in his sorry butt."

Julie winced causing Emma to take a step backwards. The brush had scored a scalp wound. "My," the old woman stammered, "you have quite a gash there, dear."

Margi sprang to her feet. "Gimme that brush, Ma." Her chair griped across the linoleum floor, sending electric bolts up Julie's spine. "You're gonna kill the poor kid."

"Don't worry about it." Julie shivered while trying to slough off the show of concern.

"Sh," Margi spat while threatening with the hairbrush. She had learned at the knees of her mother not to take no for an answer and had perfected it to the point of rudeness at times.

Julie picked at her broken fingernails and fought off sensations that kept putting her back into that flat. "Cops won't do any good now. Besides, I never want to see his ugly face again."

"Hey, listen." Margi scrunched her brow while brandishing the brush at some invisible entity. "I wouldn't put up with the likes of him either!"

Glancing at Emma, Julie gave a timid smile. "Thank God your Mom came along."

"Yeah, that's Ma for ya," Margi guffawed. "God, look at this hair. It's awesome. Like silk. And I just love the color. My hair's so pukey."

Emma shot a look at her daughter and shook her head.

"Mom says I got my father's hair," Julie said matter-of-factly.

"Her father's passed on," Emma added.

Margi's face twitched as the brush swept through a length of honey blond. She avoided the scalp.

"I had a sack full of reasons staring me in the face…" Julie began. She was reluctant to expose her stupidity. "I shouldn't of gotten involved with that jerk, but…"

"Hey, we don't give a hoot about all the gory details," Margi cut in. "We got eyes. But listen. I'll get my husband Evan and his cohorts at the police department to get on over there an' get your stuff. That sucker won't mess with them or he'll find his sorry butt behind bars, which is where it belongs anyway, I might add. Your stuff will be safe in Ma's basement until you decide what to do, right Ma?"

"Sure, the cellar's dry," Emma nodded. "It's not right for that brute to keep all your things."

"And stay here with Ma 'ntil you get your feet on the ground." Margi's brows rose to her hairline as she stared directly into Julie's eyes. "'kay, kid?"

Julie sidestepped the prodding eyes and glanced at Emma. This sweet old lady and her boisterous daughter gave of themselves so freely, yet each one was strong in her own special way. Julie had no desire to leave the presence of such wonders. Could it be that life was finally changing…for the better? From the very outset, it had always been one big negative. "Yeah…if you don't mind…I want to stay."

"I would love to have you," exclaimed Emma as she took the brush from Margi.

Spreading an arm across her mother's shoulders, Margi laughed heartily. "It's been a bit lonely around here for Ma."

Unaccustomed to witnessing such affection, Julie thought about her own mother who had always been so standoffish and reclusive. Why was it that she and Mom were one way and Emma and Margi were the total opposite?

"How much stuff ya got, kid?" Margi asked while gathering up the cups and saucers.

"Not much," Julie wheezed as she got up to help with the dishes. Instantly Emma laid a hand on the girl's shoulder, which meant for her to stay put. Giving a twisted smile, Julie relented and remained seated. "A mattress and bed frame. The sofa and kitchen set I got at Goodwill. And the TV came from a girl I worked with who moved to California with her boyfriend."

"Big whoop," Margi huffed as dishes clinked in the sink. "The guys will have that place cleared out lickety split."

"Emma?" Julie asked.

"Yes, sweetheart?" Emma replied as she wiped off the table.

"What's that song?" Julie asked.

Quite unaware that she was humming, Emma glanced at Margi who immediately winked and leaned against the counter. One leg bore her weight, which arched her backwards and made her butt jut out in an unflattering way. "That's the 'Rhapsody on a Theme of Paganini' by Rachmaninoff," Margi grinned. "Papa took Ma to see that guy a long time ago in New York City. Papa always made Ma play it on the piano for him. She's quite an accomplished pianist, you know."

Melancholy laced her voice when Emma said, "Well, I had to be. Your father loved all kinds of music."

Margi straightened up and slid her hands deep into her back pockets. "Papa passed away not too long ago."

"Oh," Julie shifted. "I'm so sorry."

Margi shuffled about a bit then blurted out, "Ma, how 'bout playin' for us?" Not waiting for an answer, she bounded off to the living room.

Emma chuckled. With a wave of the hand, she beckoned to Julie. "Come on, dear."

At the graceful archway that divided the dining room from the living room, Julie stopped short. "Wow…" Kitty-cornered in front of a huge bow window overpopulated with plants a mahogany baby grand jutted out and dominated the expansive room. Crisscrossed Priscillas draped like a bridal veil across the window that cast a golden glow upon the muted-gold fleur-de-lis wallpaper. An Oriental carpet, centered before the Italian marble fireplace, accentuated the honeyed sheen of the heavily waxed hardwood floor. On one side of the hearth, there were brass fireplace tools in a rack and on the other side birch logs stacked in a brass wood carrier. Glass doors covered the firebox, preventing heat loss up the chimney when the fireplace was not in use. Portraits littered the mantle. Like the rest of the house, the living room was spotless and smelled of lemon oil. Setting foot in this fine room seemed somehow sacrilegious. But then Margi plopped down upon one of the overstuffed, high back wing chairs as Emma lifted the cover over the keys. She patted the bench for Julie to come sit beside her.

Sheepishly, the young woman made her way to the bench. Her fingers itched to skate across the glossy surface of mahogany. She caught her image reflecting in the open lid of the piano.

Emma took great delight at Julie's naiveté, though she pretended not to notice as she sorted through sheet music racked above the keyboard. Finding the yellowed pages of the piano solo by Rachmaninoff, she opened the first two pages and started to play. After years of playing this tune, the old woman rarely looked at the notes.

Julie contemplated the aged sheet music and then Emma, who was drinking up the melodic essence as though it was fine wine. The old woman seemed to float off into some distant time and place—somewhere that had to be quite peaceful, judging from the look on her face. So Julie let the music take her away as well and found herself in her own secret world—a tranquil world—one where she had never before traveled. When the music stopped, her insides cried out for more. Moments passed. Julie took a deep breath. "That is the most beautiful thing I have ever heard."

Emma smiled. "I am so glad you like it, dear."

"You know anything about Rachmaninoff, kid?" Margi's voice shattered the moment.

"I'm afraid I don't know much about anything," Julie admitted. She wanted to confess how her life had been so empty, not only of culture and love but also of family and friendship.

"He was one of the last of the great Russian romantic composers," said Emma. "Seth and I were fortunate enough to have seen him on one of his tours. Rachmaninoff died in the early 1940s. But what a performance Seth and I saw. Icy concentration lined his face, but his music was so richly melodic. He made people feel romantic and melancholy, no matter what their mood. I always tell people that when the concert was over, I felt like I had been to church."

"Gosh," Julie whispered. She wished music and love would find her life. And family, too. She pursed her lips. She had no idea how she was going to do it, but from that moment on such things were going to be hers. But was she strong enough? She glanced at Emma. All this had come from a happenstance meeting on a dreadful night. Inspiration and hope overflowed Julie's heart. Slowly a smile lifted her cheeks that blushed like ripening peaches.

CHAPTER 4

A couple of days later, Emma was in the middle of making her bed when she cringed. "Next week is Thanksgiving Day." Her body sagged onto the edge of the half-made bed. It would be the first holiday since Seth's passing. Though she was looking forward to having the children and their families come for the traditional gathering at Grandmother's house, she had no idea where she was going to find the strength to put it all together without Seth.

Emma remembered the day that she had thrown out the last of the funeral roses. She had cried that day and had thought about keeping the roses, putting them in a plastic bag up in the attic. But no, that would be like Seth was up there, too, smothering, and she would hear him gasping for air. She would be responsible for killing him a second time.

Glancing out the window, Emma thought about winter solstice. It was drawing ever nearer making the hours pass by like faceless druids hidden beneath long colorless robes. Each day the indolent eye of morning flickered open later and closed earlier. The fire of autumn had burned out, leaving behind starkness that even daylight savings time had abandoned. A faint smile lifted her heart as she thought how the later sunrise had blessed Seth with the opportunity to savor the dawn in a more awakened state. Yet how he had always carried on so when it came to resetting all the clocks in the house.

Before Julie came along, thoughts like these burdened Emma every hour of the day as she aimlessly mucked about between one menial task and another, struggling to keep herself busy. Her life had taken on an appearance of a character set in slow motion by a cartoonist flipping the pages of a sketchpad. She felt small, irrelevant, abandoned. Even her music reflected her mood at times.

Dreary weather had added to the stifling melancholy. Emma remembered a day last week when the rain had turned into snow squalls and the wind had intruded into the old house leaving behind dankness the likes of which no heating system could drive out. As she had sunk into the recliner beside the window on the front porch, her fingertips could feel the cold air ooze in through the wooden windowsill. Idly, she had stared out at the rain-slicked street, devoid of traffic. Her heart anticipated Seth's car turning into the driveway. In her mind it did and her eyes had fled to the door. Within seconds Seth would be coming in, shaking rain off his fedora. Seconds became minutes before logic recognized that could never be.

Nonetheless, Emma had lingered there, aching for the sight of Seth, abhorring that crass remark the old biddy at Julio's Ristorante had made. Try as she might she could not put the anguish it had caused out of her head. Blinking back tears, she had looked up at the ceiling. The light rain that had been pattering on the porch roof had stopped, leaving the house so starkly quiet. Outside the window, beads of moisture clung to the junipers. She shivered and thought about the afghan draped over the back of the recliner. She refused to reach for it, for it seemed only proper for her to be cold…and old…and dead inside. Her fretting overwhelmed her. She gritted her teeth, then bracing her hands on her knees, had gotten to her feet. Her back was cold, stiff, and cramped "Come on, old woman. It's stopped raining. Fresh air will do the old bones some good."

Flexing her arms and shoulders, Emma had plodded to the closet by the back door where she had wrapped a paisley scarf around her neck. Her arms fumbled with the sleeves of her gray Chesterfield coat. Fishing black leather gloves out of the pockets, she slipped one onto her hand. As she tucked the material down between her fingers, she stopped and stared at the glove. Seth had given these gloves to her last Christmas. She bit the inside of her bottom lip. Everywhere she went, all that her eyes took in, everything her fingers touched reminded Emma of Seth. It was as if he was still there with her, his breath fanning her face, nudging away the pain.

No sooner had she closed and locked the back door when the telephone began to ring. "Margi," she puffed. Her head leaned against the doorframe. Talking to her daughter, or anyone else for that matter, was the last thing on her mind. Besides, if she went back in, that stifling old shack would surely swallow up all that was left of her. Emma needed the weight of its emptiness lifted off her soul—if only for a little while. "I will give you a buzz, dear," she muttered and turned away, "when I get back. I won't be gone long."

Watching her footing on rain-slicked leaves, Emma could smell their decay. As she rounded the corner of the house a whoosh of wings broke the silence and she looked skyward—a ragtag gaggle of geese, pointing south. Emma smiled. "Finally giving in to the onset of winter, I see. Aahh, to be going along with you." *If only to feel that free of care.*

She blinked as strands of salt and pepper blew into her eyes and raw mist peppered her face. Her hair was going to be drenched and flat against her head by the time she returned, but going back for a rain hat was out of the question. She turned up her collar and plodded along the cement sidewalk that had once been cobblestone. Her muscles loosened up with every step. Few people braved the raw elements, but the movement felt good, invigorating. She had not moved around much lately. Seth's passing had left her drained, both physically and mentally. Drawing a long, deep breath of chilled air, heavy with dampness, she expelled the air that had stagnated in her lungs for much too long.

She lifted her face skyward. The geese were long gone. She savored the fine mist, just as she had on a day so very long ago when she and Seth had just finished grocery shopping. As they had carried their purchases into the house, it seemed as though the mist steamed off her hot face like rain on August pavement. It was the only thing that had given her any sense of comfort that day. More than eight months of pregnancy had drained Emma and put her on edge. While grousing about that darned old sun that had not made one single appearance in two solid weeks, she had stepped into a mud puddle as she got out of the car. Her shoes became soaked clear through to her socks. Oh, how she detested wet socks. Then on top of that, Seth was being extremely overbearing—at least that's how Emma had seen it. He constantly got in her way, even though he was trying to be his normal understanding self. If only she had realized how irritable she was being before she had callously slammed the back door and hollered, "How come you didn't close the door? The whole house is a barn now, thanks to you!"

"But Em, I got my hands full," Seth whined. "I'm sorry."

"You are not," she snapped. "I can tell. You did it on purpose…just to aggravate me." She could see that her words had cut deep and knew that it would be better to back off, but instead she twisted up her face and remained defiant.

"Come on, Em, you're tired." He set the bags on the kitchen table. With open palms supplicating, he suggested, "Go lay down for a while. I'll get the rest of the bags."

As his calming hand reached out to Emma, her eyes seared him and she spun away. Storming off to the bedroom upstairs, she caught sight of Seth out the corner of her eye. He just stood there, smarting from her tongue-lashing. Well, after all, she was horrendously tired and sick and tired of being pregnant.

Plopping her chilled bulk onto the edge of the bed, she dug her toes into the heal of one mucked-up shoe and flipped it across the room. Then the other. The next thing was to get those socks off.

They clung to her feet like leeches. Finally she managed to roll them off into twisted masses that looked like soggy French crullers. Her feet left muddy footprints on the floor as she crossed the room to the dresser. She dug out a dry pair of socks then warbled back to the bed. Ignoring the fact that she was putting clean upon unclean, she struggled to curl each foot close enough to wriggle it into a sock.

Worming into the welcoming bed, she had pulled up the cotton blankets and lemony chenille to her chin and dropped off into dreamless oblivion. An hour later, excruciating pain jolted her awake. Clutching her belly, she shrieked, "Seth!"

Downstairs, a pan crashed onto the kitchen floor. Seth came racing up the stairs, taking two at a time. Abject terror riddled his face as he bounded into the bedroom and puffed, "Emma! What's wrong?"

"The baby," she groaned and tried to get to her feet. Suddenly slick liquid oozed down her legs. Momentarily confused, Emma gawked at Seth whose eyes were as wide as baseballs as he tried to get his breath back. "Oh my God," she screeched. "Get me some towels! Hurry!"

Off he tore, out of the room and down the stairs. Emma tried to think. Heartbeats choked her and jarred her brain. She didn't hear Seth scramble back up the stairs and into the bathroom.

"Oh, God," she whined as she looked at the floor. What a mess. If she sat down, she would make an awful mess on the bed, too. There was nothing she could do to stem the flow that was now tinged with red. She wrung her hands as her abdomen began to contract. Her teeth clenched. "Ooohhh."

Just then Seth scurried into the room with an armful of towels stacked to his chin. Jamming one in her face, he panted, "Here."

"Wait," Emma winced.

"What's the matter?" he cried.

Through shallow breaths, she said, "Contraction." When the pain eased off, Emma grabbed a towel and dropped it onto the bed. She lowered herself onto it then grabbed more towels and stuffed them between her legs. She looked up at Seth. His eyes were the size of baseballs. Tears began to flood down her cheeks. "Everything's happening so fast. Look at the mess I made."

"Don't cry, Em. It's okay." Putting his arm around her shoulder, Seth sat down next to her. "What should we do?"

Her shoulders jounced. "Call the doctor?"

"I'm on it," he puffed as he dashed downstairs. After what seemed like an eternity, he returned, trembling with anticipation. "Doc wants you at the hospital right away."

Another contraction immobilized Emma. "I am afraid I cannot stand up," she groaned. Seth filled his lungs with air and went to scoop her up. "No, wait," she cried.

He jumped back. "Whaddaya mean wait?"

"My feet…" she whined.

"Wassamaddah with your feet?" His nose scrunched up as his eyes shot downward.

"They're dirty."

"Bah! Fuggeddaboudit," Seth belched and shoveled her up into his muscular arms. Effortlessly he carried her down the stairs and out to the car. Raw mist had peppered her face that day. As Seth lowered her onto the front seat, Emma was giggling. He looked at her as if she had completely lost her mind. "Wha'?" he blubbered.

"You sounded just like your Pop." Another contraction interrupted her levity. "Whoa…"

Panic riddled his face when Seth saw his wife's face contort and become as crimson as Pop's the day he had hammered on that Boston terrier. "Holy mackerel," he gasped. "These pains are much too strong, don'cha think?"

Emma nodded. "And awfully close."

Darting back into the house, Seth returned with a blanket and quickly covered Emma. Slamming the door, he dashed around the car and jammed the keys into the ignition. His door had not closed before the car lurched backward. The door flapped back and forth, giving the car the appearance of a giant, one-winged albatross trying to take flight.

Gears ground together as Seth put the car in first. Tires screeched. The door slammed shut. He turned onto the main thoroughfare at full-bore. Horns blared as Emma rolled across the seat and into him. He nudged her upright while weaving in and out of rush hour traffic. Cutting off road hogs, the mad driver sent pedestrians clamoring for safety.

Emma whimpered. Seth shot a fleeting glance at her. Another contraction had seized her. Careening onto Commonwealth Avenue, Seth came within inches of sideswiping a patrol car going in the opposite direction. He glanced in the rearview mirror. The cop was making a U-turn. "Oh, boy."

"What's wro-*a-arch-chch*." Emma's face contorted. By this time, the pains had been too numerable to count.

With the blare of a siren closing in, traffic parted like the Red Sea. Seth's eyes shot back and forth from the road to the mirror. "I'm not stopping, bub," he howled. Slowing down was out of the question. Emma was in too much pain. And if he took his left hand off the wheel to roll down the window and signal the cop, Seth was sure he would lose control of the car as he weaved through downtown traffic. He shot a look at Emma. "God," he winced and bit his tongue. What if they didn't make it to the hospital on time? His eyes reverted to the road. Should he stop and help Emma? Keep going? What? He squinted at the mirror. The cop was a hare's breath from the rear bumper. But the blare of the siren and the bubble gum machine's blue light was just what Seth needed to clear the road ahead.

Nearing the hospital, the cop must have finally put two and two together, because he had backed off a ways. He also must have radioed the hospital, because when Seth buzzed into the Emergency Entrance ramp, horn ablaring, medical personnel were already scrambling out the door and in no time were all over Emma like ants at a picnic.

Leaping out of the car, Seth registered a double take at the cop who was sprinting towards him. "Oh, shoot," Seth winced, knowing that he had broken every traffic regulation on the books and then some. He sniveled with both palms fully extended, "Look, I had no choice."

"Aw, quitcha bellyachin', LaRosa, I got eyes," snickered the cop. He turned out to be the head honcho of the Brighton Police Department. "Jus' that when yah finish up he-ah, I wancha ta come on ovah an' look me up at the station-house. Wancha ta sign yahsef up tah break in my rookies tah the chase."

Seth snorted and dashed off after Emma. Inside, a businesslike nurse wearing a high-collared, starched uniform cut him off and pointed, "The Waiting Room is right over there."

"But..." Seth sputtered.

The nurse pursed her lips as her hands braced her hips. A God-awful scowl screwed up her face. Her black eyes skewered the man. The white cap mounted atop a severely slicked-back bun of black mane elevated and jounced with authority. "I will come and get you after the baby arrives."

His chest swelled up. He could take her on. She was only a peanut compared to him. But an inner voice let Seth know in no uncertain terms that it would be wiser not to tangle with the likes of this harpy. "Oh, for cryin' out loud," he fumed. Slinking off to the Waiting Room, Seth beat his gums. "I never even got one blessed second to kiss Em before they wheeled her down that stupid ol' hallway and through those damned swinging doors marked..." He paused. His face twisted up. "...Delivery Room," he sneered with a wag of the head. As Seth dropped onto a metal folding chair, he harrumphed and eyed the closed door. "Humanity needs delivery from that old witch out there." His eyes rolled.

Moments passed. His body would just not relax. Getting to his feet, Seth started to pace. Poor Em. She was really in tough shape. He scratched his head and plopped down onto a different chair. He looked up at the ceiling and mouthed, "I love you, my sweet Emma, more than anything in the whole world."

In a moment of clarity, Emma found herself in a sterile, colorless room. Shadowy strangers dressed in faded green surgical garb surrounded her. The table that she was lying on was hard and hurt her back. She felt her clothes being stripped off, her wrists being strapped down at her sides, and her legs being strapped to stirrups. "No!" Her voice sounded distant, small, and not her own. She could barely move as a contraction seized her. She barely got over that one when another began to build. What was happening to her? Emma was so frightened. "Seth! Where are you?"

A mask latched onto her face like the jaws of a hound. Emma struggled. A calm voice whispered, "Easy, now." Emma gagged on the stink of ether. "Breathe in…slowly." Things blurred.

When Emma awoke Seth was sitting beside her bed, holding and kissing her hand. Lost in her ebony eyes, he stroked her cheek.

"The baby?" Emma mumbled.

"A boy," Seth beamed. Tears of joy trickled down his cheek.

She smiled and murmured, "Adam."

"He's perfect." Seth leaned over and kissed Emma. A teardrop fell upon her cheek. Her fingertips gingerly picked up the droplet and placed it upon her lips.

Somewhere in the distance, Emma heard sobs, aching sobs that grew louder, more inconsolable. She squinted at Seth. His face… It was fading. The peacefulness within her ruptured. What was happening? Sobbing filled the air. What in the world…?

Shaken from her reverie, the old woman jolted back to the present. Hearing her own feet slogging along the sidewalk, she stopped. "Where the heebeejeebees am I?"

Emma searched her surroundings. The church cemetery. She had walked all this way? Those plaintive wails. Had she just imagined them? Emma listened. "No...there they go again." Her eyes skewed sideways as she turned an ear in the general direction of the sobs. Near those gravestones...behind those evergreen shrubs dripping with icy mist. "Hello?" she called and edged forward. Her heart raced. The heel of a shoe, a woman's shoe, was sticking out from beneath one of the bushes. Fighting the urge to rush in and help, Emma stepped towards the shrubs and called again, "Hello?"

No answer. The sobbing continued, unaffected. As her hand pushed aside the prickly branches, a sparrow took flight. Her hands shielded her face as Emma stepped back. Shaking off the encounter, she stepped up to the evergreen and peered around it. A woman, young, petite, all curled up, and drenched to the skin. She cowered like an animal. Emma caught one eye reflecting fear in the dim light. Honey-colored shoulder-length hair was grimy and matted against the young woman's head. "You poor thing," Emma murmured. "Why on earth are you lying here on this frozen ground?" Seeing the girl's torn blouse and ghastly bruises, she gasped, "What has happened to you?"

No reply.

"Come. Let's get you up." The old lady reached out, but the instant she touched the naked shoulder, the young woman shook her off. "You cannot stay here, dear," Emma pleaded. "You'll catch your death." Her fingers wrapped around the girl's blood-smeared hand. The girl did not pull back.

Grasping the hand, Emma gave a gentle tug. Without warning, the frozen girl fell in a heap against Emma. Speechless, Emma held the wretched human being who wept like a licked child. Rocking back and forth, she whispered, "Shhhh... It's all right. Nobody's going to hurt you any more." Emma's heart broke. What had brought this young woman to a place like this and on such a ghastly night? "Tell me your name, dear."

No reply.

Emma thought for a moment. How on earth was she going to reach this stranger? What should she do? She glanced around the cemetery. There was nobody to help. Mist was turning to rain. There was no time for delay. "My name is Emma LaRosa," she offered quietly. "Please, tell me your name, dear."

"Julie," mumbled the young woman hiding her bruised face in shame. "Sp...Spencer"

"Everything is going to be all right now, Julie," said Emma. "I am here and I will not allow anybody to harm you, I promise. Come on, let's get you up."

Emma had all she could do to get Julie to her feet and hide her horror when she saw additional bruises ripening on the young woman's sodden face and arms. Blood caked in the corners of her swollen mouth. She wore jeans and a navy blue sweater that dangled off one arm. No coat protected Julie against the November elements.

"Who did this?" Emma pressed as she pulled the sweater onto the girl's other arm. "I am going to call the police when I..."

"No! No police," Julie screeched, cutting Emma off. "Please!" She pulled away, her face dead white. "He'll kill me if the police come. I just know it!" Her eyes scoured the gravestones as if an insidious monster known only to herself lurked behind one, intending to do her further harm. Julie looked as if she would bolt at any second.

Emma scanned the cemetery. Nobody was there. Not knowing what to do or say, she decided that the best thing to do was bring the half-naked girl home with her. There would be enough time later on to figure out what should be done about the brute who had done this terrible thing. Right now, Julie had to get warm and dry or she was going to come down with a nasty case of pneumonia. Emma, too.

Taking off her Chesterfield, Emma stuffed Julie's arms into the sleeves. She spied the girl's purse and scooped it up. Snagging it over her shoulder Emma led Julie out of the cemetery. Rain slanted down in the semidarkness. In the distance, a dog barked and there came a whistle and then only the sound of rain that was turning to sleet. Soaked and frozen to the bone, the two women slogged along in and out of diluted streetlight.

The telephone was ringing off the hook as Emma and Julie rounded the front corner of the house. Sliding the key into the lock of the back door, Emma said, "Hold your horses, Margi."

At the kitchen table Emma pulled out a chair and gasped for air. "Here, Julie. Sit."

Julie lowered herself onto the chair. "I can't," she whimpered. "It hurts."

Emma tried to fathom the kind of brutality that caused such pain. The telephone nagged her. Leering at it, she scowled, "For heaven's sake."

"Go," Julie muttered. "Answer your phone."

No sooner had Emma lifted the receiver than her daughter's hysteria spewed forth. "Ma! Where in the world have you been?" Margi demanded.

"Margi…" Emma started.

"I've been going nuts. I've been calling you for hours! Even called next door to old man Johnson. He says he saw you take off hours ago, hot-footin' it towards town. I almost called the cops!"

"Margi, please. I am all right," Emma vehemently interrupted. "Listen, sweetheart, I am all right. Let me do a couple of things right away and I will call you back in twenty minutes."

"But, Ma…" Margi countered.

"I really have to go, Margi," insisted Emma. "I will call you in twenty minutes." Hanging up the phone, she turned her attention back to Julie. "Come on. Let's get you warmed up." Peeling off the waterlogged Chesterfield and letting it drop to the floor, Emma led the shivering girl upstairs to the bathroom and drew a warm bath. She poured in some of her treasured honeysuckle oil, figuring that the aroma and warm water would make Julie feel better. The fragrant steam that billowed in Emma's face made her realize how chilled she was. But taking care of herself would have to wait until after Julie got settled into the warm tub. A dreadful wince drew Emma's attention. Seeing that Julie was having an awful time taking off her blouse, Emma offered, "Here. Let me help you with that."

Julie backed away clutching her blouse to her chest.

"It's alright. I'm not going to hurt you," Emma whispered.

Julie hesitated then loosened her grip on her blouse.

Emma slowly extended her hand. As the tattered blouse dropped, she gasped. Cigarette burns dotted the girl's back. Emma's stomach tightened. "What kind of person mutilates another in such a manner?" she spat.

Julie buried her face in her hands and started to cry. Emma squelched the fury rising within her. This was neither the time nor the place for anger. Support and understanding, not prodding, were of the utmost importance at this moment. The only one who could give Julie what she needed right now was Emma.

"Oh," Julie whined as she lowered herself into the bath water. "It hurts so bad." Her face contorted as if the water was battery acid. "Shhuute…oh…mmm…it really…burns."

Emma pulled the shower curtain, partly to give the girl privacy, but mostly to hide her own revulsion. If only there was a way to make all this suffering disappear. Gathering up the soiled clothing from the floor, she left the bathroom and headed to the bedroom. She grabbed Seth's old sweater off the hook on the closet door and wriggled into it as she hurried to the kitchen. She picked up her filthy, waterlogged Chesterfield and slung it over the back of a chair. Water pooled beneath it on the floor as Emma waited for water in the teapot to heat. Too tired to mop, she stared at the growing puddle until the teapot started to whistle. She took two mugs out of the cupboard and unwrapped two bags of chamomile tea, hooking one on the rim of each mug. She leaned against the kitchen counter and took a deep, quivering breath, trying to shake off the sight of tobacco burns on skin, hoping that she would not have to see such a sight again. She shut off the flame and poured the water into the mugs. After dunking the bags several times, Emma returned to the bathroom with one mug and knocked on the door. "I made some tea. Can I come in?"

No answer.

Emma knocked a little louder. "Are you all right, Julie?"

"Uh-huh," came a muffled voice.

"I made you some tea. Would you like me to bring it in?"

An unsteady "Sure," came from beyond the door.

Opening the door, Emma slowly stepped inside the bathroom, careful not to frighten the girl. Much to the old woman's relief, Julie looked a little more at ease though her hands trembled as she took the mug. Emma stepped over to the linen closet. Taking out a fresh towel, she placed it on the commode. "Here, whenever you're ready, wipe off with this, and here's a nice warm flannel nightgown. Help yourself to the robe hanging on the back of the door. If you think you will be all right for a few minutes, I am going downstairs to call my daughter."

Julie nodded. A faint smile lifted her swelling cheeks.

"You have a nice smile," Emma winked.

Julie quickly turned away.

Closing the bathroom door quietly behind her, Emma shrank against the doorjamb. She had not meant to upset the girl. Why had a simple compliment riled her up so? Was she that unaccustomed to ordinary niceties? "Good Lord, what a nightmare this whole thing is."

Margi answered her phone on the first ring.

"I am truly sorry I was so rude, dear," Emma apologized and took a sip of tea.

"What's going on, Ma?" Margi demanded. "This is not like you at all."

"I found someone…a girl, uhm, young woman named Julie."

"What?" Margi screeched.

"She was huddled under some shrubs in the church cemetery, beaten and half-dressed."

Margi gasped. "Ma. What the heck were you doing way over there?"

Recounting the long walk home and the nerve-wracking experience in the bathroom, Emma asked, "Who could have done such a thing?"

"Call the cops, Ma," Margi spouted. "Right now."

"I can't," Emma winced. "Julie got awfully upset when I suggested that. But I sure wish I could get my hands on the brute who did this."

"Be careful, Ma," warned Margi. "This is the eighties. You never know what kind of sicko is out there. Not only that, whoever did it might be stalking her."

Emma thought for a moment. She had looked around the cemetery several times. "No, dear...not a soul was around. If there had been, I surely would have asked for help. Believe me, I had all I could handle."

"Well, I don't want you going out alone again, hear me, Ma?" Margi said. "I never know what the heck you're gonna get yourself into."

"I guess you are right about that one," chuckled Emma.

"Ma, this ain't no time for jokin'...come on," snapped Margi.

"I know, I know..." Emma glanced up at the ceiling. "Oh, sounds like Julie's out of the tub. The water's draining. I better go."

"I'm comin' over, Ma," said Margi.

"Don't do that, dear," Emma said. "We'll do just fine."

"Listen, Ma. Call me if the least little thing happens, hear me?" Margi demanded.

"I will."

"Be over first thing in the morning," said Margi. There was a pause, then came a low voice, "Love ya, Ma."

"I love you, too, sweetheart," returned Emma. Hanging up the phone, she smiled. Just then the bathroom door creaked and Emma hustled up the stairs.

Julie was standing in the middle of the landing with the robe slung over her arm and her wet hair dripping onto her nightgown. Emma grabbed a towel and while blotting out the moisture, asked, "Would you like to lay down, dear?"

Julie gave a scant nod.

"You can sleep in my daughter's room," said Emma and led the way. "Well, it used to be her room before she got married." Taking the robe, Emma laid it across the foot of the four-poster bed that was always made up in case of unexpected guests, especially grandchildren. She pulled the covers back and the frail young stranger crawled in and instantly fell asleep.

Covering Julie, first with the sheet scattered with blue cornflowers and then the matching comforter, Emma stared at the face that was much too young to know such pain. Tiptoeing to the door, she noiselessly closed it behind her. Her fingers went to her lips, kissing them, then touching the bedroom door the same way she had done when her Margi was growing up.

Throughout the night Emma remained alert. Several times when Julie had cried out in her sleep, Emma went to the door to listen, but all was quiet beyond. As the night wore on, Julie stirred no more, becoming lost within insidious darkness until morning.

CHAPTER 5

*G*etting back to making the bed, Emma picked up the sound of water running in the bathroom and glanced out the bedroom door. Julie was taking a shower. Then, to the old woman's surprise and delight, her ears perceived a small voice humming the Rhapsody. This was the first time she had heard Julie do that. Seth would have loved Julie, especially the way the girl's cheeks balled in rosy apples whenever she smiled. And smiles were coming more often now. How nice to see a little life in the girl's eyes. Emma had to chuckle, thinking about the way Julie buzzes about in the kitchen, wanting to know all the whys and wherefores of cooking. Apparently cooking, holidays, birthdays, and other such things had not been a part of the girl's short life. A warm, supportive family had been virtually nonexistent. But how did a child who lacked any solid base at all grow up to be as polite and sensitive as Julie? Emma began to compare her relationship with Seth to that of Julie and Jim's.

"This bedroom is awesome," Julie gushed.

Emma pressed a hand against her chest and gasped, "Oh, my." She turned and gaped at Julie. "You gave me such a fright!"

A flutter of eyelids sent a silent apology as Julie fluffed the moisture out of her hair with a towel. She was wearing white, skin-tight stretch pants and an oversized peach-colored cable-knit sweater that covered her down to mid-thigh. She was barefoot. "Wish I had a room like this." Taking a heavy breath, Julie skimmed her fingers across the surface of the antique mahogany dresser. There wasn't so much as a scratch anywhere. She counted herself lucky that the old lady had come along when she did. Julie bit her lip, knowing for sure that she would have been out on the street. Her life had certainly hit an all time low. There was no doubt in her mind that she didn't have a job, since she refused to go back to work at the restaurant for fear that Jim might hunt her down there. She had not even called to quit. Right now, that maniac had no idea where she was and Julie wanted to keep it that way. Margi and Emma had insisted that she allow her bruises to fade before looking for another job.

"You will have the things you want if you keep working at it." Emma said while giving the girl's shoulder a reassuring pat. "Put all those dreadful things behind you and keep hope in your heart. And don't stop trying no matter what. Time has a way of working things out, just wait and see."

What are the chances, Julie felt like saying. While rolling her eyes, she spotted a black and white photograph ensconced in an oval wood-grain frame embellished with three-dimensional roses. She stepped over to it and asked, "How long were you and Seth married?"

Emma finished smoothing out the chenille bedspread then patted it fondly. "Fifty-two years last spring."

"Gosh, you look so incredibly young."

Incredibly young, Emma thought. With hands on her hips, she straightened her back and stretched. Glancing at Julie who was closely inspecting the staged setting that lent dignity renown to most photographs taken in those days, Emma said, "I was seventeen."

"Your husband was very handsome," Julie mused.

Emma stepped next to Julie. How straight and tall Seth stood in that superbly-cut black tuxedo embellished by a white rose on a bed of baby's breath on the lapel. Her chest tightened. "Seth was thirty.

Funny, I still feel like that young bride, but when I look in the mirror, there's an old lady gawking back at me."

Julie shook her head and mumbled, "I can't imagine being married that long. Shoot. I never had one relationship last even a year. I don't think I'll ever share fifty-two years with a man."

"The right one will come along, dear," Emma said while patting Julie's arm, "when you least expect it."

Julie gave a lame smile and followed the old lady out of the bedroom, "How did you two meet?"

"Seth noticed me with my sisters at a park that was near my parents home in Cambridge. I saw him there several times and thought he looked nice." Emma flushed. The vision of their beginning still enchanted her. "Seth and his parents were immigrants—so were my parents. But I was born in this country. Well, Seth told his father that he liked me and asked him to talk to my father about courting me. Somehow, his father tracked down my family and my father agreed. So the next Sunday afternoon, our parents visited in the kitchen of my parents home and kept a good eye on Seth and me sitting in the parlor."

Stars filled Julie's eyes. "Did you go out a long time?"

"Oh, my goodness, we did not go out on dates," Emma chuckled. "No, no, no. Being alone was not allowed, not until after marriage. That was the way of the old country."

"Wow," said Julie. "And that was okay with you?"

"I did not know any other way," Emma shrugged. "But, it was fine with me though. Seth was such a perfect gentleman…and I liked him. He turned out to be a wonderful husband and father."

"You didn't love him when you got married?" Julie asked incredulously.

Emma felt an all-consuming heaviness in the pit of her stomach. When did their love start? At first sight? Had her heart fluttered ever so slightly at that moment? Or when she saw him nervously waiting for her at the altar, looking so handsome? Or the wedding night when he had been so gentle? "Love came in good time," Emma sighed. "We became friends first."

"You miss him very much," Julie observed.

"Yes, dear, I do. He is here…" The old woman checked her thoughts as her hand covered her chest. "…uhm…in my heart all the time." Sadness veiled her face. If only she could tell Julie how Seth returned to this room whenever she got sad and blessed her with visions of better times that made her strong again. She even heard his voice, although no words were ever spoken.

Seeing her old friend so silent and withdrawn, Julie placed a hand on Emma's shoulder. "I think it's good that you have a room like this to go to. Wish I had that luxury when I feel bad."

Emma cleared her throat. "This will be our first Thanksgiving apart in fifty-two years. Seth always lent a hand."

Spying a gold chain lying on top of the bureau, Julie went to pick it up. "I thought men of his generation didn't help out around the house," she mused while fingering the heavy links. She turned it over and over, trying to figure out what kind of jewelry it was.

"Oh, that's true of men even now—and even some women—but Seth was different." Emma glowed. "He made it a point to get in my way, pretending to be helpful…and he was, most of the time. But there were times that he pestered the daylights out of me when I had too much to do. The little devil would sneak up behind me and grab me around the waist and lift me up and twirl me around until I got dizzy. But when I was pregnant, Seth knew better than to do that. So instead, he would nudge in between me and whatever I was doing and grab my hand. Well, off we would go in a tizzy, waltzing around with a spoon held high in the air, dripping all over the place. He was such an imp." Emma could still see Seth in his chef's apron and his white shirt with rolled up sleeves. "I always pretended to be irritated and impatient, but really, I loved it. And you know what? Seth knew that I did."

Julie tried to imagine what it must feel like to dance around a dumb old kitchen like that. How positively romantic. How very sexy. "Wish I could find someone like that."

Emma patted the young woman on the back. "You will, dear. You will."

Holding up the gold chain, Julie twisted up her face and asked. "What is this?"

"Oh, that's Seth's watch fob chain," Emma said as she took it from Julie. "He liked to wear gray, pin-striped suits. This end clipped inside one pocket of the suit and a pocket watch was attached to this other end. The chain draped over to a fob pocket where the time-piece was placed. A trinket of some sort was attached and dangled outside the fob pocket. The chain was mostly for decoration, but it also helped when taking the watch out of the pocket. Here, let me show you."

Emma went to the closet where she selected one of Seth's suits. As she drew it near his essence wafted up into her nostrils. She held it close to her bosom and sensed that he was near. She smiled. Draping the suit across the bed, Emma attached his pocket watch onto one end of the chain and the other to the inside of one of the breast pockets. She wedged the watch into the fob pocket, letting the chain drape between the two pockets. She stepped back and with a cock of her head, admired what she had done.

Julie clasped her hands over her heart. "Oh, I like that very much. You don't see anything like that anymore." She ran her fingers across the chain. "Where's the trinket?"

Emma shrugged and studied the chain. "This chain once belonged to a priest. A cross was attached to it, but it was awfully big and heavy. Seth had a smaller version made and had it attached to the chain." She fished through the pockets. "Here it is. I'll have to get Adam to reattach it to the chain."

Julie studied the cross. "It's beautiful."

"Hmph," Emma thought aloud. "I can't imagine what happened to that big cross."

"It's a shame that men don't dress up like that anymore." Julie pursed her lips.

"Mmm, and women too," Emma nodded. Detaching the chain, she tenderly arranged it in a wide circle on top of the bureau and toyed with the miniature cross until both were perfectly displayed. "Sure was nice when people got all guzzied up just to take a walk." She stepped back to the bed and picked up the suit. She smiled at it and breathed in his essence one more time before hanging it up in the closet. She cleared her throat. "Listen, Julie, I want you to call your mother today. Ask her to come for Thanksgiving dinner, will you?"

Something inside Julie flip-flopped. "How come? You don't even know Mom."

"Well, I would like to have her here anyway," Emma insisted. She pinched Julie's cheek. "She must be a nice person to have a sweet daughter like you."

Julie flushed. "But all your family will be here," she stammered. "Mom won't know anybody."

"My family gets along with everyone. Besides, the men always settle down in the parlor after dinner and watch the football games while we women clean up. After that we just sit around the dining room table and gab. We can all get to know each other then. Don't you worry. I just know your mother will fit right in."

Though Emma was very convincing, Julie's mind raced. Her relationship with her mother had always been distant for some unknown reason, yet there had never been any real problem between them. It was just that Mom never opened up. Julie rubbed her palms on her hips. "Maybe it would do Mom some good to get out of the house on a holiday—for a change." She bit the inside of her lip. "And I've never experienced a traditional Thanksgiving before." She sighed. "Be kinda nice to find out what that's like." Suddenly she slapped her hip and puffed, "It's worth a try. I'll give her a call tonight."

Emma was pleased.

At six-thirty that evening, nervous fingers dialed the phone. A small, hushed voice filtered through the line, "Hello?"

Julie hesitated.

Another "Hello?"

"Hi, Mom." Julie cleared her throat. "How's it goin'?"

"Why...Julie...how are you?" gasped her mother. "It's been a long time. Where are you? You okay?"

"Yeah, Mom. I'm living with a friend of mine—Emma. She, uhm, we want you to come for Thanksgiving dinner." Julie blurted out. The other end of the line went silent. Julie panicked. She had worked herself up all day over all this to the point that now she wanted her mother to come for Thanksgiving more than anything else. "Mom? You there?"

"Well, I don't know, Julie." There was another pause. "I'm not good company," her mother stammered. "And Emma doesn't even know me."

"I told her you'd say that," Julie chuckled. "Come on, Mom. You don't have anything going anyway. And you'll just love Emma. Okay?"

"Well, let me think about it," said her mother. "So, tell me, what have you been up to? I haven't heard from you in such a long time."

Avoiding the subject of Jim and not having a job, Julie said, "Nothin' much. Emma's keeping me in line. Sorry I haven't called. I...I guess I just, uhm, just got wrapped up in some stuff. How 'bout you?"

"Oh, same old, same old," her mother sighed. "Working every day. That's about it."

"I really want you to come, Mom," Julie whined.

"All right, all right," winced the mother, giving into her child. "I'll be there. Let me get a pencil and paper, so I'll have the directions."

❦   ❦   ❦

Julie rolled over and squinted at the clock radio. 6:10 AM. The illuminated numbers hovered over the night table like the sun over the horizon just after dawn. She heard activity downstairs, the same activity that nudged her from sleep each morning. Sleeping-in just didn't happen in this house. But that was okay, since lately she had been going to bed with the chickens anyway. Yet Julie noticed that she felt stronger and healthier with this early-to bed, early-to-rise lifestyle. It gave her more time to learn stuff from Emma. Suddenly it sank into Julie's brain. "Today's Thanksgiving!" She gasped. "Emma's already in the kitchen." Tossing off the covers, she yanked her jeans on and wriggled into a sweatshirt. It was incredible how tirelessly that dear old lady worked at making everything perfect for others, never once thinking of herself. It was simple as that. "Wish I was that way," she huffed. Pulling on socks decorated with pilgrims, Julie was amazed that she even had such thoughts. How quickly things had changed. Not too long ago, she was living with Jim Martin, resigned to living under a dark cloud of fear. God knows how long that would have gone on. She felt as if she had no other alternative, what with Jim moving in and taking over her whole life. How was she supposed to get him out of her home? She thought her world had come to an end that night that he had pummeled her senseless. Thank God, he had passed out on the bed, so she was able to get away. Julie shuddered. How incredible that Emma had come along when she did. Opening up her arms and heart, that old woman had gathered Julie up as if she was her own. Now the young woman was actually trying to figure out what kind of person she wanted to be. What kind of life did she want? What does life really mean? Yes, thanks to Emma's positive influence, Julie was looking forward to a future brighter than she had ever imagined. The dark sinister cloud had lifted and Julie would do anything to keep that dark cloud from blanketing her life ever again.

Julie shuddered. *Where is Jim?* Was he out there somewhere, hunting her down? She glanced at the window and almost went over there to peek out and see if Jim Martin was lurking down in the yard. Casting that impulse aside, Julie rushed out of the bedroom, hurtled down the stairs, and skidded into the kitchen glowing with the early morning light and reeking with the aroma of onion, celery, and sage. Emma was straining to lift a huge, uncooked turkey off the table. "Oh, Julie," she puffed. "You are just in time. Open the oven door, will you dear?"

"I can't get over how big that turkey is," Julie exclaimed.

"Ol' Tom's a beauty, that's for sure." As Emma slid the bird into the oven, she held her breath. She gasped for air as she stood up then picked up her yellow gingham apron and wiped her hands with great gusto while Julie closed the oven door. Then the old lady squatted in front of the oven dial and squinted like a surgeon over a delicate operation while her old fingers performed precise maneuvers to set the oven temperature just so.

Julie took in every last detail, her fingernails clicking together with anticipation. She wanted to cook like that. She wanted to be just like Emma. Itching to get started, she asked, "What can I do?"

"Oh, my goodness, dear, let me see," Emma said while brushing away beads of sweat bejeweling her brow. Once again she wiped her hands on her apron. "Well, the turkey should take a good seven hours, I suspect." She winked at Julie then stepped over to the counter. Jabbing an index finger into one of several loaves of rising bread dough, she said, "Let's stuff the bread! Grab that one, and let's bring these to the table." As she lifted a loaf off the counter, the cup that she had her morning coffee in crashed to the floor.

"Oh, no, the handle fell off," Julie cried. With a worried looked on her face, Julie picked up the handle and the bowl of the cup and offered both pieces to Emma.

"Oh, don't worry about it, dear, Seth will..." She bit her tongue. Her hands froze in mid air. Alas, her brain finished the thought. *Seth will fix it.* Heartbroken, Emma gently took the pieces and put them on the counter, butting them up against the backsplash where there was no chance of further damage. She swallowed hard then picked up a loaf of rising dough and brought it to the table. "Bring that other one over here, will you, dear?" Using a butcher knife, she split the tops of the loaves lengthwise and down halfway. She carefully separated the sides while giving directions. "Spoon equal amounts of that onion and bacon mixture that I chopped up while you were still in dreamland."

Julie flushed, flattered to be entrusted to the task. When she had finished, she glanced dubiously at Emma.

"Now pull the sides up over the mixture and pinch them together like this." As Emma demonstrated all was quiet. Seconds later, her hands flew up into the air as she crowed triumphantly, "Tah dah! Now we will let the dough rise one more time and then we will bake them. When they are done, we will brush melted butter all over them."

Julie grinned from ear to ear. Her face shimmered with delight as her head scrunched down into her shoulders. Never in her entire life had she ever had so much fun and learned so much at the same time. For days the two women had worked on this project and now Julie thirsted for more. "What now, Em?"

"I know it's a bit early, but we should see to the dining room. That way, if we're missing anything, we'll have time to make a call to someone for them to bring it. I already know I don't have enough chairs. Why don't you call Margi and ask her to bring a few." But as Julie started for the telephone, Emma peered at the clock. "Wait one moment, dear. It's too early. Margi's not up and about yet."

In the dining room the two women pulled apart the oval table and then Emma took three table leaves out of the coat closet near the front door. Placing the leaves in the center of the table, she then opened one of the drawers of the massive hutch of early 40s vintage and took out a starched ecru tablecloth that she had crocheted herself many years ago. As wrinkled ivory hands, twisted slightly at thickened arthritic finger joints, flattened out the folds across the table, Julie pondered, *How many people did those old hands comfort and love over the years?* That was the beauty that only age and devotion wrought. Emma's face was thoroughly engrossed in the task at hand, determined that everything must be just so. It seemed as though Emma didn't have a worry in the world. Drinking up every action and every word, Julie could not help wondering, *how does a person get that way?* Determined with all her being to pattern herself after Emma, Julie started to hum.

"I do so love when you do that," Emma sighed.

Julie squinted at Emma. "Huh?"

Emma smiled. "You were humming, dear."

"Oh…" A silly grin sheeted over the girl's face. Her pearly teeth clenched the tip of her tongue.

"Please, continue. You have such a soft lithesome voice. It fits Paganini."

Lithesome? Julie was amazed. She had never dreamed that she would ever be connected to such a word. "You are going to play that song today, right? I know Mom will love it."

"If we can get the guys to turn down their football game for a couple of minutes," Emma chuckled. She placed two silver candelabras on the table and said, "Go get that flower arrangement we bought yesterday." She joined in the humming while centering a scalloped orange and brown doily on the table. Julie set the flowers in the middle of it. They both stepped back to scrutinize the creation that reflected in the immense wall mirror. Emma jammed her hands into her hips and gave a decisive nod. "Not bad. Not bad at all."

"Wow," was all Julie could say.

The morning sped by. Julie's head spun watching the old lady scurrying from here to there, from there to everywhere. Emma knew exactly what to do, when to do it, and where everything should go. She was an old hand at this and very patient with the young interloper. Around noontime, Julie changed into a maroon pantsuit and matching pumps that Margi had bought for her, special for this occasion. And for good luck, Emma let her wear a gold chain with a small crucifix that she had worn on her wedding day over fifty-two years ago. When Julie came out of the bedroom, Margi, Evan, and their children were just arriving, bringing extra chairs with them.

"Hey, take a gander at the kid, Ev," blustered Margi while elbowing her husband.

Julie was beside herself with excitement. Not knowing what to say, she trailed Evan into the living room where he went directly to the marble fireplace. Julie listened and watched intently as he explained in a voice, which still echoed an English ancestry, all the intricate details of how to make the perfect fire. He was a calm, logical sort with a personality that aimed to please. Rarely did he speak ill of anyone or use colorful language. A heavily beeswaxed handlebar mustache drew attention away from his balding pate and bulging midriff attributed to daily doses of Merlot. Both kept folks from taking the man too seriously. He carried himself with the self-assurance and pride that came from a successful career, a beautiful home, and adoration for and from Margi and his children. Weekends found him doting over his wife after she had smacked headlong into another one of her self-made catastrophes or at the office with one or two of the kids zooming around his desk while he tried to catch up on a busy week. It was easy to see why Margi bragged so much about falling head over heels with him the first second she laid eyes on him.

A cheerful fire glowed in the hearth as diners began to arrive. The place became chaotic. Everyone spoke at the same time. From the corner of her eye, Emma watched Julie pace from one window to another, nervously awaiting her Mom's arrival.

The doorbell rang. As the girl darted to open it, a sense of relief came over Emma. *At last.* The old woman had been worrying that Julie's mother might shy away at the last moment. She peeked around the corner. There was Julie's Mom, slender and pale, smiling in her own reserved sort of way. A slight tremor stifled her voice as she said, "Hi, Julie. I've missed you."

Julie threw her arms around her mother. From the way they hugged, it was obvious how much they meant to each other. "Missed you, too, Mom. Come in. You gotta meet Emma." Grabbing her mother's hand, Julie tugged her along. "Oh, here you are, Em," she gushed. "This is my mother, Elizabeth Spencer."

Elizabeth hesitated. She half-expected to see a person of more Julie's age. She was caught off guard when the old woman embraced her then kissed her cheek as if they had know one another all their lives.

When a faint smile erupted on her mother's stoic face, Julie grinned. Mom wasn't one to smile much. Hopefully that was going to change, starting today.

"Take your mother around and introduce her, dear," Emma spouted as she rushed off to the kitchen.

Acknowledging her mother's befuddled stance, Julie shrugged her shoulders and said, "Let me take your jacket."

Slipping off her tailored blue jacket, Elizabeth smoothed out her white silk blouse accentuated by a cameo locket that harbored an ancient picture of Julie's father. She looked down at her black slacks and jammed her hands into her hips. "Look at these pants. That darned cat needs a good brushing."

Julie broke into a broad grin. "You look great, Mom." Linking arms, she dragged her mother from one person to the next until Elizabeth had been more than adequately introduced and hugged. The LaRosa family had an earthy style that Julie absolutely adored. And what a big family it was. The girl had never seen so many people all related to each other and all seated at the same table. Her senses vibrated with all the jabbering and laughter.

Emma scurried in and out of the dining room, producing more and more food for the already overstocked table. At the insistent urgings of the crowd, Emma finally sat down. But her bottom had hardly settled on the chair when she started to get up again. "Oh my, I forgot the cranberry sauce."

"Ma! Sit down," everybody chimed. Laughter broke out, for more than enough cranberries had already been placed on the table. Still, this was all a part of the ritual. Without it the day would not be complete.

Joining hands, the group bowed their heads in prayer. Each person took a turn expressing what he or she was thankful for during this past year. Emma started. "I am thankful to God and Seth for giving me such a wonderful family and also these new friends here today."

Julie felt her mother's hand twitch. She looked at her, but her face betrayed no emotion. Suddenly the room went quiet and Julie discovered it was her turn. "Oh. Uhm. I'm thankful for Emma. And Mom." Her heart pounded. "And all you guys."

Muted laughter filled the air and then once again all was quiet. The clock on the mantle ticked. Julie glanced at her mother. Everyone waited. Elizabeth cleared her throat. She gazed at her daughter. Moisture glazed her eyes. "I'm thankful for Julie."

"Dig in," howled Margi and pandemonium broke loose as platters of food sped around the table. Afterwards, gorged men retired to the living room to watch the football games as the women cleared dirty dishes from the table and took them into the kitchen. Evan tried to help. Instantly henpecked into submission, he retreated to the parlor. Energetic children scurried between the living room, dining room, and kitchen until Margi shooed them all outside.

Still the kitchen was overrun with women. With wide-eyed excitement Julie declared, "There's still too many people in this kitchen! I can't hear myself think!"

The other women purposefully ignored her observation, all but Margi who went out of her way to bump into Julie. "Oh, sorry."

Julie squinted at Margi. Detecting a squelched chortle and shoulders shaking with silent laughter, Julie immediately concluded that the bump had been no accident. "Yeah, right, Margi," she guffawed while jamming her hands into her hips.

Margi feigned innocence. "Whaddaya mean, kid?"

When the dishes were done, the ladies reassembled around the dining room table and yakked about jobs, shopping, child rearing, recent events, whatnot. "So, what do you do for work, Elizabeth?" Emma asked.

"I'm a nurse at City Hospital."

"Oh my," said Emma.

"You live near there?" Margi asked.

Elizabeth nodded. "Just a stone's throw away. I walk to work most days." Opening up a little, she revealed trivial things about herself. It was more than Julie had ever heard her mother speak.

Margi turned to Julie and asked, "You decide what you're gonna do for work, kid?"

Julie fidgeted as her mother shot her a confused look. "I'm not sure," Julie stammered. "I know I've got to start looking sooner or later, but I just don't know what kind of job I want." She scratched her head and felt a scar. Quickly she folded her hands. "I do know I'm not into waiting on tables anymore."

"Evan!" Margi hollered, Everybody jumped. When he came running, she barked, "You got a job for the kid at St. Anne's, don'cha?" She elbowed Elizabeth and said, "My Ev's an administrator over there at St. Anne's Reg."

Elizabeth smiled awkwardly.

Evan nodded and twisted the ends of his mustache.

"Gee, that sounds okay," said Julie with a bounce of her head. "But I'm afraid I don't have much experience in anything."

"Big whoop," phshawed Margi. "Lots of things need doin' in hospitals. Besides, I seen ya workin' with Ma. You're friendly and smart and catch on quick…hey, you'd like an environment like that. Trust me."

A bit embarrassed from all that flamboyant flattery, Julie said, "Well, uhm, sure. Thanks." Still, Julie was unable to avoid Elizabeth's curious eyes, so she took her mother by the hand and said, "Come on, Mom. Let me show you my room."

"My room," Margi postured.

Julie shrugged and said, "I stand corrected."

Upstairs, after hearing about her daughter's ordeal at the hands of Jim Martin, Elizabeth said, "You should move back with me. You can take your time looking for a job. And go to college if you wish."

"I don't know, Mom. I kinda like the idea of working at St. Anne's. Besides, I don't have a car, so I couldn't get there from your place."

Elizabeth glanced down at her hands. "We could make a fresh start of it…"

Julie rubbed her forehead. Living here felt so good. She really hated the thought of going back to Mom's gloomy apartment. Besides, what about Em? What would happen to her dear old friend if Julie left?

Rolling her eyes across the ceiling, Elizabeth cleared her throat. "Maybe it's time to give up that old place. We've been living there much too long—years," she muttered. Looking directly at Julie, Elizabeth seemed to beg. "We could look for a place between my work and St. Anne's."

"You know, Mom," Julie stuttered, "I kinda like that idea. We can start all over again."

Elizabeth gave a sigh of relief. "I have some savings. We could buy some new things. How 'bout that?"

There was a look of hopefulness in her mother's eyes that Julie had never seen before. "You mean it, Mom?" Julie asked.

Elizabeth nodded.

Julie's brows lifted to her hairline. "Wow, Mom!" She jumped up and locked her mother in a bear hug. Unprepared for such a show of emotion, Elizabeth slowly encircled her arms around her child. Oh, how good it felt to hold her daughter. Backing away, Julie noticed a tear trickle from her mother's eye. Wiping it away, she said, "Geez, I'm glad I took Emma's advice and invited you for Thanksgiving dinner."

A broad grin broke on Elizabeth's face. "I'm glad too."

CHAPTER 6

On the second Saturday in December, Emma awoke to the season's first snowfall. While coffee brewed, she pulled back the curtains and watched a multitude of flakes scurry here and there, seeking the perfect spot to set down upon the white blanket that cloaked the barren landscape. *Nobody will brave weather like this just to drop in on an old fuddy-duddy like me,* Emma thought.

Heaving a sigh, she went to pour herself a cup of coffee. How empty the old house felt now that Julie had moved out. She had become very attached to the girl and felt the loss of not having her around anymore. Emma stared into the coffee cup. Her sad eyes reflected back at her. "It's good that Julie and Elizabeth have patched things up." Their apartment was not far away, and Julie, now working at St. Anne's Hospital, called quite often, sometimes several times a day, with news of small discoveries or successes that never failed to warm the old woman's heart. Lingering over the empty cup, Emma mused, "Maybe being alone won't be all that bad." The past few weeks had been very busy, what with Thanksgiving and all. The hubbub had done her some good, though it did tucker her out some. "Well," she puffed, "today is as good as any to start sorting through Seth's belongings." She got to her feet and as she placed her empty cup in the sink, a thought crossed her mind. *Perhaps Seth will come back…and be with me…for just a little while…maybe.*

So it was with mixed emotions that Emma set about her day. After making the bed, she emptied the closet, folding the clothing into stacks on the bedspread. Her children had already taken what they wanted and the rest would go to charity. She stared at the stacks. How she hated to part with any of these things. Emma tsked. "What good will it do to keep any of these things, Seth? That won't bring you back, will it?"

An eerie feeling rippled across her flesh. Emma froze. Was Seth behind her? She spun around. Her eyes fell upon his button-down V-neck sweater hanging from a hook inside the closet door. The bedraggled blue-gray knit had been his favorite. He wore it around the house whenever there was the slightest chill to the air. He would have hit the ceiling if she even thought about getting rid of it. Suddenly the night that Emma had brought Julie home flooded back. After settling the girl into the bath, Emma had warmed herself with that sweater. Emma stood there, staring at it. Slowly her hand reached for it. Unhooking the sweater as if it was some sort of religious relic, she held it against her face. The smell of Seth clung to every nub of yarn. It toyed with her senses as she buffed her cheek with the sweater. Her eyes closed. Clearly she could see Seth sitting at the kitchen table, his arms folded across his chest, dozing off after a hectic day, and he was wearing this sweater. Oh how she hated to wake him. Seth looked so peaceful.

Drawing the sweater away from her face, Emma searched the nubby yarn, her thumbnails separating the stitches as if somewhere in its depths she would surely find her dear lost Seth. She bit the inside of her cheek. Oh, if only he was in there. If only she could pluck him out and hold him tightly to her bosom. Never would she let him go again. *How cruel time is. It has a way of aging young lovers, then separating them with death. But is it cruelty or benevolence that time has left behind the scent of Seth?* Emma sighed. Unable to part with the old sweater, she hung it back on the hook. Her fingertips caressed the nubby yarn once again. She took a step back. Seeing the sweater there gave her a sense of solace and strength. She touched it once more then closed the closet door and walked away.

Sorting through his bureau drawers, Emma took out the hordes of matches and toothpicks that Seth had pilfered from restaurants and vacation destinations. "Momento," he had insisted. There were golf balls, tees, baseballs, pens, chocolate mints, and programs from shows they had attended through the years. After filling an entire coffee canister with the matches that he had taken from Julio's alone, Emma chuckled. "You certainly are quite a pack rat, Seth."

"Ma! Ma? Where are you?" Margi bellowed.

"Oh my," Emma gasped. The coffee canister crashed on the floor as her hand covered her mouth. The back door slammed. Her eyes skimmed over the matches strewn across the floor then fled to the bedroom door. "Margi?" she breathed. Relief sheeted over her. Companionship would lighten this dreadful chore.

"Ma?"

"I am in the bedroom Margi," Emma called.

As Margi pranced into the bedroom and planted a kiss on her mother's cheek, she bubbled, "Look what the cat dragged in!"

"Well, well, well. Julie! What a nice surprise," Emma sang out and rushed over to her young friend. Almost in tears, the old woman said, "Oh…I am so pleased to see you, Julie. And Elizabeth! This is a surprise."

Julie and Emma kissed and squeezed each other like long lost souls. "I missed you too, Em," gushed Julie. She gave her old friend another bear hug before releasing her to greet Elizabeth with the same gusto. Embarrassment flushed Elizabeth who was still unaccustomed to such physical contact.

"Whattaya doin', Ma?" Margi clucked while eyeing the piles of her father's clothing on the bed. She gawked at the bureau where the top drawer was pulled out and men's socks and underwear were dangling over the edge. Suits were strewn over an old chair or had fallen onto the floor. A gray one that had a gold watch fob chain dangling out of one pocket was hanging in the doorway. "What's all these matches doin' on the floor, Ma?"

As Emma stooped to pick up the matches, a twinge of sadness returned to her. "I thought today might be a good day to sort through your father's things. I must admit though, it has become quite a chore."

"Here, Em, let me get those matches," said Julie.

"Well then, let's get this business over and done with," Margi pressed. "Lemme scoot up the attic and get some boxes to put all this stuff in." Margi could not bear this type of activity especially because it made Ma depressed again. Ma had perked up during the Thanksgiving holiday, but she was the type that tried to hide her sadness from the world. "I talked to Adam this morning. Him an' Janice an' Elliot will be along shortly. An' they're bringin' those gigundous muffins from the bakery, so we hafta make shur we got lots o' coffee!"

Watching Margi dash out of the bedroom, Julie giggled. "She's too much to take all at once." She put the canister full of matches on top of the bureau then turned around to see Emma taking suits off the chair. "Let me help you with those, Em." *How awful to have to do this after fifty-two years with a man. It's sad, yet…if only I could know that kind of sadness.*

"Well, thank you dear," said the old woman. Laying a suit on the bed, she commanded, "Here Elizabeth, sit."

Elizabeth dropped into the overstuffed chair. It wasn't fair. That old woman had fifty-two years with her man. Fifty-two. Elizabeth had only a few precious months with Peter. There should have been more—a few of Emma and Seth's years. And look at all those clothes. There was nothing like that after Peter left, nothing for Elizabeth to decide whether to hold on to or let go. Where did that old woman find the strength to make such decisions? Elizabeth put her head back and closed her eyes. The weariness went beyond the physical.

Confusion blurred her mind as something swelled up in her throat, choking her, as if wanting to be set free.

The raucous in the attic above them was quite distracting and even more so when it ceased. Moments later Margi catapulted into the bedroom and tossed several boxes onto the bed. Immediately she began to jam clothing into them. As she lifted up one pile of under-shirts, she suddenly became quite subdued. All eyes fell upon her when she wheezed, "Oh…geez…here's Papa's wallet."

Emma swallowed hard. Margi missed her father so much. They had been very close. In many ways they were like two peas in a pod. "Go ahead, Margi. It's okay."

Gingerly, Margi picked up the weathered black leather wallet. She turned it over several times. Years of riding in the back pocket of Seth's pants had compacted and rounded the wallet, and the edges were devoid of color. "Know what, Ma? It's like Papa's still with me," Margi muttered. She took a deep breath and gulped. "I swear he kisses me goodnight every night like when I was a little girl. I see his face, soft and smooth, like after he shaved, and I touch it, and he smiles at me. He listens to my day and I hear his voice whispering in my ear, telling me that he'll always love me—and you too, Ma. When I wake up, he's gone."

Emma nodded. Softly clearing her throat, she murmured, "I know sweetheart. We keep your father alive in our hearts that way. He will always be with us."

Margi cautiously opened the wallet, exposing the pictures that Seth had placed there, as well as his license, social security card, and the family picture taken at his and Emma's fiftieth anniversary cele-bration. Remembering the day it was taken, Margi smiled. Little did she or anyone else know that there was so little time left to spend with him. Well, she had known it in her gut, but no way was she going to admit to it. But now, looking at that picture, it was quite apparent how frail Seth was at that party.

Behind the anniversary picture was a faded picture of Emma and Seth taken on their wedding day over fifty-two years ago, a copy of the one on the wall. Margi's baby picture was there along with those of her siblings. Tears welled and flooded over Margi's eyelids.

Putting her arm around her daughter, Emma said, "You can have those pictures if you wish—and the wallet. I know your Papa would have wanted you to have them."

With the sleeve of her sweatshirt, Margi swiped away her tears. The cuff was now a handkerchief. She managed a smile as she separated the pictures, placing the baby pictures side by side. While she pried the old wedding picture off the fiftieth anniversary picture, Elizabeth and Julie stepped over to study the array. Unexpectedly, a yellowed piece of paper dropped onto the bed. Margi shot a questioning glance at Emma, who was just as startled. Picking it up, Margi gingerly unfolded it. The fragile paper split in half. Holding the pieces together Margi handed it to Emma. "It's addressed to you, Ma."

"Me?" Emma gasped. Margi nodded. Taking the pieces, Emma looked down at the words, My Precious Emma."

"Ma," said Margi. "Read it to us."

Emma swallowed hard. Her voice cracked as she read,

My Precious Emma,

Ever since that day in the park when I first saw your lovely face, you have meant everything to me. Having you to love changed my life forever. You gave me more joy than any man could ever hope to have. I want you to go to the attic where I have hidden a boot box. It is beneath the insulation near the entrance to the front garret. Think of me. I will always be thinking of you.

Yours for all eternity,

Seth

The room was silent. The man had spoken from far away, from beyond the grave. Emma desperately tried to compose herself. When she spoke, her voice sounded small and fragile. "Well…I think…" She took in a deep breath and peered at Margi. "Let's go get it."

As her old friend led the way out of the room, Julie spoke up, "Mom and I'll wait in the kitchen. We'll make the coffee." Getting no reaction from her preoccupied friends, Julie knew that this was a private time for Emma to share with her daughter. Whatever they discovered in the attic should remain between the two of them.

Entering the cold, musty attic, Margi trumpeted, "Can you imagine Papa doing such a thing? Wonder what's in that box?"

"We will soon find out, dear," replied Emma. She heard the storm raging outside the house. The rafters groaned. Her entire body trembled with anticipation. Was her beloved Seth reaching out to her again? Loving her again? Maybe he was hiding there in the attic. Maybe Seth was not really gone at all. She should have expected this sort of thing from him. But as Emma and Margi rummaged about the attic, reality set in. Seth was not there.

"Look, Ma. Over there," Margi pointed. The pink insulation at the front of the house had a slight rise to it, unlike the rest beneath the garret. Clearing cobwebs out of her path, she made her way to it and burrowed into the insulation. "Ma," she howled. "I got it!"

Emma gawked at the boot box that Margi held high in the air and then at Margi. Her eyes seemed to question her daughter. Margi pursed her lips as she let the boot box sag. She shrugged and offered it to her mother. Emma stared at it. She clenched her fists then dried her palms on her housecoat. Reaching for the box, her hands trembled. She lifted the lid. Beneath was an assortment of pictures, trinkets, and other paraphernalia. Selecting a photograph, Emma held it up to the light and squinted. It was a picture of a shaggy dog named Brandy that had been the family pet back when the children were growing up. Margi, who was five years old at the time, had both arms wrapped tightly around Brandy's neck. The crooked-toothed animal good-naturedly tolerated the stranglehold.

"Will you look at that," exclaimed Margi. "You couldn't ask for a better dog. Hey. What's this?" She held up a red tie and an armband with the printed words, Remember! Justice Crucified August 23, 1927. And inside the box were lapel pins bearing the likeness and names, Sacco and Vanzetti.

A tremor shot through Emma. She swallowed hard. Getting to her feet, she winced, "Your father had a flair for all kinds of strange things. Come on, dear. Let's take this downstairs. We'll take a look at what else is inside at the kitchen table." As Margi scampered on ahead, Emma stuffed the tie, armband, and lapel pins behind a pile of old books. Putting the lid back on the box, she clutched the box close to her breast, cradling it as if it was a newborn infant while descending the attic stairs.

"Guess this shouldn't surprise us, huh Ma?" Margi commented.

Emma nodded, though this strange chain of events bewildered her. Why in the world did Seth leave a boot box? And what if there was something else in it that might knock her for a loop? She could not imagine why he would do a thing like that. Not Seth.

Adam, Janice, and Elliot were taking off their snowy jackets as Emma and Margi came into the kitchen. The youngster rushed to his grandmother's arms. Tossing off his hat, his curly tresses sprang to life like Jumping Jacks. "Hi, Nana," he panted. "I made two baskets! That means I scored *four points!*"

As the young basketball player in a green Celtics sweat outfit snuggled up under his grandmother's arm, she was forced to loosen her grip on her precious cargo. It fell onto the table. Forcing pleasantness out of her confused state, Emma said, "Why, Elliot, that is wonderful. Did you win the game?"

The boy's round face turned down. "Nah…" he stammered as one foot raked back and forth on the floor. "But that's okay." Suddenly Elliot started leaping about. "'Cause I still scored *four points!* My bestest *ever!*" His hand flew high in the air and he gave his Grandmother a high five.

A tap tap came on the back door and it creaked open. In strolled Evan and the kids. "Surprise," they whooped. "We knew you'd be home!"

"What happened?" Emma laughed. "I thought company was out of the question on such a snowy day."

"Shows you a thing or two, Ma," said Margi with her chin jutting forth.

Rachel, Margi's twelve-year-old daughter, came up to the table while shaking the snow off her jacket. Twin ponytails exaggerated the roundness of her rosy cheeks. Her eyes widened into nuggets of black coal as she pointed to the boot box on the table. "Hey, Nana. What's that?"

"Grandpa left this for us. We were just about to see what's in it. Why don't all of you pull up chairs," Emma motioned. "Julie and Elizabeth were so sweet to make the coffee. Adam, Janice, bring those goodies over here. Come on now help yourself. Sit…eat!"

Margi could no longer contain her curiosity. "Ma! Get over here. Right here, sit next to me." Her hand slapped the chair beside her. Shoving the lid off the cardboard box, she ogled the things inside then slid the box in front of her mother.

Hush came over the kitchen as Emma sagged onto the chair. For a moment she stared at the array. Her heart melted. A boutonniere, preserved in wax paper. The white rose had turned to rust-brown and the white ribbon was now ocher. As she took out the boutonniere, Emma said, "Your father wore this on our wedding day." She choked back the tears, not wanting her children to see her cry.

She held up a shriveled cigar. The band wrapped around it proclaimed, "It's a boy!" Two more of the same were in the box and one that read, "It's a girl!"

Emma peered into the boot box. Trying to decide what to bring out next, she spied a yellow rose, part of a bouquet that Seth had given her when she had miscarried. How much he must have hurt from the same things that had hurt her. But Seth had always hid his pain, trying always to be strong for her sake. She wished she could hold him again and comfort him in her arms.

Adam scooped up a yellowed document folded in threes. As he flattened out the folds, his eyes grew wide and his mouth dropped. "Look at this," he gasped and passed the papers around the table. "A stock certificate! This is worth a bundle. I thought Papa had detailed everything in his will. He must have forgotten about it."

Emma shrugged. "Take it and find out if it's any good, will you Adam?"

"I'll look into it first thing Monday morning," Adam said. He was an attorney in Newton, making big bucks since graduating from Harvard. Dressed in a larger version of the green outfit his son was wearing, Adam was not one to forget his roots.

Elliot held an old news clipping. "Who's this, Nana?"

"Bartolomeo Vanzetti," Adam spoke up. His eyes locked with Emma's. She sensed something in his eyes. What was it? She dared not ask, for something inside warned her against it. She looked away and quickly took a fishhook out of the box. A green plaid ribbon was caught on its barb. The inquisitive children closed in.

"Holy Moses! That's my hair ribbon," Margi squealed and snatched it up. Several strands of dark curls were entwined in the mess. "I wore this the day Papa took me fishing. I got so upset 'cuz he always took the boys fishing and not me. I complained that he was not being fair and never wanted to do anything with me. I teased and teased until finally he broke down and took me fishing, just the two of us…and no boys. Big whoop…I never asked to do that again. What a disaster."

"What happened?" Janice asked.

"We were fishing with bamboo fishing poles. Papa was great at casting. The line always dropped exactly where he wanted it, but I just couldn't get the hang of it. I tried and tried. He kept watching, telling me what to do, and trying to encourage me to do it by myself. Finally, he stuck the end of his pole into the ground and came over to give me a hand. Over and over again, he showed me how to cast that line." Margi sucked in air. She was on a roll. "Well I tried, but I just couldn't do it. So Papa came up behind me and wrapped his arms around me. He positioned my hands on the pole and held them there while we swung back and forth until the line hit the water. I was so happy 'cuz it actually landed in the water. But it wasn't where Papa wanted it—no, no, no! He insisted that we had to try it again. Boy, what a mistake that was! This time I was bound and determined to show him that I knew what I was doing. The line went out of control and the hook got stuck in the plaid ribbon of one of my ponytails. My hair got all knotted up in it and look! You can still see some hair in it! Well, I started to cry because it was pulling my hair and when it wouldn't come loose, Papa got so frantic that he cut it out with his army knife. It was always our little secret. Ma never knew. He even convinced Ma that he had taken me to the hairdressers on the way home so I could have the pleasure of my hair being cut in the latest do. Hey, everyone was wearing short hair, right Ma?" Margi roared with laughter. Tears streamed down her face.

The children screeched with delight. Emma tsked a couple of times as the other adults joined in the hilarity.

"In the meantime, a bass took Papa's bait," Margi continued, "and pulled his pole out of the ground. Well, off goes his pole, this way and that, right out into the very middle of that pond," screeched Margi as her hand clutched her side. Uncontrolled laughter reverberated throughout the kitchen as everyone watched her writhe in gleeful pain.

"So, what did he do?" Julie asked, wishing she had a father like that.

"Dove into the water and swam after it, what else?" Margi blared.

"Of course," Adam sang out, "that's exactly what Papa would have done. *No* fish was gonna steal *his* rod! Imagine the indignity!"

"Did he catch the fish, Mommy?" Rachel asked as she picked up the ribbon and held it close to her face. Her expression became intent while examining the barb that refused to release the impaled ribbon. The other children clustered around her as she pulled at one of the dark hairs that still refused to budge.

"He sure did. A bass. *And* a nasty cold. I never *ever* even suggested that we should go fishing again after that," concluded Margi. Grinning from ear to ear, she got up to get herself more coffee. She raised the pot, gesturing to others, who wanted more?

Thoroughly enjoying the reactions to the contents of the boot box, Emma said, "Well, let's see what else is in here."

Adam chuckled when she took out a picture of a basketball team that Seth had coached when Adam, Timothy, and Samuel were children. He reached for it and after studying it for a moment, turned the picture around for everyone to see. Pointing to a lanky kid with red hair who was noticeably taller than all the other team members, he said, "See this tall guy here? Papa got this kid in the second round of the draft. It was Papa's first year at coaching basketball. He couldn't figure out for the life of him why the other coaches didn't scoff up this tall guy right away. Red should have been a real asset to any team. Papa thought he struck gold when he got him. First day of practice, he set up a maze of plastic cones and had all the guys practice dribbling through them. When it came to Red's turn, Papa found out in one big hurry exactly why the other coaches had shunned the kid. Red started off, hitting the first cone with one big, clumsy foot and totally missing going around the second. At the third cone he fell head over heels right flat on his face. He picked himself up and continued knocking down cones, ricocheting the ball off others…you name it. When he was done, only the second cone was left standing. The guys were rolling on the gym floor, laughing so hard. Papa just patted the kid on the back and said, 'Good job.' Then he turned away and blew his nose. Remember those big white handkerchiefs? Well, I'm positive that he was just hiding his laughter behind his. Anyway, he turned back to the guys, so cool, calm and collected, and asked, 'S'pose cavemen blew their noses?' Oh, my God. The place went nuts."

And Emma's guests followed suit. Elliot laughed so hard that he was forced to run to the bathroom while clutching his crotch.

"Papa got caught with that one, but the next season he got the shortest kid in the draft." As Adam continued, admiration for his father was written all over his face. "That kid shined like a new penny. He got right in there and stole the ball right out from under the other player's noses. And got them to foul him too. He scored the most points of anybody that year."

As the box emptied, stories continued, allowing each loved one to come to grips with the kind of a man Seth was. His power, humor, and imagination lived on. Emma found peace in the process, knowing that he had left this boot box for his family as a message. Yes, Seth wished that everyone would get on with life and do their best in spite of human imperfections. He wanted them to remember that he loved them all very much.

That night Emma knelt at the bedroom window and gazed up at the stars that twinkled in the December sky. "Thank you, Seth," she whispered, "for your priceless gift."

And his spirit filled her.

CHAPTER 7

❀

*E*lizabeth twitched in and out of sleep. The dismal cloud that she had been living under for so many years had been shredded to pieces by a simple boot box. Suddenly, she wanted no more part of the past. But how unfair she had been to Julie all this time. Elizabeth threw off the blankets and got out of bed. "I've got to tell Julie. I have to explain…make it up to her…somehow. But what if she doesn't understand? What if she can't forgive me?" Slipping into her robe, she went to the kitchen and made herself a cup of tea. Her head was pounding. How could she have stubbornly held on to Peter's memory for so long? So self-absorbed in heartache, she had failed to notice the child who had her father's eyes grow into a beautiful young woman. "Oh Julie," she murmured. "I'm so sorry."

Dropping onto the recliner, Elizabeth sipped her tea and stared out the living room window. Sure, she had provided for Julie, but she had never been a true mother. No mother could be that heedless of her child's existence. Elizabeth thought about her own mother who lived in Arizona. She had never been close to Mother like Emma and Margi. Perhaps Mother resented her not only for having a better standard of living during childhood but also for the increased educational and career opportunities that had come along for women following Mother's generation. Mother was forced to put her interests aside and take on the thankless job of housewife in a small out-of-the-way Massachusetts town, which must have been terribly stifling. Family economics had played a role in her leaving school after the eighth grade, but the decisive factor was that in those times, women were not thought to need any further education. Too bad too, because Mother was an excellent student. Elizabeth had seen several withered report cards. Yet it seemed that Mother had always put as many obstacles in Elizabeth's path as she could. And spending any kind of quality time with Mother was never a valid consideration, for she professed that children were lucky that they had been given life in the first place and a roof over their heads in the second. Not only that, Mother strictly adhered to the axiom that children should be seen and not heard. No, her family and the world had to pay for Mother's lot in life.

The sun was coming up, and Elizabeth was still agonizing over the right words to explain how much Peter had meant to her and how his loss had turned her into a recluse. She raised herself off the recliner and tromped to the kitchen to make coffee. How very old she felt. It wasn't long before Elizabeth heard Julie. She sat down at the table and waited, sipping on a cup of coffee but not tasting any of it. How many times had she thought and rethought her words during the long restless night? Suddenly Julie was there, kissing her cheek and saying, "Good morning, Mom."

Julie set about making herself a bowl of cereal, pouring milk and sprinkling blueberries on top. She wolfed down a spoonful before sitting down.

A tremor shot through Elizabeth. Now, with daylight streaming into the kitchen, the only thing to do was just to let the words happen. She heaved. "Julie. I must talk to you."

Julie stiffened. Glancing at her mother who looked pale and agitated, she asked. "Everything okay? You look like you didn't get much sleep."

"Yesterday, when we visited Emma..." Elizabeth's voice was choppy. Her eyes focused on her coffee cup, avoiding her daughter's.

"I realized how unfair I've been." Her heart thumped. She had never spoken of Peter to anybody. It had always been too painful to even think about him, let alone to speak of him. But now she wanted to. Now, she must.

Julie patted her mother's hand. "Don't worry about it. We're okay now. That's all that matters."

Elizabeth grabbed her daughter's wrist and exploded. "No, Julie. It's not all right! You have to let me tell you this! It's been pent up inside of me for much too long. I've got to get it out. Now!"

Julie pushed her half-eaten bowl of cereal away. This was not like Mom at all. Mom never raised her voice. Whatever she had to say must be dreadful. "Mom, it's all right. Go ahead. Tell me."

"Your father's name?" Elizabeth quivered, for surely Julie was going to detest her.

"Peter Spencer," Julie whispered.

Elizabeth got to her feet and took her empty coffee cup to the sink. It hovered above the porcelain as she choked back the dread. "No. Blair was his last name."

Julie's brow wrinkled. "Blair?" The coffee cup crashed into the sink as Julie thought back to the time she had asked about her father. The question had visibly shaken Mom and then when tears had welled, Julie had become frightened. All her mother said was that Peter had died in Vietnam before Julie was born. Julie had never asked about him after that.

Elizabeth came back to the table and stood behind Julie. "Your father and I were not married. We were planning to marry after he graduated from B. U., but his reserve unit was activated. He went to Vietnam…" Elizabeth's voice trailed off. Only the sound of her body collapsing onto a chair interrupted the silence. Her fists balled up in front of her lips. Once again her heart broke as visions of Peter leaving played in her head. Oh, when would she stop thinking about him? She fought back tears. Moments passed. She took in a deep breath and plowed on. "We talked about going to Canada. Other guys who didn't believe in the war went there to avoid the draft. No matter what his personal feelings were, Peter thought that if he ran off to Canada it would disgrace his family. He said he'd be copping out because his father had fought in World War II and his grandfather had fought in World War I. So he convinced me to wait and get married when he got back. We thought he'd be gone no more than a year." Elizabeth chewed her knuckles. Her eyes rolled away the moisture welling there. "But two weeks after he got to Vietnam, his platoon was ambushed while on patrol in the jungle near the Cambodian border. A few guys made it out, but not your father. Nobody knows for sure what happened and since there was no proof that he was actually dead, he was listed as missing in action." Tears streamed down her stricken face. "I relive all of it over and over again, as if it happened only yesterday."

Seeing her mother in so much distress and wringing her hands, Julie cupped her hands over hers. As tears overflowed the girl's eyes, the atrocities of the Vietnam War visited yet another generation. "It's okay, Mom," Julie whispered. "How terrible that Peter never came home."

Elizabeth withdrew a hand and swiped away tears. "There isn't even a grave…a place to go…grass to kneel on to talk with him." Her hand dropped on top of Julie's, the warm moisture dampened both. "I loved him so much. I refused to believe that he was not coming back. I still see him, over and over again, walking away from me the way he did that morning. He turned and waved to me and with that silly little grin of his, he called, 'Don't worry, Bethie. Nothin's gonna to happen to this bod'. I'll cherish you in my heart, my little morning eyes, forever.'"

Her voice was so soft and real that Julie felt as if she was standing at her mother's side, reliving the scene at that very moment so long ago.

"His words have echoed in my head every day since he left," Elizabeth continued. "I was convinced that somehow, someway he was going to come back to me. I prayed to God to please, please, bring my Peter back. I would wait forever. But he didn't come back… No… Peter never came back to me." Elizabeth fell sobbing onto the table, releasing the pain and sorrow that she had carried for so many uncertain years.

As Julie stroked her mother's shoulders, Elizabeth looked into her eyes. "I didn't know I was pregnant with you until after he came up missing. Your father never knew about you." Searching her daughter's young face, Elizabeth sought out reaction—now that the truth had been laid bare.

Julie was silent, though she was becoming more agitated with every passing moment. Finally Julie got up from her chair. She paced from the stove, then to the sink, back to the stove, then to the refrigerator, back to the stove, to the kitchen counter. She leaned against it and crossed her arms.

"You're angry," Elizabeth muttered knowing full well how much she deserved her daughter's wrath.

"Kinda," Julie sputtered. Her eyes rolled then zeroed in on her mother's. "What about his family? Why didn't they step in and help you out?"

Elizabeth hung her head and picked at her fingernails. "They lived in Virginia. I never met them, but when I heard that Peter was missing, I called them. But it seemed like they wanted no part of me. I was hurt by their coldness, so I never called back. They didn't know about you either. Out-of-wedlock pregnancy in those days was a social disease."

"What about your mother and father?"

Elizabeth turned away. *God, Mother would have hit the ceiling if she had known.* "They moved to Arizona before I met Peter because my father had lung cancer. He died just after you were born. My mother and I were never close, so when I did talk to her, it was easy to cover up things."

Julie stood there in silence. The families could not be blamed if they did not know. Julie ran her hand through her hair. *Geez, no wonder Mom was always so far away while I was growing up. Nobody was ever there for her. And being so withdrawn all these years, it's obvious how much she loved Peter.* Julie gnawed the inside of her cheek. "My birth certificate?"

"Here," Elizabeth muttered handing Julie the document.

Julie took it and zeroed in on the space marked Father. Unknown was typed in capital letters. The feeling of being a nonentity washed over her.

"I meant to tell you," Elizabeth muttered, "but there was never the right time. Then you moved out, so…"

Julie cringed, for it dawned on her that her own seemingly disinterested actions did not help matters one bit. By not asking questions or pushing Mom a little harder, she had cheated the both of them of the love and support that only they could give each other. "Gee Mom. I should've never moved out. That was the worst thing for both of us."

"But I never did one blessed thing to stop you," cried Elizabeth. "Even that's my fault."

Julie shook her head. "It's mine, too. I was mistaken when I thought you just didn't care. I should've known better." She came back and sat down beside Elizabeth. "Well," she sighed and gripped her mother's hand, "we can't change the past."

"I'm sorry about everything," Elizabeth moaned. "It's just that…yesterday? When Emma opened that boot box full of her family's memories? It really hit me hard. I saw how all of them were able to put Seth's death into perspective…just by talking about him. Remember when Margi said that she talks to him every night? And he kisses her in her sleep? I think that I was so entrenched in my dark world that I didn't let Peter in to comfort me like that. Was he there all the time and I just didn't see him?"

"Emma sure brightened up from the memories," Julie mused.

Elizabeth nodded. "She didn't get sadder thinking about Seth the way I do when I think about Peter. I always avoid thinking about him, but subconsciously I guess I do anyway. Whenever Emma said that's how we keep our loved ones alive in our hearts as we get on with life, it really floored me."

"Gosh," Julie winced as she thought back to yesterday. "The whole family was there for each other, laughing and remembering Seth. That was kinda neat."

"Yeah," Elizabeth said whimsically. "I didn't feel much mourning going on there. It was almost like, well, like a celebration. If I had that kind of support, maybe our lives would have been different...much different."

"Too bad your mother lives in Arizona," sympathized Julie. "Why didn't you move out there?"

"I was convinced that someday your father was coming back and when he did I was going to be in the same place so he could find me right away...but I guess that if he hasn't come back by now, he never will..." Elizabeth broke off. She stood up and dragged her chair to the refrigerator. Climbing up, she opened the cupboard above the refrigerator and took out a miniature cedar chest. "A furniture company gave these to all the girls in my graduating class," she said as she got down. Placing the miniature chest on the table, Elizabeth took out a tarnished ring. "Your father made this for me out of buss wire. It's a peace ring."

Julie rolled the gnarled and pitted piece of wire over and over in the palm of her hand. She examined the way it had been soldered together and imagined how much love her father had for Mom to do such a thing. She imagined her father actually touching it and now by touching it herself she hoped that somehow she would magically know the man. She slid the ring onto her pinkie finger and could almost feel his love. She smiled at her mother whose face was blanketed with resignation. A kind of peace was growing there, a look that Julie had never seen. Sadness mixed with elation when it came to her that Mom was finally putting her lover's absence behind her, ready to face the future.

"I think that all this time, Peter has been in heaven, looking down at you and me," said Julie. "I know that he's very proud of the way you loved him and waited for him for such a long time. He still loves you, Mom, I really feel that way, and he always will. I'm also sure that now he wants you to get on with your life. Maybe he met up with Seth in heaven and they talk about us all the time. Wouldn't that be neat?"

Elizabeth smiled. "That would be something." Reaching into the pocket of her sweater, she produced his class picture and another picture of the two of them taken at the observation area at the top of the Prudential Building in Boston. She flattened the pictures, yellowed and defaced by time, on the table. How many times had she fallen asleep looking at them and found them the next morning mangled in the sheets?

"My father was very handsome," Julie said ruefully. If only saying that would magically bring him back. How nice it would be to talk to him, if only for just a little while. She fingered the picture, trying to comprehend the man who had always been missing from her life. She could not help but see her resemblance in him. She had his cocoa brown eyes and the same tilt of the head. And that silly grin. Grief suddenly overwhelmed Julie. Peter would have made the most perfect father, if circumstances had been different. If only he had survived, her life and Mom's would have been so very, very different.

"You look like him in many ways," said Elizabeth. "That comforted me more than you know. I would have died for sure if I didn't have you. If only I had the sense to let you know that. I should've been a better mother, but I was so wrapped up in my own sorrow that I failed to give you the love and support you needed. You were such a good little girl. You deserved so much better than me. And now look at you, a beautiful young woman. I just don't want you to throw away your life the way that I did."

"I won't, Mom," Julie whispered.

Elizabeth scrutinized her daughter. "I know the things that Jim did were terrible, but find a way to put it all behind you. He controls your life if you give him any more thought. There's a good man out there…I just know it. He's waiting for you. Your whole life is ahead of you. Don't waste it drowning in self-pity or fear the way I did. I was so, so wrong."

Julie nodded, but she wanted to tell Elizabeth that Jim was different. He was not the loving, gentle individual that Peter was. And Jim was still around. Julie could feel it in her gut that she was going to cross paths with that creep again. Aarch, she didn't want to think about him any more.

Gazing at the picture of the two young lovers, Julie said, "You looked so radiant Mom. I hope you can look that way from now on."

Elizabeth leaned over and looked at the picture. "We made a very handsome couple. And we were quite fashionable for the times, too. See those bell bottom, hip huggers? And those wide, black patent leather belts fastened by huge pewter buckles?"

"I like those green, funky flowers plastered all over his shirt," said Julie. Mom was wearing a handkerchief-sleeve blouse splashed with lavender flowers and elasticized under the bosom, exposing a bare midriff. "Mom," Julie chuckled. "I can see your belly button!"

Elizabeth grinned sheepishly.

"I should've been there for you," Julie mumbled.

"Listen, none of this was your fault, understand?" Elizabeth demanded.

"We both made mistakes, Mom," said Julie.

"But all that's over," insisted Elizabeth. "Right?"

Julie nodded. "We're going to be happy from now on. We can do it."

Elizabeth threw her arms around her daughter, relieved that Julie did not hold any grudges about the past. "Yes we have each other. And our dear friend Emma and her wonderful family. From now on,

I vow to do everything in my power to make a better life for the both of us."

Julie glanced at her watch, "Oh!" She jumped to her feet. "I gotta get to work!" She grabbed her jacket and asked, "What are you up to today?"

Elizabeth thought for a moment. She was not quite finished with the past. "I'm going into town. I should be home before you."

"Don't forget, we're going to Emma's for ice cream tonight," Julie said. Her tongue lapped her lips. "Banana splits!"

"I'll pick up the bananas on the way home," laughed Elizabeth.

"Can't wait," Julie called as the door closed.

Elizabeth pictured a sumptuous array of sundae items on Emma's kitchen counter. "Better watch out, there Bethie. The way you eat at our old friend's house, you're gonna weigh a ton before you know it."

Julie raced back through the kitchen and into her bedroom. "Forgot my keys." As she returned she panted, "Emma told me that Bostonians eat more ice cream than any other people in the whole country."

"I believe it," Elizabeth chuckled. "That Emma. She can find the simplest excuses to get people together."

Extending a hand towards the illuminated Express to Skywalk button, Elizabeth hesitated. Her hand trembled uncontrollably. How many years had gone by since she last stood on this spot? The express elevator doors slid open. Her hand dropped. She stood there, peering inside the gaping chasm. Was she sure it was the right thing to do? A sinking feeling came over her. If she went up there, it would mean the end of Peter forever. She rolled her eyes. Should she or shouldn't she? The doors began to close. Suddenly Elizabeth bolted into the elevator. She just could not go on any longer living in the dreamless stupor Peter left behind.

Elizabeth pressed the top button and the car rocketed upward fifty floors. Alone, she sped towards the observation area, her weight compressing against her feet until she was unable to lift either one of them. There was no going back now. Her ears popped. Twice. And then again. The sensations seemed to liberate her from the darkness within her soul and reminded her that she was still alive. From here on out her life was going to change.

Disclosing the truth to Julie had given Elizabeth the strength to finally accept that Peter was not coming back. It cleared the way to sort out her relationship with him and the impact it had on her life—and their daughter's life. So for the first time since that dreadful day when she had learned that Peter was missing in action, she was ready to face his memory. Emma had made all this possible. Single-handedly, that old woman had transformed Elizabeth's life from bleak emptiness to the promise of better days, today and tomorrow. Julie had come back to Elizabeth—because of Emma. Somehow the old woman had to have known how lonely life had been without Julie. And she didn't even know Elizabeth at the time. Mothers and daughters should be together. That's why Emma had hatched out her covert scheme for Thanksgiving. And because of that boot box, Elizabeth had come to the realization that grieving empowered loved ones to accept loss and go on living. This journey today was a sort of boot box, a way to sift through the times Elizabeth had spent with Peter, times she might have forgotten, but mostly, times she had resisted in remembering because losing Peter had been much too painful. The elevator door slid open—and so did memory.

Blinking out the sunlight that streamed in through wall-to-wall windows, she stepped into the observation area. The splendor of Massachusetts in winter, framed by the snow-capped mountains of New Hampshire and an endless sky of cerulean, lay before her. Boston had changed drastically since the last time she had come here with Peter. Back then the only structure competing with the Pru's height was the old John Hancock Building and that was not nearly as tall. Now, a new Hancock Tower of reflective glass dwarfed the old and added to the innumerable skyscrapers that dominated the skyline. From this height Commonwealth Ave. resembled a toy village. Cars, the size of thumbnails, scooted about the busy city streets where people were mere dots that bespeckled the sidewalks.

Wandering along the Cambridge-side windows, Elizabeth recognized the Charles River and the Hatch Shell. And the ancient Longfellow Bridge with its salt-and-pepper towers of stone. An MBTA train was slithering across it, heading towards the Charles Street Station. "Oh," she gasped. "MIT..." A smile lifted her lips. She pointed to a grassy spot next to the river. "Peter came into my life there."

"You talking to me?" grumbled a longhaired security guard while teetering on a chair braced against the wall. His index finger held up the visor of his cap.

"Oh...no..." Elizabeth covered her mouth, surprised that she had spoken out loud. "I'm sorry. Guess I was talking to myself."

The guard shrugged it off. His mouth rounded into a gaping yawn and finished with several smacks of the lips. He then pulled his cap down over his eyes and resumed his siesta.

Elizabeth quickly put distance between her and the security guard, just in case she unwittingly spouted off again. She spotted Fenway Park, then Quincy. She slowed. Following the shoreline eastward, she murmured, "Castle Island." She and Peter had picnicked there one hot summer's day. While listening to the Red Sox lose another game, they had carelessly fallen asleep and later awakened to unpleasant sunburns.

A shadow crossed her face. Elizabeth looked up at a 747 that was on final approach to Logan Airport. How often had she and Peter gawked at the underbellies of other aircraft that had descended over the harbor entrance while sailing eastward to Cohasset, Scituate, or Plymouth? Twenty years had gone by since then. On this winter day no sailboats plied the water, for the windy December temperatures had created the kind of chop that discouraged most fair-weather sailors. Near the World Trade Center, tugboats were nudging a mammoth cargo ship into a dock to unload foreign automobiles. Next to the Aquarium, small sailboats that were used in frostbite races tugged at their moorings. Their masts swung bare above booms covered with blue tarp. The port had changed quite a bit, coming alive with renewal projects that enhanced access to the shoreline.

Elizabeth loved Boston Harbor, even in its dirty disarray of the 60s. She remembered the brown water with litter floating on it, washing listlessly against decaying pilings. Funny, she could still smell that dirty salt water. Things were different now. What a pleasure to sit on the benches or on the seawall behind the Aquarium and watch planes take off over a modernizing harbor.

Settling on the window ledge, Elizabeth took a cleansing breath and raised her face to the warm sunshine. In this same spot back in the 60s, a stranger had taken the picture of her and Peter—the one she had shown to Julie this morning. Glancing down at her hands folded upon her lap, she stared at the peace ring that Peter had made, a heartbreaking substitute for a wedding band. From a senseless stupor of loss and pain, her soul awoke and the memory of Peter began to live in her mind. It was a warm, spring Saturday in the late 60s. She had been jogging along the Charles River in Cambridge when in front of her near MIT, Vietnam protesters blocked the sidewalk, raucously expressing opposition to the war. Across the street, supporters of the United States involvement in that small Southeast Asian country were just as rowdy. Noticing that the gathering was becoming volatile, Elizabeth opted to avoid the noisy confrontation, so a safe distance away, she had thrown her backpack onto a grassy spot near the sun drenched Charles and sat down. Hugging her knees, she squinted at the Prudential Building looming on the horizon on the opposite shore. Still new to the skyline, it was a wonder to behold. Ever since someone had told her that the view from the observation deck was spectacular, Elizabeth had designs about going up there some day.

Stretching out her legs, she picked at blades of grass. Tearing them in half, she tossed them one by one into the water while listening to bubble gum rock on her transistor radio. Beyond, a sailboat drifted lazily with a bikini clad sun worshipper sprawled upon the bow. A pair of ducks guided a brood of seven along water's edge, guarding their safety while searching for food in the shallow water. When a dragonfly hovered then lit on her sneaker, she studied its psychedelic blue and green wings.

"What a drag. There's no escapin' Nam."

The insect flitted off and Elizabeth glanced up. Her hand shaded her eyes against the sun's glare. A stranger was standing there with his hands on his hips. Off one arm a light jacket looped. His shirtsleeves were rolled up to his elbows, exposing sun-darkened forearms. Elizabeth squinted for a clearer look. Sunbeams picked up the amber brindled in his cocoa eyes as the breeze toyed with his honey-colored hair. Her heart skipped a beat. Gazing into those eyes for the rest of her life would be no huge chore. As his hand reached out to her, his mellow voice sounded like music. "I'm Peter Blair. Mind if I hang out a while?"

Elizabeth glanced at his outstretched hand for a moment then pretended to check out the surroundings. Gesturing to the ground beside her, she stretched like a cat and said, "Shur. Why not? Nice to share this bodacious day with somebody." But there was no way for her to ignore his silly grin as he squatted next to her. She felt her face redden. Her blood flowed through her like liquid fire.

"Saw you turn back from the protest." His head swung over his shoulder. "Hey, check it out. It's turning into a shoving match."

"Shiish," Elizabeth winced. "I don't want anything to do with that kind of stuff."

"You're not taking sides?" Peter asked as sirens whined in the distance.

"There's good and bad on both sides I guess," said Elizabeth. "Thing is, I really don't like guys getting wiped out in Nam. Sure wish that would stop. They're too young."

"I can relate to that," Peter agreed. "I'm in the reserves. The way the government's activating everyone these days, I might get forced to the line, though I figure I'm safe 'cuz I'm a student at B.U. and they usually don't take us college kids."

Elizabeth sighed. How many nice guys like this one came back from Nam in body bags? By now the sirens and other commotion had made it impossible to carry on a conversation. She continued to throw grass blades into the sparkling water. A sculling team rowed past. Usually she could hear the crew captain marking cadence, but today the noise made that impossible and even seemed to be a problem for the rowers, too. Swiping away pieces of dirty blond hair that the breeze tossed in her face, Elizabeth felt Peter's eyes. She glanced at him.

"You have the most gorgeous eyes I've ever seen," he hollered.

Elizabeth quickly looked away. Her skin tingled with excitement. Nobody had ever told her that. Why, considering her pale skin and dirty blond hair, her eyes were much too dark of a brown. She thought she looked totally weird. If only she had her father's blue eyes, then she might think that she was at least a little bit attractive. But then again, this guy Peter had a way of making her feel like the most beautiful woman in the world.

"Uh…um…" he stammered as the noise abated. His movements were harried and clumsy. "You haven't told me your name you know."

Amused by his childlike nervousness, she lay back on the fragrant carpet of green and closed her eyes to the springtime rays. He liked her too. "Elizabeth. Elizabeth Spencer."

Propped on his elbow, Peter chewed on a blade of grass while studying her every detail. "Elizabeth. Perfect name for a love goddess."

"Huh?" Elizabeth shot a look at him as though he was nuts. She started to giggle. He was so silly, so handsome.

Ignoring her reaction, he said, "Haven't seen you around here before, Bethie."

Peter spoke her name in a way she had never heard it spoken before and something stirred inside her. She was drawn to him like gravity during a fall. She felt warm, wonderful, and special, just like the sunshine and fresh air that whispered across the water after a long harsh winter.

Peace finally returned. Stuffing her backpack behind her head, Elizabeth listened to the rhythm of the water lapping upon the shore, accompanied by crickets. Both harmonized for the gulls that circled overhead in thermals as though part of a giant mobile.

"I just moved into my own place, not far from here," said Elizabeth. "My parents moved to Arizona 'cause my Dad's sick. Lung cancer. The doctors say that the dry climate might do him some good. I couldn't go 'cause I'm in training at City Hospital." As her mind conjured up the last time she saw her father, she felt a lump in her throat. His body was so thin and frail that his clothes hooked on his shoulder bones, making him look like a wind-ravaged scarecrow. His eyes were dull and his once-rounded jowls were mere outlines of bone beneath pallid skin. She detested cigarettes. She did not expect to ever see her father again.

After a while, the cops had disbanded all the protesters and left the area. Elizabeth started to get up. Peter sprung to his feet and offered her his hand. "Mind if I tag along?"

Elizabeth smiled and took his hand. How strange it would be to have company, but it would be terribly disappointing if Peter left. "Shur," she said.

Nearing the ancient Longfellow Bridge, she pointed. "That bridge is known as the salt and pepper bridge."

"Come on…" Peter laughed.

"Really," she insisted. "See those four support towers? Tell me what they look like."

Peter stopped and squinted at the bridge where a seagull coasted down and perched upon one of the granite towers. "Salt and pepper shakers! Cool!"

Elizabeth giggled. His laughter blended with hers, which was a rarity in itself. She grabbed his hand and dragged him onward. How wonderful all of this was. As they passed beneath the tower where the gull had landed, she looked up. An opaque eye stared down at them. She pointed and Peter looked up and they both laughed and the gull flew away.

Meandering along the esplanade, the afternoon faded and a short time later, thunder exploded. Totally engrossed in each other, they had failed to notice the approaching storm. A sudden torrent of rain and lightning bolts forced them to scurry to the Hatch Shell for shelter. Drenched to the skin, they acted like giddy school kids. Peter took his handkerchief from his pocket and dabbed the rain from her face. As she gazed into his eyes, an incredible fullness swelled within her until she thought she was going to explode. Blood pulsed through her veins as if before now, none had ever been there. His fingers laced through hers and pulled her close. She fit so perfectly in his arms. And oh...how right it felt. The moment his lips met hers, she fell in love forever. Life would never have meaning without Peter.

They spent the following days and weeks together, idolizing each other. It seemed as if there had never been one single moment that they had not known one another. They felt comfortable together and were able to speak about anything on their minds. During the long Fourth of July weekend, Peter chartered a forty-foot sailboat. He was a skilled yachtsman, having sailed most of his life off Chesapeake Bay with his father who had been a Navy man all his life. Two college chums came along as Peter and Elizabeth set sail for Plymouth. Before they left, he braided her hair that billowed across her face. "Good sailors don't let their hair get caught in the rigging," he teased as he tied it off with a string he found below deck. Teaching Elizabeth to sail, Peter boasted that she was the quickest learner he had ever seen. She was at home on the ocean and loved the wind whispering in the full sails after the rumbling motor had been shut off. Peter became exasperated when Elizabeth untethered her hair and flounced her head side to side.

Much like the great humpback whale that hovered near the boat, the wind, waves, and sun set Elizabeth free. She twirled round and around like the mammal, unhurried, sinuous, whimsical. One time it stopped its game and a small beady eye fixed upon her for what seemed like an eternity. She laughed with glee. Then the humpback continued to cavort, though from time to time it paused on its back and flapped its fin as if waving to her. And Elizabeth returned the gesture.

Docking near the Mayflower, Elizabeth and Peter dangled their feet off the afterdeck while watching fireworks illuminate Plymouth Harbor the night of the Fourth. Under a million winking stars, Elizabeth filled her lungs with salty air while snuggling with Peter inside a double sleeping bag on the bow. The others bunked below. The constant sweep of the lighthouse beam overhead and hypnotic motion of the waves beneath them lulled away all care. Only endless words of love rustled the crystalline silence until dawn slowly brightened the pale darkness and a blazing orb perforated the horizon.

On Sunday they sailed through the misty morning out of Plymouth Harbor headed for Boston, meeting with a moderate chop that was driven by winds off the open Atlantic. Peter tethered himself to both sides of the helm and as the bow pounded the waves, he looked like he was riding a wild bronco. Elizabeth had taken a picture of him. It was one of those that had gotten mangled between the sheets throughout the years.

An hour later the wind and seas had changed and they sailed downwind, wing on wing. Mist turned into a gentle shower, but the sailors refused to consider any form of rain gear. It was much too warm for that. When their souvenir tee shirts adhered to their skin, sending purple, yellow, and green dye streaming down their legs they laughed. Peter pulled Elizabeth to him, saying, "Come here my little purple people-eater." She clung to him and he murmured, "I'm hung up on you, Bethie. I need you in my life, now and forever."

Smiling up at Peter, Elizabeth whispered, "You're the best thing that ever happened to me."

As they rounded Minot's Light, off Cohasset, the sun came out from behind the clouds and cast a shimmering trail upon the surface that, along with three dolphins leaping in unison through the waves, led the way into Boston harbor. They followed returning vessels of all sizes and description and passed ships that motored out with cargoes of tourists all eager to behold the sunset over the city of Boston. Envious passengers waved exuberantly. As Elizabeth leaned her hip against the rail, she muttered, "Wish this perfect weekend didn't have to end."

From the helm Peter smiled that silly grin of his and nodded, "Yeah. Me, too."

Devastating news came in mid August. The Defense Department activated Peter's reserve unit. Just like that, their summer of love ended. Their last evening together, Elizabeth and Peter plodded along the River Charles to the place where they first met on that warm spring day not so long ago. As they sank to the ground, no words could console them. Aching, abysmal numbness suffocated them as they held each other tight, not wanting to believe that they were being torn apart. The sky blackened and evening stars twinkled overhead. Moths bombarded streetlights. In the trees insects rattled. Trekking back to her apartment, they were oblivious to cooking smells, voices, and sounds of television sets that drifted out open windows. Unable to imagine a world without Peter in it, Elizabeth fumbled the key into the lock. Her eyes invited him in, knowing full well that after this night Peter would be gone. She gave herself to him in anguished tenderness forced upon them by government business thousands of miles away. Defiantly she kissed and loved him throughout the brief night, praying that in the morning it would all be a bad dream. How in the world could she ever let Peter go? She hated this monstrous war for taking away her love, her life.

Dawn arrived much too soon and her world came crashing to an end. "Please," she pleaded as she fell to her knees. Her arms reached out to him. "Don't leave me here all alone. Peter. Please. Don't go."

"Don't worry Bethie," he called over his shoulder, faking that silly grin of his. "Nothin's gonna happen to this bod'. I'll cherish you in my heart, my little morning eyes, forever."

And…he was gone. Her muscles went limp. As her body rumpled into a heap upon the floor, her mind went blank. And so went the years.

Elizabeth heaved a sigh as that last night with Peter so very long ago faded in her mind. Somehow she had made it through all the pain and sorrow. But as Peter lived on deep within her heart, the hopeless pain that had plagued her all these years now lifted. Clasping her hands in front of her lips, Elizabeth felt blessed to have known Peter. "You were the best thing that ever happened to me."

Tears of joy brimmed in her eyes as she raised herself up off the ledge and slipped the peace ring off her finger and dropped it into her pocket. Elizabeth glanced one more time upon the riverbank where they met. "Good bye, Peter."

CHAPTER 8

*T*he steeple bells of Brighton's Catholic Churches were in the midst of tolling twelve when Margi parked her car in front of the bank on Washington Street. The neighborhood drugstore was located to the left and next to that, the hair salon where Margi got her hair cut and Emma got her hair washed and set each week. To the right of the bank was the woman's boutique where Elizabeth liked to shop. Next door was the health club. All were a block away from Julio's Ristorante. As Margi got out of the car, her hands started flailing to get the attention of her sister-in-law who was sitting in her car down the street. "There's Janice, Ma. Janice, yoo-hoo, Janice!"

Emma squinted into the bright sunlight and waved. She scanned the street and said, "Looks like Julie and Elizabeth have not gotten here yet."

Janice got out of her car as they approached. Exchanging hugs, Emma shivered, "How dreadfully cold, isn't it?"

"Certainly is," Janice nodded while clenching her gloved fists. "Is this weather ever going to warm up?"

"It's s'posed to a bit I guess," said Margi. "Humph. Know what that means, don'cha? Shur as shooting, we're gonna get slammed with a blizzard."

"The radar on the weather report this morning showed a big storm system headed in our direction. The weather man didn't know exactly how much snow we are in for, but it could be upwards of six inches."

"This winter won't ever end," Janice huffed as the wind whipped the length of her auburn hair that cascaded halfway down the back of her black suede jacket. Blue corduroys covered her legs and disappeared within knee-high black leather boots. She shoved her blue knit scarf over her shoulder then pulling the matching tuque down over her ears, scurried off to Julio's.

The winter did feel a lot longer than any Emma had ever experienced, though she figured it was only that way because Seth was gone. Her chest tightened. The aching loneliness that his absence created was at times too much to bear.

"Emma," Julie called as she bounced up to the group. "You look so nice."

"Kinda hard to tell under all those clothes, kid," Margi countered as she looked back to see that Julie had parked a couple of cars in front of hers.

Hustling up behind Julie, Elizabeth was yanking the collar of her sable coat over her nose. She managed a muffled, "Hello," before most of her face disappeared below the collar. Only one eye was left exposed to find the way to the restaurant.

Elbowing Julie, Margi motioned with her head, saying. "Hey, kid, I like your car."

Julie returned Margi's jab. "Yours ain't too bad, either."

Janice shot a quick glimpse at the two cars while making a beeline for Julio's. Emma had used the stock certificate found in the boot box to buy Margi's two-year-old car as a Christmas gift for Julie and then had given Margi a little extra so that she could go out to buy the car she had had her eye on for quite some time. From the unexpected bounty the old woman fulfilled a major fancy of each family member. It was not hard to do so, since she had a good memory for such things.

Emma recalled the Monday after the boot box was discovered. Mesmerized by mundane moments of crocheting and the drone of the early news report, she had jumped when the back door buzzer blared. "Heaven's to Betsy," she had exclaimed as her hand fled to her chest to calm her racing heart. She had squinted at the clock. 4:45. Odd. By this time on Mondays, things usually got pretty quiet. The buzzer sounded again. "Be right there," she hollered in a squeaky high-pitched voice. Stuffing her needlework on the seat beside her, she lowered the footrest of the recliner. The buzzer sounded again, this time more prolonged and insistent. "Yes, yes, I am coming!" At the door she pushed aside the shade and peeked outside. "Why, Adam. What on earth are you doing here at this hour?"

Clutching the folded documents that had been discovered in the boot box, he waved. His face resembled that of the excitable child Emma had known him to be years ago. Hastily she unlocked the door and opened it. "Come in. Come in."

He pecked her cheek and gave a quick hug all the while gushing, "I just had to stop by on my way home from the office. Good news."

Her brows arched. "Good news?"

Adam darted past Emma and plopped onto a kitchen chair. He spread open the folded yellowed documents and trumpeted, "Get a load of this, Ma. You're a wealthy woman!"

Her hands steadied her weight on the table. "For heaven's sake, Adam," she stammered, "what are you talking about?"

"These stocks are worth a bundle! I can't believe Dad overlooked them in his will."

Staring at the yellowed paperwork, Emma sagged onto the chair next to Adam. He shot a questioning look at her. "What're you gonna do with them?"

Emma shrugged. "I have more than enough to live on," she mumbled. The only thing that came to mind was, "How 'bout a bite to eat?"

Adam hesitated. Eating had not even crossed his mind. He looked down at himself still dressed in a three-piece navy blue suit and red power tie. "Uhm, sure," he said. "Janice knows I'm here. She and Elliot are at their karate classes."

Emma got to her feet and rubbed her palms on her apron as she went to the refrigerator. Up until now she also had not even considered supper. Most nights it was well on to nine o'clock before her insides let her know that she had not eaten. By that time, she only munched at best because eating made her sleep too restless. But this was kind of nice having Adam drop in. She selected several covered dishes and set them on the counter. She had not had a chance to be alone with her oldest son in ages. As he got up from the table, he loosened his tie then took it off along with his suit coat. Emma smiled and squeezed his cheek. "How handsome you look."

Adam flushed and half-heartedly swiped away her hand. "Come on, Mother." While rolling up the sleeves of his white shirt, he asked, "What can I do?"

"Pour the drinks, dear. Juice and soda are in the fridge."

As he poured two glasses of cranberry juice, he said, "You could sell the stocks and set up trusts. Proceeds will be tax free if you do it that way."

"I could do that," Emma nodded. She tilted her head thoughtfully while setting a slow flame under a frying pan of precooked eggplant, sandwiching slices of mozzarella cheese between them. She added cut-up sausages and mushrooms and heaped tomato sauce onto the concoction. She put the lid on the pan and turned to Adam. "But you know what?" she said as she wiped her hands on her apron. "I think I want to use some of it for a few other things, too."

As they ate, Emma spelled out how she wanted to distribute the proceeds. Adam was proud to have a hand in seeing that her wishes were realized. But then as he got up to help clear the table, he cleared his throat and said, "Ma, there's something else."

"Yes dear?" Emma asked while covering a plate of leftovers with plastic wrap. When he did not answer, she shot a quizzical look his way. His eyes avoided hers. "What is it, Adam?" she asked.

He hesitated, trying to find the right words. He went to the chair where his suit coat was draped and fished about the pocket. Pausing for a moment, he looked into his mother's eyes. Slowly his hand raised a time-ravaged photograph up to eye level. Emma took a step back. That photograph had come up missing ages ago. She swallowed hard as their eyes locked. "Where did you get that?"

"The wind blew it off the dressing table in your bedroom."

"Dressing table?" Her hand trembled as she reached for the photograph.

"You know, the kidney-shaped one with the yellow checkered skirt next to the window."

"Gingham?" She sputtered as she looked into the eyes of the man in the photograph. She had never known him, but yet…she knew all about him.

Adam nodded. "I snuck up there one day while we kids were playing hide and seek."

Her top lip quivered. "You had this picture all this time?"

Adam nodded dubiously, "I heard what you and Papa said."

Emma covered her mouth. Her eyes widened. The cosmetic drawer…that was where she used to hide it—beneath the black velvet lining. But then one day, it came up missing. She had searched high and low, but it was nowhere to be found.

"I was hiding under the dressing table," Adam mumbled.

Emma looked away and bit her lip.

"I heard you say that the man in this picture was your father. It was supposed to be a secret, but Grampa, er, Andrea Benedetto spilled the beans to you just before he passed on."

Emma cleared her throat. "All this time you knew?"

Adam rolled his eyes.

"Grandpa and Bartolomeo Vanzetti were great men," she murmured as she sank onto a chair.

Adam nodded. "I researched the Braintree heist in one of my law classes. What a set up. Whoever did it did a great job. There's virtually no trail."

Emma shook her head.

Adam sat down next to her. "You look like him...and Grampa, too."

Her fingers went to her lips then to the picture. "My Papa told me that I am like the both of them in many ways."

"I never doubted that."

"What do you mean?"

"You knew it since 1941 and never once mentioned one word of it to a single soul, not until that day with Papa in the bedroom. You kept your mouth shut just like Bartolomeo Vanzetti did. He sacrificed his life for what he believed—and for you and your Mama...and all the rest of us. Imagine what the press would do if they found out about us?"

"Have you told anyone?"

Adam shook his head.

"Not even Margi, Timothy, or Samuel?"

"What would be served by doing so?"

Emma shrugged. The secret was safe. That gave her comfort. A thin smile lifted her lips.

"But I would like to know..." Adam started.

Emma scratched the back of her neck. "My father—my biological father—was an immigrant. A fishmonger...a poor man without family who fled the tyranny of the old country only to find more in the new. He became a pawn between factions that for right or wrong had their own ends in mind. He went to his grave knowing that by doing so would force all sides to examine their own failings, but more importantly he did so to protect my mother and me."

"He certainly accomplished that," Adam winced. "Nobody has a clue about us. Not only that, to this day, the mere mention of Sacco and Vanzetti makes people stop and wonder if there is a better way to solve strife."

"My father made a pact with a person who was not so good. He would keep his mouth shut in return for keeping my existence a secret forever."

"Who was this other person?"

"I cannot say."

"Cannot or will not?"

Emma looked away, rolling her eyes. "Both my father and this person suffered greatly. My father knew that it was God's will for him to die. And there was no taking back the harm that the other man had done. My father wished to have something good come of his death…" Emma took a deep breath and looked directly into her son's eyes. "So the other person granted my father's wish."

Adam stared at her intently. He shifted. He glanced up at the ceiling.

Emma got to her feet and tried to distract herself by cleaning up the supper dishes. But that failed miserably. "You know, Adam, I am the luckiest person in the world. I had two fathers who cared about me and my Mama very much—a notorious martyr and an ordinary man who was a good husband to my Mama." Emma paused. "My Mama paid dearly for the past but was also blessed."

Adam got up and put his arms around his mother. "You are their blessing…and ours." He looked into her eyes. "That's why nothing can be gained from anyone else knowing."

Her hands suddenly felt clammy. She swiped them across her apron and said, "I was thinking that maybe after I pass on you should tell Margi and your brothers."

"That's not going to happen in the near future, so let's not even discuss it," Adam said flatly.

Emma took off her apron and laid it across the back of a chair. "Come with me," she said. Taking Adam's hand, she led the way to the attic where she shoved aside a pile of old books. She picked up a tie, an armband, and lapel pins and handed them to Adam.

"Look at these pins," he gasped. "They've got Sacco and Vanzetti's pictures on them—as if they were political candidates." Squinting in the inadequate light, he read aloud, "'Remember! Justice Crucified August 23, 1927.'"

Emma got to her feet. "Your father collected all kinds of strange things—even me."

"Come on, Ma. Let's go, let's go. I'm starved," exclaimed Margi while giving Emma's arm a tug.

The old woman gave a blank look at her daughter.

"Ma, you daydreamin' again?" Margi asked.

A shudder ran through Emma as she shook off the encounter with Adam. "Uhm. I'm sorry dear. Are you hungry?"

Margi looked at her mother as if she were from the planet Zebulon. "Shiish-yeah!"

"Well we should go then, shouldn't we, dear," Emma muttered and pulled Margi along.

Shaking off bewilderment, Margi said, "The special had better be portabello mushroom chicken. I'm gonna have linguini with it. And for dessert, maybe rum cake or spumoni, or...or maybe even both."

"Margi, you eat too much," Julie chided. "How do you stay so thin?"

"It's running after Ma's grandkids," Margi retorted.

Seth's old friend Anthony swung open the door and stood aside while the women rushed in from the cold. Taking Emma's arm, he seated her and the others at a table next to the plate glass window that overlooked the wintry street. No sooner had Emma removed her green knitted gloves that matched her coat when the handsome young waiter Pauly set fresh-baked rolls and butter in the middle of the table. Margi leaned over and sniffed the steam. "Mmm," she breathed. Immediately she started rummaging through the bread-basket while hollering over her shoulder. "Bring on the coffee, Paulie."

"For heaven's sake, Margi," scolded Emma as she handed her coat to Anthony.

Without a clue that she had done anything ill-mannered, Margi squinted at her mother while wriggling out of her coat. "Whatsamadda Ma?"

Ignoring the squabble, Elizabeth piped up, "Make that two, Paulie." Making no attempt to take off her gray coat, she shrank onto a chair and shivered. Her teeth chattered as her gloved hands warmed her cold nose.

"What a sight you are," laughed Emma as she smoothed back the tendrils that the wind had strewn across her forehead.

"I'm definitely not a winter person," Elizabeth blustered while waving off Anthony against any ideas of taking her coat.

Emma chuckled. She had grown quite fond of Julie's Mom. It seemed that both Julie and Elizabeth were so much happier now that they were together again and all settled into their new apartment. A recent conversation had revealed that Julie's father had been missing in action in Vietnam for years. How difficult that must have been. Losing Seth was hard enough, but at least Emma had him around for more than fifty years. Imagine raising a child alone. That was no easy task. Not only did that terrible war over there in Asia tear so many families and friends apart, but it had also changed the way Americans looked at war. Future armed conflicts would never again be accepted without question.

After Paulie took their order and left, Margi leaned over to Julie and whispered, "That guy's kinda cute, wouldn't cha say?"

"Don't even go there," spouted Julie while spreading a white cloth napkin across her lap.

"Aw, come on." Margi elbowed Julie. "Lemme fix ya up."

"Margi," Julie whined. "You don't even know him. Listen, I'm not about to meet anyone that way again." Chugging down half a glass of ginger ale, she shook her finger at Margi. "The next time I meet someone, it'll be through a formal introduction by someone who really knows what the guy is all about. I'm not getting myself into another bad situation. Uh-uh. Never again. I learned my lesson."

"Good," said Emma as she gave Julie's hand a squeeze. "You be careful."

"Aw, Ma. You're such a worry-wart." Margi blustered while dabbing her bread into spiced olive oil. She gnawed off the saturated spot then dabbed some more.

"Well, I worry too," Elizabeth spoke up. She was finally peeling off her coat. A gold locket adorned the pale yellow turtleneck beneath her gray pantsuit. "Julie's been through too much. She deserves someone who will be good to her."

The expression of concern surprised Julie, especially coming from her mother in public. Julie took her mother's hand and squeezed. Things had really changed since that conversation about her father. Elizabeth smiled, contented that she had done the right thing about revealing the past.

"These days, you have to be careful," added Janice. "There's so many weirdoes out there. You never know who to trust anymore."

Julie fiddled with her fingernails. "There's this guy at work...Ken Waters. A woman who works with me was his daughter's nanny."

"Ellen," Margi jumped in as she popped the last bit of bread into her mouth.

Julie's eyes widened. "You know her?"

"Margi knows everybody," Janice taunted.

Sloughing off the comment, Margi went on with her mouth still full. "You could do worse, kid. Ken owns the computer company that services the hospital.

Julie shrugged. "I bumped into him at a hallway corner one day last month. I was so embarrassed...I didn't know what to say. When

I told Ellen about it, she told me how his wife Regina and little one had died four years ago. They've had a tough time getting over it. Anyway, ever since then Ellen's been buggin' me about letting her fix me up with Ken. I keep telling her that I'm not ready yet. Actually, I'm kinda scared to get involved. It's too soon."

Like a wise old sage Emma said, "You have to look deep into your heart."

"You're gonna be scared for a long time," Janice winced as her sapphire eyes revolved. She carefully wiped her fingertips with her napkin. "It took quite some time before I trusted anybody after my divorce. I told myself never again and gave up looking for Mister Right. I was bound and determined to build my life the way I wanted it to be. And then out of the clear blue sky, Adam came into my life." She snapped her fingers. "Just like that."

Julie and her mother shot raised eyebrows at Janice. Divorce? In this family? But Emma's family was so perfect. There couldn't possibly be troubles in this ideal family. Reading their minds, Emma said, "Every family has its skeletons."

"If that's what you want to call them," Margi chortled.

Emma frowned. "The way I look at it is, the Good Lord put us all together on this earth whether in good circumstances or bad. It is better to make the best of it and accept each other. Life is too short. Janice had a very bad time, but my son loves her and I would never stand in the way of the happiness of any of my children. And you know, Adam dearly loves Elliot. The three of them adore each other. What more could anyone want?" Emma looked fondly at Janice.

Humbled from her mother-in-law's unsolicited praise, Janice braced her elbows on the table and rested her chin on her folded hands. "My ex was an alcoholic. He didn't care one bit that Elliot and I got thrown out of our home because he didn't pay the bills. The almighty bottle landed us deep in poverty. One day I had enough. I was going to make it on my own and get back a little dignity."

"I thank God that Adam and Janice found each other," said Emma, reaching over and patting her daughter-in-law's hand. "That child deserves a loving father, even if his real father doesn't want him."

Wishing that she had a family of her own that radiated so much love and strength, Julie sighed, "Gee, I thought all this time that I was the only one with man troubles."

Emma laughed. "When it comes right down to it, all we have in this world is each other. How many unconnected people do you know who are truly happy? Not many, I would say. We all need somebody."

"What about you and Seth?" Elizabeth blurted out. "How do you manage to go on without him?"

The question caught the old woman off guard. Not even her own children had ever asked anything so personal. Emma glanced across the table. Elizabeth was toying with her salad. Sensing a cry for help, the old woman said, "I miss my Seth with every part of my being. But he is with me in everything I do. There will never be anyone who can be all that he was to me," Emma paused fighting back emotion. "I go on even though sometimes I don't know where to find the strength…" she hesitated. Her loss thumped in her throat.

Margi frowned. Setting down her fork, she braced her hands on the table and got to her feet. She lumbered to Emma's side. Her arm encircled her mother's shoulder as she laid her cheek on her head. "I miss him too, Ma."

Emma drew a deep breath and patted Margi's hand. "I know you do, dear." Smiling up at her daughter, she continued. "Seth and I had a good life together. I wish he hadn't gone yet, but that was God's will. We will be together again, I am sure of it. We raised a wonderful family and I am still here, a part of it. I need Seth, but my family needs me just as much. I go on for the sake of my family, because that is what I know he wanted me to do. If I had gone first, I would have expected him to do the same without me."

The women at the table were silent, imagining themselves in Emma's situation. Elizabeth patted Julie's hand, realizing that even though Peter was gone, Julie needed her the same way as Seth's family needed Emma. Too bad that old woman had not come into their lives a long time ago. With that kind of support, perhaps life would have been better.

As Margi sat down again, Paulie arrived with lunch. After he left, Julie spread her napkin on her lap and said, "It sure is hard to trust again. I'm afraid to even talk to another guy, never mind getting into another relationship."

"It's not easy," Janice mused while staring at her plate of food over the rim of the glass she held in her fingertips. "I thought Adam was too good to be true, but he's stayed the same all this time. He's always kind and considerate." She winked and whispered behind her hand. "Don't tell Ma, but he's also very romantic. Every so often he brings me yellow roses. Adam says yellow roses mean friendship and I'm his best friend."

"My Seth was such a ham. I see it in our children every day," Emma quipped. "Look at Margi, here. She eats just like he did and never gains an ounce."

Margi looked up with a mouth full of pasta. A napkin was tucked into her blouse and caught a speck of sauce as she slurped, "Geez, Ma."

Emma laughed and squeezed her daughter's hand. She handed Margi a napkin to wipe off her face then turned and playfully wagged her index finger at Janice, saying, "And as for being romantic, young lady…where do you think Adam learned that?"

Crimson glazed Janice's porcelain face. With a comical grin she said, "From Seth, ma'am."

Her hand braced her hip as Emma shot a quizzical look at Janice and asked, "And while we are at it, when do you suppose I can expect another grandchild?"

Janice shrugged.

❧   ❧   ❧

An hour or so later, the women exited Julio's Restaurant just as a sharp blast of air whipped leaves and paper into a gritty spiral in front of the door. At Janice's car they hurriedly said good-byes and as they trailed Margi down the street a deep male voice came out of nowhere. "Stop! Police officer! Put your gun down! Now!"

Gunfire cracked, breaching the frigid winter air as a burly thug in black garb and ski mask hotfooted it out of the bank foyer. One poorly aimed bullet ricocheted off the parking meter behind Margi's car. Elizabeth crumpled. Julie grappled for her, but her mother slipped through her grasp. Blood gushed onto the sidewalk and Julie choked. Where was it all coming from? More gunfire! Julie sprawled on top of her mother in a vain attempt to shield her from the harm that had already been done.

The bandit darted by while firing over his shoulder at the pursuing police officer. Gunshots missed their mark. "Damn," the thug cursed and turned abruptly to continue the flight. But there was Emma. Their faces cracked together. The gun flew into the air. Rebounding off one another, two bodies splattered upon the frigid cement. The only one left standing was Margi. Confused, she gaped at her mother lying helpless, bloody, and unconscious. Just then the bandit's gun hit the sidewalk and misfired. Margi dove to shelter her mother as the aimless bullet struck the ensuing police officer. He dropped his gun and fell to the pavement. Crushing one hand against the pulsating wound on his upper thigh, he gripped his phone in the other and screamed, "Officer down! Officer down!" Giving the location, he commanded, "Ambulances and officers respond. Citizens down… Citizens…down…" He fought to maintain consciousness, but the phone sagged away from his ear.

Down the street Janice had just fished her keys out of her pocketbook and was about to unlock the car door when the gunshots rang out. Instinctively she ducked. Terror shot up her spine. The shots had come from the direction that her luncheon companions had gone. She leapt to her feet and ran for all she was worth until she came upon Emma and Elizabeth lying motionless on the sidewalk clouded by putrid gun smoke. She stopped short. Her hands covered her mouth, containing her horror. Margi was lifting her mother's head onto her lap, screaming, "I don't know how to stop the bleeding! It's coming out her nose! I don't know what to do! Oh my God! Ma's choking! Somebody help Ma! Help!"

Elizabeth was barely conscious, bleeding from the bullet wound in her stomach. Her eyes had begun to glaze over. Abject terror had drained the color from Julie's face as she cried, "Oh no. Oh no. Oh no."

Several other unfortunate people were crouching down close to buildings. Not one bystander made a move to help. In a window above the hair salon, a Doberman was barking wildly. The bank robber started to come to. Janice's eyes grew wide. He yanked off his bloody ski mask. Clawing at his bushy black mop, he had spotted the officer who was no longer in control. Janice's breath had become increasingly shallow. The thug staggered to his feet and began limping towards the cop's gun. Janice's tongue ran across her bottom lip. Her heart thumped. She was the only one who could stop further bloodshed. Her feet felt like lead as she raced toward the gun. Scooping it up, she sidestepped the thug and took a spread-eagled stance. Both hands gripped the gun and her eyes narrowed. "Stop," she bellowed. "Stay right there! Or I'll shoot!"

The bandit hesitated. Steel gray eyes pierced hers. A severe underbite made the scowl that plastered his face even more sinister. "Gimme that gun, sweet cakes," he slurred and warbled towards Janice. His forefinger cocked an invisible gun and his thumb snapped down.

She willed her finger to squeeze the trigger, but it just wouldn't. She glared at the gun that refused to fire. It appeared enormous and out of place in her hands. Tremors shot through her. But then a rumble boiled up from deep within Janice. Slow-motion obscurity befuddled her senses as her arm, palm up, sliced at the thug. "Arghugh." Sweeping into a high-kneed lunge, the heel of her boot torpedoed a decisive kick to the groin. As the bandit folded, she landed in front of him. The back of her clenched fist hooked under his jaw, catapulting him backwards. In a bristled pose she watched him land in a heap. Her nostrils flared and the fires of hell blazed in her eyes. The incapacitated thug flattened out. He managed to brace himself up on one elbow. His eyes slitted sideways at the woman towering over him like the mighty Colossus of Rhodes. Her teeth gritted as once again she pointed the gun at him and seethed, "Don't get up or take it from me, the next time you will be one dead man!"

Falling back onto the sidewalk, he cursed, "Bitch."

The blare of sirens reverberated off city buildings as a police cruiser screeched to a halt. Two uniforms, a male and female, bounded out of the still-rocking cruiser. Guns drawn, they took direct aim upon the only other person with a gun—Janice.

"Put down the gun," howled the male officer.

Janice failed to respond. Her gun remained cocked and aimed at the thug, her finger paralyzed against the trigger. Adrenaline and instinct for survival locked her away from all reason.

"Put down that gun!" This time, both officers bellowed, followed by the screech of mouth whistles. And voices exploded again. "Put the gun down… Now!"

Janice's head twitched. Her eyes zeroed in on the cold, metallic viper ensnared in her hands. Her finger relaxed and her arms sagged falling limp at her sides. Her grip loosened and the gun dropped onto the sidewalk. The female officer raced to Janice, barking, "Calm down, ma'am. Calm down. We'll take it from here."

Janice stood there, numb. Vomit bubbled up in her throat as the male officer picked up the gun butt-first with a piece of cloth that he had taken from the back pocket of his pants. Her hands clenched and she jammed them into her pockets as she surveyed the bloody scene stinking of gunpowder. Things looked bleak. Those she knew and loved the most were in peril and there was not one blessed thing she could do to make any of it better. Margi was rocking her unconscious mother back and forth, sobbing hysterically, "Please, God. Please don't take Ma, too." And Julie, with her mother lying across her lap, was pressing on the wound, trying to stem the flow of life's fluid. Janice turned away. Her legs were about to give way under her.

Paramedics rushed up with black bags and gurneys. Cops were everywhere. Some kept the surge of curiosity seekers at bay, away from the crime scene, while others cordoned off the street and rerouted traffic. Only emergency vehicles were allowed access. One instant of inexplicable insanity had torn everybody's world to shreds. As Janice watched the EMTs lift Emma onto a stretcher and wheel her into a waiting ambulance that jutted out into the street, she detested herself for taking for granted the well-ordered life she had come to know.

Margi stuck to her mother's side, wailing over and over again, "You're going to be all right, Ma." Metal doors slammed. Sirens wailed and faded in the distance.

Julie was in a state of shock as she searched her mother's fading eyes. "Hang in there, Mom, okay? Mom? Please. I love you. Hang on."

"Julie," Elizabeth whispered. "Julie, I...I'm sorry. I...all that time..."

"It's okay, Mom. Everything's going to be okay," Julie cried and kissed her mother's forehead.

Janice's stomach churned as one paramedic shouted, "The bleeding's as good as we're gonna get. Come on. Let's get her outta here." The attendants hastily lifted Elizabeth onto a stretcher and wheeled her to a waiting ambulance. Julie got in. The doors slammed behind her. Sirens shrieked and blinding lights revolved as the ambulance sped off to St. Anne's Regional Hospital. Another followed right behind, transporting the wounded cop. Bloody devastation was left behind…and so was Janice LaRosa, standing there, empty inside, fists clenched in her pockets. Tears stung her eyes in the wintry air. Noise and lights fled into oblivion. She stood there so, so horrendously alone.

❦   ❦   ❦

The doors of the emergency room burst open. A triage nurse commanded, "Take this one to O. R. One." A second nurse grabbed Julie's arm.

Trying to shake her off, Julie screeched, "Leave me alone. I'm going with Mom."

"Let the doctors do their job," insisted the nurse. She shook the girl's arm. "We need some information about your mother so the doctors can do the best they can. You do want to do everything you can for your Mom, don't you?"

"But," Julie shook her head then looked into the prodding eyes of the nurse. Her heart wanted to follow her mother, but logic dictated otherwise. "I've never known Mom to be sick." Julie broke down and cried. "Oh gosh, I know so little about any medical problems she might have."

The nurse tugged her arm, asking, "Where can we contact her husband?"

"She doesn't have one."

"And her mother?"

"Arizona."

"We'll need her telephone number."

"I don't have it."

The nurse stepped back and frowned.

"I've never spoken to her…" Julie whined, "and I don't know if Mom ever has."

"So there's no one but you?" gasped the nurse.

Julie shook her head. "No one."

The nurse hesitated, "Well, you and I will just have to figure this thing out as best we can, now won't we?" She wrapped Julie's forearm around hers and led her into an information booth. Afterwards, the nurse told Julie to take a seat in the hallway, but instead, Julie searched out Emma and Margi. Unprepared for what she saw, Julie froze. Emma was unconscious, ashen. Her lips were blue and puffed up beneath the oxygen mask. An intravenous line was taped to the back of her weathered hand where a rivulet of blood had not been swabbed and had crusted. A machine beeped out heart rhythms as fluorescent lights illuminated green-capped heads of doctors and nurses hovering around Emma. Margi was standing off in the corner, swaying in a psychotic oblivion. Her mother's blood smeared her tear-streaked face. Margi had dressed to the hilt this morning, which was a rarity in itself, but now her snow-white blouse with puffy sleeves, her tan vest and skirt, her nylons and shoes were a bloody mess. A student nurse tried in vain to soothe Margi's hysteria. Worming through the concerned crowd, Julie trembled. What on earth was she going to say? "Margi? Margi, it's me. Julie."

Margi's eyes were blank. Julie cupped her friend's face in her hands and looked straight in her eyes. "Don't you recognize me, Margi?"

Margi's brows came together as her eyes explored Julie's face.

The beep of the heart monitor slowed. "BP's dropping," a voice warned. Beeps mutated into one long, ugly wail. Panicked eyes shot at the machine. Terror riddled Julie and Margi's faces.

Margi grabbed Julie's coat. Her entire being quaked as she shrieked, "Ma won't wake up! Julie…Ma won't wake up…"

CHAPTER 9

*W*eightlessly Emma drifted, upwards, meandering this way and that through a milky puff that refreshed her soul like morning dew upon the rose. Ethereal lilt infused the air sweetened by jasmine and orchid. Serenity such as she had never before encountered overflowed and enlightened her soul. Sheer luminescence swelled before her. Her eyes strained to see as she was drawn ever nearer and nearer. Her heart hastened the journey that could only progress in its own due course. Eventually resignation quelled her being and languidly she glanced back from whence she came. Whirling lights sliced the smoky haze that muddled the stage below where chaos reigned. Unexpectedly the scene faded. Nothing remained…only the figure of a solitary woman, aching, desolated. Emma strained to see. Janice? A second vision arose, that of beloved Margi, her white blouse soiled with crimson, standing in the corner of a sterile emergency room. She was swaying to and fro. And there was Julie, also covered with blood—Elizabeth's. Emma watched as the young woman took tenuous steps towards Margi. Emma sensed her struggling to muster strength enough to comfort her despairing friend as well as herself. Words were muffled. An alarm whined. Horror sheeted all the faces. Julie and Margi clamped on to one another and held tight sharing moments of utter fright. Was destiny to dictate the unspeakable commonality of losing both their mothers on the very same day?

The distinct light tugged at Emma. Expanding larger and larger, it filled her with mystical anticipation. A shadow slowly emerged, resolute. Closer, ever nearer it came. She squinted through the intense brightness, willing her eyes to see. Her soul exploded, "Seth!" Her arms cast off the cloak of loneliness. Reaching out to him, she cried, "It's you! It's really you! Oh, my dear Seth."

But arms went unfulfilled as through unmoving lips the shadow whispered, "Emma…"

Longing to touch him, hold him in her arms, she whimpered, "Oh Seth, I have missed you so."

"Emma." His voice was clear, direct. "You must go back."

"But Seth," she cried. "I have been so lonely without you."

His head swung side to side. Sadness dripped from his eyes. "It is not your time."

"Please," she begged. "I need you."

"You must go back."

"No," she protested. "It cannot be any other way. I will stay here…it can be no other way. I…I need you so."

A hand elevated from beneath hallowed robes. One colorless finger pointed downward. "Our family and friends need you."

Emma shook her head. "Not anymore."

"There is still so much that only you can give. Look."

"No," she moaned as her arm covered her eyes. "I won't. I want to stay here…with you."

"Our own sweet Margi suffers so," the spirit continued. "She has not fully accepted my passing. She is incapable of losing you so soon."

"She will be fine…" Emma choked on her heartless words. "…in time." Shame overwhelmed her until suddenly her eyes were opened. "Wait. The reason you don't want me here is Margi Bascuino. You wish to spend eternity with her."

His smile was devoid of pleasure. "Margaret Bascuino released my heart the moment the eyes of God beheld my love for you. Nobody but you will walk eternity with me. My heart cries out as yours does because our walk together cannot yet begin, but now is not our time." Emma peered up. Eyes tender, the spirit gazed down, deep into hers. "Now is not our time," came a soft echo.

Her heart broke, for such an unhappy happenstance devastated her to the core. Reluctantly her gaze retreated downward.

"See Julie," he murmured. "Over there. She needs you now more than ever. She and Elizabeth still have a long road ahead of them. Only you can lead them through the darkness. That task has been given to you. It is part of your destiny. You have already accomplished part of it. But you are not finished. Go back. You must go back."

Her head wavered side to side as Emma peered up into the eyes that had been taken away from her. "But my dreams, Seth," she whimpered. "My dreams are filled with you. And no matter where I go, no matter what I do, you are there. You are so much a part of me, Seth. I cannot let you go… No, not again. How can you ask this of me?"

"I *am* with you, Emma. That is the reason that you see me in your life. Take comfort in that," he whispered, "for my devotion to you remains ever constant. You will come to me…in due course. But this is not the moment." His arms extended and beckoned her. "Feel my presence with them…just as you feel my presence now."

Without mortal touch, the spirit enveloped her entirely, creating wholeness, enrapturing, bestowing peace within her. Her chest filled. Involuntary breath issued forth. And once again her heart beat with the rhythm of life. Her essence spiraled downward…down…as the light of Seth lingered behind…down… As she disappeared beyond drifting clouds, his honeyed voice called out from the fleeting glow. "Emma. Go to the room." His voice became so dreadfully faint. "You will always find me there, my forever love."

"Seth," Emma wheezed. Rancid air exploded from her lungs. Her eyelids flickered. Her eyes heavy and dry, she blinked through searing light. But Seth was gone...

The shadow of a concerned doctor clad in green garb hovered over Emma. He hesitated then handed shock paddles to a nearby nurse. A toothy grin brightened his face. "She's coming around." Placated that all the intense work had finally paid off, his body heaved. His fingers grazed her cheek and then her forehead. "What is your name? Can you tell us your name?"

Emma cleared her throat. It was so dry and foreign matter gritted like sandpaper against her teeth. Her voice refused to come. A nurse dripped fluid in her mouth and Emma swallowed hard. "Emma...Emma LaRosa."

"Yes," exhaled the doctor as his fist rose victoriously into the air. He spun around to concerned family and friends and said, "She's back!"

Sighs of relief and jubilant whispers echoed throughout the disheveled emergency room. Margi fled from Julie's arms and defiantly shoved her way through medical personnel, bellowing, "Ma! Ma!"

As her daughter fell sobbing onto her bosom, Emma lifted a weak hand and let it fall upon the blood-caked head. Stroking her child's anguish away, Emma smiled, her heart crying out, *You are right, Seth. I am still needed.* "Shh...I am here, Margi. I am here." It was at that moment that Emma spotted Julie peering from behind the faces of family members. Tears of relief streamed down the girl's drawn and bloodied face. The old woman beckoned, "Come here, dear."

Waddling to her blessed old friend, Julie trembled uncontrollably. "Emma," was all she could get out. Salty tears baptized the wrinkled hand that stretched out to her.

"Julie, what happened?" Emma mumbled. "Your Mom...?"

"It was a bank robbery, Em. Mom was shot...bad. She's in surgery. I don't know anything..." Julie choked on her terror. "...and nobody's telling me a thing." No longer able to hold back the dread she felt for her mother nor the relief of her old friend's return, Julie turned away and broke down.

Emma tugged on Julie's hand. Again. And again. At last the girl made eye contact with the old woman. "Your mother's going to make it," Emma whispered. "I just know it."

"Emma?"

Glancing toward the foot of the bed from where the small, hushed voice had come, Emma squeaked, "Janice! My hero. Janice."

And Janice smiled, her eyes dropping to the floor.

As family members engulfed the matriarch's bedside, Julie inconspicuously withdrew. In the hallway, powerlessness laced with relief overpowered every last fiber of her body. Her legs were no longer able to bear her weight and Julie collapsed onto a chair. She took a tremulous breath. Her mouth was parched and tasted of grime laced with gunpowder, blood, and hospital. While sitting there, waiting for news of her mother, Julie heard Emma's words repeat over and over again in her head "Your mother's going to make it. I just know it."

Somewhere within the haze, there were footsteps. The metal chair beside Julie griped as weight settled upon it. A mellow voice broke through the numbness. "How's your mother doin'?"

Slowly Julie lifted her worry-sick eyes. It was Ken Waters. His face was sullen. His square jaw loose. His warm cocoa eyes invited trust. "I don't know." She shivered beneath her winter coat.

"Want me to find out for you?" he volunteered.

Her eyes grew hopeful. "Oh...please? Could you?"

"Shur thing." Ken sprang to his feet and taking purposeful strides down the corridor, disappeared around the corner. In no time he returned. A nurse was with him. She gave Julie a reassuring smile as she passed. Ken sat down and took Julie's hand. Squeezing, he said, "She's gonna find out what's going on."

Julie nodded. Her eyes followed the nurse down the hall where she shoved open swinging doors labeled No Admittance. Julie gave Ken a faint smile and said, "Thanks."

Eternal moments passed. The nurse burst through the swinging doors and made her way directly to Julie. "They're finishing up as we speak. The doctor said he'd be out in about fifteen minutes. Can I get you anything?" Ken shot a questioning glance at Julie. She shook her head no. Noticing the girl's blood-caked face, the nurse held out a hand. "Why don't you come with me? I'll get you a face cloth so you can clean off your face. You don't want your mother seeing you like that."

Julie stared at the nurse's hand.

"Go," Ken urged. As she gazed at him, he nodded. "You got time. And I will be waiting right here just in case the doctor does come out. I'll come and get you right away. Promise." He patted her hand and nodded some more.

Something deep inside told Julie that she could trust this man. Pulling herself together, she got to her feet. The nurse put an arm around her shoulder and slowly led her away, all the while whispering words of encouragement. At the nurses' station she produced a face cloth and several towels from behind the counter. Just down the hall, she knocked on the door of a restroom. There was no answer. She pressed the metal handgrip down and shouldered open the bulky door. "Here," said the nurse, confidently. "Nobody will bother you here. Take all the time you need. You know where you can find me if you need anything, okay?"

Julie stood there as the door closed behind her. Alone in the cold, expansive room, she took a trembling breath. She looked around. Toilette. Wash basin. Shower. No, she was not going to take off her clothes. That would chill her even more than she already was. She stopped short. There, in the full-length mirror that was clamped to the back of the door…was that her? Her hair was matted with filth and blood. Tracks of tears streaked through the dry blood splattered on her face. Grimy crimson smeared her camel-colored coat. Suddenly warmth no longer mattered as defiantly she ripped off the coat and stuffed it into the trash. Her teeth gnashed as some of the thick material stuck out of the covered container. "Get the hell out of my life," she screeched as her foot jammed the damned thing into the container. As the cover swung back and forth, she panted and looked down at herself. There were gaping holes in the knees of her nylons. Blood and sidewalk grime caked her legs all the way down to her shoes—her shoes…they were mutilated. Remembering the time that Emma had scrounged around the closet on her hands and knees looking for shoes, Julie rolled her eyes. "What's with me and shoes?"

Inspecting her plaid wrap-around skirt, Julie was amazed. It was only slightly soiled. Her heather-colored mock turtleneck had gone unscathed. She pulled it over her head and hooked it on the doorknob. She stuck her head in the sink and ran the water full force as if that would take away the trauma. Squeezing out soap from the wall dispenser, she lathered up her hair. As she did, broken fingernails gouged her scalp, making her remember one other God-awful day. Rinsing endlessly, she grumbled, "I should shave off all this ugly mop." She scrubbed her face until it stung and after rinsing, dried it with a hospital towel that smelled of pine disinfectant. Blotting the dampness from her hair, she looked around for a comb or brush. She had a small brush in her pocketbook…but where was that? Having no clue, she crossed her arms and groaned, "Oh, great." Seconds later, her arms uncrossed and she rushed to the trash container. She tugged out one side of her coat and fished around in the pockets. She grasped her keys and held them up so she could see the attached heart-shaped ornament that bore a picture of Mom and her. She held them to her breast and sank to the floor. Nausea brought bile to her throat. She was going to throw up. She crawled to the toilet. Nothing happened.

After a while, Julie got to her feet and splashed water on her face. Without toweling off, she tussled her hair into place with her fingers.

When a broken nail snagged, she struggled to remove it and discovered that virtually every one of her nails had been mangled. Geez, they had just grown out from that melee with Jim. The despicable events of last November and the past few hours embroiled her. Biting off a piece of fingernail, she began to pace. Her shoes clacked on the tile as she shook out her arms and legs and leered at the mirror every time she passed it. She spun around and jammed her hands into her hips. Glaring at herself, she yelped, "Chill out, you. This is not doing you or Mom any good." Her fingers covered her lips. *Mom! Oh, God. Mom. I gotta get back!*

Shaking out her wrists, Julie took deep breaths while flexing her shoulders. She felt a little better. She took another deep breath and without letting it out grabbed the door handle and left the bathroom. A faint smile lifted her lips when she rounded the corner and Ken instantly rose to his feet. Her breath came easier now.

"Nothing new on your Mother," he said. "But a cop came by with your pocketbook."

Her smile disappeared. She wasn't sure she wanted it. It was scraped up and would always remind her of this day. It was as if Ken could read her mind, for he placed it on the chair next to him, the chair on the opposite side from where Julie was going to sit. As they sat down together, she heaved a sigh, "Nice of you to stick around."

"I had to. I've had more than my share of this stuff. Nobody should go through it alone." His voice drifted off as his head turned sideways. Four years had come and gone since the loss of his wife and child, but he felt as if it all happened just yesterday. He doubted if he was ever going to get over it.

Reading his pain, Julie whispered, "Ellen told me about…" She looked down at her fingers laced upon her lap. "I'm terribly sorry." How could anybody survive that kind of tragedy? How could she survive the loss of her mother, now that she and Mom understood each other better? Gosh, what Mom must have gone through when she lost Peter…hum, Peter, Dad? What would she have called him?

How would it have felt to have a real live father? Especially at a time like this. Noticing Ken's knees, only inches from hers, Julie froze. She could not speak as a chill swept through her, making her skin crawl. No man had gotten that close to her since…since Jim. Then Ken's scent drifted her way. It was light, pleasant, and somehow reassuring…just like his voice when he said, "It's okay."

A middle-aged surgeon with a wiry beard and graying brown hair that was disheveled after pulling off a surgical cap, exploded through the O. R. doors. Still in green scrubs, he tromped up to Julie. She searched his face for signs—any sign—positive, negative—anything. His tone was straightforward when he spoke. "Your mother's doing as well as can be expected. The next several hours will tell the story. We've done all we can do. There's extensive damage to internal organs. We patched them up. Now we wait. As soon as your mother is settled in the recovery room, a nurse will be out to get you. I'll be checking in from time to time. Any questions?"

Julie shook her head. There should be questions, but she could not think of any. As the surgeon turned and walked away, she got the feeling that his words had been well rehearsed under the fire of experience. But still she wanted to call him back. She wanted to hear some words of reassurance.

Ken patted her hand. "Your mother's halfway there."

CHAPTER 10

"*I*'ll take you to your mother now," said a nurse in blue scrubs.

Julie gave a sigh of guarded relief. Supporting her elbow, Ken helped her to her feet.

"She's still sleeping," the nurse continued as she led them through the swinging doors warning No Admittance. Julie cast an anxious look at Ken. He smiled reassuringly. The nurse patted Julie's shoulder and said, "The anesthesia won't wear off for several hours. We don't want her waking up too soon and moving around too much."

As they weaved through the never-ending maze of halls and several more swinging doors, Julie wished Ken or the nurse would say something, anything to take away the sound of her heart thundering in her ear. There must be some meaningless topic. The weather? Sports? How awful what happened to Mom? They entered the recovery room where only monitors and the scuffing of their shoes on the tile floor disturbed the silence as they passed cubicles created by light blue fabric hanging from ceiling tracks. The nurse stopped in front of one that was half-opened next to the observation station and yanked open the drape. Julie stopped in her tracks and gasped at the sight of her pallid, gaunt mother lying there so frail with tubes and monitors violating her body. Mom did not stir. Her face was expressionless, deathlike. Her eyes showed not even a hint of movement.

Her lips did not smile that almost undetectable way that only Julie had the privilege of knowing. A tube was coming out of her mouth and was taped to her right cheek. Her arms lay parallel to her lifeless body, limp, unmoving, while intravenous tubes dripped hydrating fluids and medication into the top of her right hand. At intervals the blood pressure armband automatically filled and relaxed, relaying numbers to a monitor at the head of the bed. Another monitor echoed heart rhythms. Julie reeled and Ken grappled to sustain her. The nurse quickly pulled up a chair and said, "Here. I'll get another chair."

But Julie remained standing as the drape slid shut. Searching for signs of life, she enfolded her hands around her mother's left hand. Helplessness overwhelmed her. She sank onto the chair and began to weep.

"Your mother is going to be okay." Ken's voice was subdued as his arm wrapped around her shoulders. "She's a survivor." When the nurse returned with another chair, Ken dragged it close to Julie. He made sure that she never lost contact with her mother's hand. "The worst is over," he whispered. He took off his jacket and draped it over the back of the chair. Loosening his tie, he opened the top button of his shirt. He rolled up the sleeves of his v-neck sweater and sat down. "We'll be right here when she wakes up."

Julie bit the inside of her cheek. She glanced at Ken who was leaning back in his chair, studying her mother. An inner suffering was prevalent on his attractive face, yet there was hope there too. It was so hard to believe that he had come here out of nowhere and without ever being asked. He stood by her, strong and confident, just when she needed someone the most. A hint of a smile lifted her lips, the first since this whole awful mess started.

An hour passed. Nurses came and went, checking this device and that. Monitors seemed to hypnotize Julie into the same trance that had turned her mother to stone. At long last a nurse's voice rattled the stupor. "She's coming out of the anesthesia."

Julie raised herself up as her mother gave a slight moan and her eyelids flickered. Slowly her eyes blinked open. Her brows arched as she filtered out the glare that made shadows of the figures that surrounded her. Facial muscles refused to cooperate as her parched lips attempted to form, "Julie."

Leaning over the bedrail, Julie drew her mother's hand to her cheek. Long, slender fingers were limp and cold as they touched the girl's face. Tears of relief overflowed as Julie whimpered, "I love you, Mom."

"Here," said the nurse while gently spooning ice chips into Elizabeth's mouth. "This will help to moisten your mouth. We don't want you drinking too much water all at once." The ice melted quickly and after another spoonful, the nurse dampened a face cloth and dabbed it on Elizabeth's face and neck.

"Feels good," Elizabeth breathed.

"Glad to hear it," smiled the nurse. "Can you tell me your name?"

Julie watched nervously while her mother cleared her throat in small coughs. "Hmm, uhhm…Elizabeth…Spencer."

With a sigh of relief, Julie smiled at Ken. He winked. She felt herself flush and quickly looked back at her mother and contentedly patted her hand. "It's heaven to hear your voice, Mom."

The nurse took her patient's pulse then said, "My name is Anne." She picked up the call button and waved it in front of Elizabeth. "If you need anything, just press this." Placing the device on the bed near her patient's hand, Anne patted her arm and said, "Be back in a while."

Gazing at her beleaguered daughter, Elizabeth savored the image. She managed a faint smile as her eyes closed. Drifting in and out of medicated sleep, she found comfort in Julie's vigilance. She was unconcerned about the stranger. It was good that Julie had someone to lean on.

Julie was indeed thankful that Ken was there. She was becoming accustomed to his reassuring smile and nod and when he squeezed her hand, she felt as though she could face just about anything. "How did you find out about all this?" she asked.

"Someone came into Ellen's office saying they had seen you run into Emergency behind a stretcher and that your clothes were all bloodied up. Ellen called me at my office and I hopped right over here. Hope you don't mind..." Ken searched Julie's face, adding, "But I'm kind of glad I did. When I saw you come out of Emma's room alone, I knew right then and there that you needed someone to stick it out with you. Everyone else stayed with Emma and that's to be expected, but that didn't do you much good."

"Well, I am glad you're here." Julie frowned. "Mom and I don't have family like Emma does." She clenched her jaw. "Someday..."

"Did you get hurt, Julie?" Elizabeth wheezed.

Julie and Ken shot startled glances at the bed. "Mom," Julie exclaimed and rubbed her mother's hand.

"You hurt?" Elizabeth repeated.

"Scraped my knee, that's all." Julie shook her head, minimizing her wounds. They were nothing compared to Mom's. What's a few broken nails? They would grow back. She picked up the paper cup and spoon and asked, "More ice?"

Elizabeth gave a slight nod then cast a questioning glimpse at the stranger who immediately stood up. "I'm Ken Waters. I know Julie through work." He shifted as if to shake her hand but then backed off.

"Ken stuck it out with me since everyone else stayed with Emma," said Julie as she spooned ice chips into her mother's mouth.

Remembering the lifeless old woman lying in Margi's arms, Elizabeth became agitated. "Emma? She okay?"

"Don't get yourself upset, Mom." Julie set the spoon and empty cup down on the bed tray. Toying with her mother's hair, she said, "I saw Em a couple hours ago. I'm sure she's just fine by now." She glanced at her watch then at Ken.

"Hey, listen," he said with a cough. "I'll go check it out and bring back coffee. Something to eat, Julie?"

Julie smiled. "Coffee's good."

As his footsteps faded away, Elizabeth whispered, "He's nice."

"Yeah," Julie said wistfully. "I talked about him at Julio's, remember? I can't believe he's been here all this time." Noticing that her mother was rustling about with a distressed look blanketing her face, Julie asked, "What's the matter, Mom?"

"Been lying this way too long." Elizabeth let out a faint groan. "But it hurts too much to move."

"I'll get Anne," said Julie, pressing the call button.

Together, Julie and Anne adjusted Elizabeth's position and attended to her needs. Then Anne picked up the spoon and empty paper cup and said, "How about some water?" Without waiting for an answer, she filled a fresh paper cup from the water pitcher and stuck a straw in it. She held it as Elizabeth took several gulps.

Elizabeth coughed and said, "Thanks."

"Let me know if there's anything else," Anne said. As she yanked the drape aside, she came head to head with Ken. She jumped back. "Oh my goodness. You startled me."

Ken was just as shaken as she was and they both laughed it off. He handed a cup of coffee to Julie and said, "Emma's doing great. Everyone but Margi has left." He reached into his pocket. "Here's the fixin's for the coffee. I didn't know how you take it."

"I really appreciate everything you've done," said Julie.

"Glad to help," he said. Embarrassment reddened his face as he shot a sideways look at Elizabeth. Noticing that color had returned to her amused face, he stammered, "You're looking a lot better, ma'am."

"Elizabeth," she chuckled. "I want to thank you for hanging out with Julie through this awful mess."

Ken nodded and gulped the rest of his coffee. "I gotta go. Time to get back to work."

Julie looked at her watch. "Oh my God! It's morning!"

Acting as if he did not want to leave, Ken said, "Anything else I can do before I go?"

"No. You go get some rest," Elizabeth said. "And you too, Julie."

"But Mom," Julie whined.

"I'll be all right," her mother insisted. "You gotta go home and feed the cat."

Julie chuckled and Ken looked confused. She poked his arm and said, "We don't have a cat."

"Oh," Ken nodded. "You're quite the joker," he said as he squeezed Elizabeth's hand. He put on his jacket and as he left the cubical said, "I'll be back."

"I'll go home and freshen up," said Julie as she bent over the bed rail and kissed her mother goodbye. "And feed the cat...but I'll be right back right after that. I don't feel like sleeping. I want you rockin' 'n a-rollin' by the time I get back, you hear?" Before pulling the curtain, Julie gazed at her mother one last lingering time. "Love you, Mom," she said and looked up. *Thank you, God, for not taking Mom.* As she glanced back at Elizabeth, Julie paused for a second then went back and kissed Mom again. "See you in a little while."

Ken was waiting outside. "Where's your coat?" he asked.

Julie lifted her index finger to her mouth, "Shshsh," she whispered. She tugged him away from the curtain and again whispered. "It's in the trash. The sight of that filthy thing makes me want to puke. I never want to set eyes on it again."

Ken took off his jacket and said, "Here, take mine. This sweater's heavy enough." Helping Julie to put it on, he said, "Where's your car?"

"Oh no," Julie gasped. It had not occurred to her that she was without transportation. "It's still parked in front of the bank. Drop me off?"

"It's on the way," Ken laughed and took her arm.

❧   ❧   ❧

Yellow police tape had been stretched around the crime scene. Two men in suits were hovering within, jotting down information in notebooks. Margi's new car was still there. A bullet had punctured the rear window, spider-webbing the glass. Emma's green knitted gloves lay on the sidewalk where she had fallen. And not far away was one of Elizabeth's one-inch heels. Seeing the color drain from Julie's face, Ken said, "Don't look." He pulled up behind Julie's car and cut the engine. His fingertips lifted her chin towards him. "It's over, okay?" His eyes coaxed a nod. "I'll wait right here until you leave."

"I'd like that," she said and lightly kissed his cheek.

Surprise blanketed his face. As she reached for the door handle, he said, "Wait."

She glanced back at him.

"Don't forget your pocketbook." As she reached down on the floor to get it, he stammered, "If you need anything…anything at all…call me at work…or home. Here's the number." He grabbed a business card from the ashtray and scribbled his home number on the back of it. Gazing at her tenderly, he handed it to her.

"Thanks," she murmured and slipped it into her pocketbook.

He grabbed her other hand. Their eyes met. With a wistful smile, he winked and gave her hand a light squeeze. Feeling herself flush, she quickly opened the door. The air had a sharp edge to it and the smell of spent gunpowder was faint. Neither pierced her senses as she hurried to her car.

Ken rolled down his window and called, "See you at the hospital tonight." He started to roll the window back up, but stopped. He rolled it back down and hollered, "And don't forget to feed the cat!"

Julie waved a hand high in the air and hastily unlocked the door. As she turned the engine over, she peered into the rearview mirror. Ken was back there giving her a thumbs-up sign. As she drove away, she peered into the mirror. He was still there, sitting in his car, watching. When she rounded the corner at the next block, she looked again. He wasn't there anymore. Suddenly, she missed him and had the urge to turn the car around.

CHAPTER 11

$\mathcal{J}$ulie slouched over the kitchen counter and leaned on her elbows. Cradling her chin in her palms, she stared vacantly at the mug of water revolving inside the droning microwave. She had just gotten up from her mother's bed where she had crashed after arriving home. She had gone straight there. Her own room never entered her mind. But lying on Mom's bed, she felt so alone. How hard it was not to hear Mom moving about the tiny two-bedroom apartment. Most times, it wasn't easy to hear her anyway, but at least Julie knew she was there. It seemed as though Mom never slept. She was up late at night and before the crack of dawn, yet rarely did she watch television or read a book or listen to the radio.

Twenty-one seconds were left on the microwave timer. Julie stood upright and stretched her back. How on earth was she supposed to sleep? Everything that had happened in the last twenty-four hours still had a hold on her. She remembered grabbing Ken's jacket from the foot of Mom's bed and dragging it up around her shoulders. The smell of him was all over it. She had thought about his business card she had chucked into her pocketbook. She had grabbed her pocketbook off the night table and had fished it out. Studying his writing on the back of it, she pictured how he had given it to her. As her fingers ran across the number, the thought of him warmed her through and through. Her eyes closed, envisioning his face. Her heart told her she could trust him. She wanted to… She shivered. But…well, her track record as far as men were concerned was not all that good to say the least.

The wall phone next to the microwave jarred Julie upright. She snatched up the receiver and banged it against the side of her head as she said, "Hello."

A subdued voice on the other end said, "Hey kid. It's Margi."

Julie shook herself out of her daydream. "How's it going?" The microwave squawked and its light went out. She unwrapped a tea bag then took out the steaming mug.

"Hanging in there, I guess. Dreadful thing, huh?" Margi's voice melted away as if mentioning the bloody melee might bring it all back to life.

Mindlessly Julie dunked the tea bag in the water and muttered, "Yeah…"

"How's your Mom? I didn't get to see her," Margi mumbled. "Wouldn't have done her a bit of good seeing me all bloody and all."

Julie shuddered with the thought. Taking a deep breath, she said, "Mom was pretty much out of the anesthesia when I left. The nurse told me she would probably sleep off and on for the next twenty-four hours."

Margi took a deep breath. "I'll poke my head in when I go back, promise."

"I came home to get cleaned up. But I'm stuck in this God-awful funk," Julie cleared her throat. "I can't sleep, but I can't seem to get going either."

"Know wha'cha mean," Margi said dryly. "I am so tired, I could just drop, but I just can't bring myself to sleep."

Julie walked away from the cup of tea, leaving the bag in it. "I can't believe that we had such a good time at Julio's and then a thing like that happened to spoil it all. How in the world can anyone do such a thing?"

"Bet that schmuck ain't the least bit concerned at all about how many lives he messes up," Margi spouted.

Julie winced. "Thank God everyone made it."

"You don't know what it's been like," Margi grumbled. "First my father and now… Anyways, Ma's worried about cha, kid. And your Mom too. I told Ma to simmer down, everybody's doin' fine. But you know Ma, she's gotta fret about somethin'."

"Well, tell her to stop," Julie said. "I'll peek in before I go to see Mom. I know she will grill me for all the latest info on your mother." Julie also knew that once she was with Mom again, she would not want to leave until they kicked her out. "What time you goin' back?"

"In a bit. Ev's driving me back, 'cuz the cops kept my car for evidence an' all.

Julie didn't have the heart to tell her that her new car had a bullet hole in it. "I can pick you up if you want."

"Nah. I wanna talk to the kids and make sure they're dealing okay with this. They're still asleep," said Margi. "Ev says they did just fine. He took them to the chapel during the worst of it 'cuz he didn't know what else to do, since I was such a wreck and there was such a commotion."

Julie bit her lip. It wasn't fair that such a terrible thing could happen to such a nice family. She shuddered with the thought of how much worse it could have been. "Well, give Evan and the kids my love."

"Whaddaya think about Janice?" Margi chuckled. "Pickin' up that gun an' all? We oughta name her 'Sure Shot Janice' or somethin'. Did you see her haul off and kick that guy? And of all things, the way she stood over him spread-eagled with the gun pointing straight at his head? I never heard anybody holler like her. Can you believe all that?"

Unable to resist her friend's humorous narrative, Julie giggled. Tears of relief welled. How wonderful it was to hear that boisterous voice. And for that matter her own levity. "Have you seen Janice since your mother woke up?"

"Nah. She ducked out shortly after Ma came out of it. Didn't say so much as good-bye," Margi said. "Bet by now though, the reality of it all has set in."

A shiver shot up Julie's spine. "Yeah, I'll bet."

"Anyway, don't forget, ya gotta stop in when ya get back. I can't take it when Ma gets all nerved up."

Julie gave an uneasy chuckle. "Sure will. I'll get my act together and be there soon." Suddenly Julie wanted to see her Mom and Emma. She needed their reassuring presence.

"By the way…that friend of yours…Ken?" Margi gushed. "He popped into the emergency room lookin' for ya and then again to check up on Ma. Whatta hunk!"

Julie felt her face redden and at that moment was glad that nobody else was around to see. "He stayed with me all the way through till Mom woke up."

"Ma's really takin' to him. And you know that when Ma takes a shine to someone, she gets involved, or, um, maybe I should say, meddles? So watch it, girl."

As her friend twittered on and on like a schoolgirl Julie mused, yeah, Ken was quite a guy. He said he would be at the hospital later, but would he really show? Or was he too good to be true? How about that…Janice had said that very same thing about Adam at lunch yesterday.

A short time later, Julie stepped into the shower. The stream of water felt glorious, routing out the stress from her aching body. Again her long blond hair became caught in torn fingernails. After drying off, she clipped her nails to the quick and decided to call Margi back to get her hairdresser's number. Time for a change…a big change. Visions of Ken mingled with thoughts of her mother. Julie had a feeling that her brain would never again separate the two and that life was definitely going to get better from here on out. As she reached for the phone, she spied the tea she had made earlier. She had not taken a single sip. Shrugging it off, she dumped the strong liquid into the sink, tossed the bag and wrapper into the trash, and then made a hasty call to Margi.

Afterwards, Julie set about packing a few things for her mother. Plucking a faded terry cloth robe off the back of the bathroom door, she held it up. "Too ratty." She bit the inside of her cheek. "I'll just have to get her a new one," she said and hung it back up. In her mother's bedroom, she slid open the top bureau drawer and selected underwear. In the closet, she found a sweat outfit for Mom to come home in. The suitcase on the floor of the closet was much too big for so few things, so Julie rustled about the closet and spied a flowered overnight bag on the shelf behind some hats, scarves, and other things. "Perfect!" Opening the bag on the bed, Julie stepped back. Her fingers pressed against her lips. Inside was a mishmash of schoolwork—hers—preserved by a mother who had never shown the slightest sign of interest. Julie started to pace. Every so often she stopped to squint at the overnight bag that vomited schoolwork. How much Mom had suffered, not only from losing Peter or being rejected by his family or even by her family leaving her alone, thousands of miles away, but also by having an illegitimate child born when that was such a social stigma. Julie loved her mother but had her mother loved her back for no other reason than she was her child? Julie sank to her knees. Softly she sobbed grieving for a lost father and all the goodness missing from her life that his loss had stolen. Raising her eyes heavenward, her voice transgressed the silence of the empty apartment. "Why wasn't I ever good enough to make Mom forget?"

As Julie steered her car onto Washington Street, it was a stroke of luck that a car was just pulling out from a parking spot right smack in front of her mother's favorite store. She avoided looking at the bank where mayhem had broken loose. In the middle of parallel parking, she bit her cheek. "Money. Gosh, do I have enough?" After shutting off the engine, she fished through her wallet. "Eight bucks." She stared at the bills in her hand then remembered a secret stash. Emptying the contents of her pocketbook on the front seat, she yanked back the torn lining in the bottom. "Great!" Taking out several twenties, she kissed them then chucked all the money into her jacket pocket. Leaving the pocketbook and its contents on the seat, she jumped out of the car. A sharp wind assailed her. Her hair tossed wildly about as she locked the door. Brushing her hair aside, she dashed around the car and looked up.

"How ya doin' lil' lady?"

Her body turned to stone, for she stood face-to-face with one of the guys who worked with Jim—the squat pulpy one who sported a buzz cut and always needed a shave. His grimy, washed-out work khakis looked like the same ones he had on the first day she had set eyes on him. His hand clutched a beat-up metal lunch box. Julie stopped short. Her blood went cold. As her eyes darted about, a crooked, yellowy leer smeared his face. His breathing was hard and heavy as he inched closer. "Lookin' for Jimbo, honeeh?" His alcoholic eyes lusted beneath spindly eyebrows while his forehead furrowed repeatedly and he gnawed on a wad of gum.

Julie backed into the trunk of her car. Jim and this guy had staked her out, waiting for the right moment to close in on her. Heartbeats throbbed in her throat. The guy leaned into her. "The ol' cuss's been braggin', ya know. How he got outta ya what he was aftah. Humph. An' now, he ain't got no more use fer ya, honeeh." He snickered. His gum snapped. "Nah. Yer butt is out in the cold now."

So Jim wasn't looking for her. She steadied herself and glanced around. It was a toss-up whether that stink was coming from this guy or a skunk that had just shot off in a back alley. Strangers passed by. All gave wary expressions, but nobody stopped. Not one got involved. Not one said, "Hey, what's going on there?"

"Kinda means yer up for grabs, don' it?" The back of his filthy hand swiped his lips as he gave her a sidelong glance. Was he giving her the finger? "How 'bout givin' me a tussle?" He chewed with anticipation.

Red anger flushed her face as every muscle in her body tightened. Julie straightened and shoved him away. White-knuckled, her fist threatened the jerk inches from his face. "What do you think?" she growled. "I'm a piece of meat?"

As she skirted around him, he grabbed her arm and spun her around. The tips of his ears were scarlet. His other hand shook the lunch box at her. "Wassamattah wit' cha? Think yer too good fer me or somethin'?" he slobbered.

Hatred impaled him as her teeth gritted. Her voice came as a steady seethe. "Get your filthy paws off me!"

He froze momentarily then dropped her arm and raised his hands, lunch box upside down in one. "Okay, okay. Only askin', honeeh," he chortled while backing away. His jaws rolled as his back teeth masticated gum. As Julie made a beeline for the woman's shop, the slime-ball slouched down and with one hand on his knee, roared with laughter that echoed among the buildings.

Blasting through the door at a dead run, she slammed it then leaned against the doorjamb. Tremors shook her body as she gasped for air. She leered up at the convulsing bell overhead.

A saleslady peeked out from behind a rack. "Can I help you?"

Swallowing hard, Julie pulled herself away from the doorjamb. Her hand brushed back the hair on her forehead. She reached into her pocket and held up a wad of crumpled bills and said, "A robe…I…I hafta buy my Mom a robe."

❦   ❦   ❦

The sight of Emma curdled Julie's insides. She had squelched the terror she had experienced on Washington Street, deciding not to mention it to anyone. Everybody had enough on their minds. Still, her legs began to quake again. But a weathered hand hungrily reached out to her and the touch stabilized her. She gazed at her old friend whose face had swelled so badly within a mass of black and blue that her eyes had become mere slits. Gauze and pink medical tape covered her nose. The flowered Johnny she wore seemed too flippant. Julie wanted to kiss Emma, but where? A peck on the cheek would sure cause pain, so instead the girl kissed the old hand. Emma gripped Julie's hand and pulled her near. "I'm so glad to see you, sweetheart. Come here, come here. Don't I look a frightful mess?"

Julie winced. "Geez, Em. You don't know how good you look to me."

"Your mother…how is your mother?" Emma implored. "Margi tells me they took out a bullet?"

"Yeah, in her stomach. It was touch and go there for a while. Gosh, I thought she'd never come out of the operating room." Julie unloaded pent-up terror. "Oh Em, I don't know what I'd do if I lost you or Mom."

Teardrops moistened the old woman's hand as she caressed the girl's cheek. "Here now, don't cry, dear," said Emma. She stroked Julie's blond hair. "We all pulled though and will all be the better for it. Now come on. You're much too pretty to cry. What if that handsome young man comes in? Now what is his name? Ah, yes, Ken."

Glancing at Margi who was grinning sheepishly, Julie said, "You guys are too much." Collecting herself, she changed the subject since she dared not to speculate on Ken's intentions. "How about you, Em? What's your doctor got to say?"

"I have a concussion and a batch of other medical mumbo jumbo. They want me to stay here tonight, for observation they say, but I don't want to." Emma's lips pursed.

Margi shook her index finger. "You're staying right where you are Ma, even if I have to sit on you."

Just then Janice walked into the room and Emma beckoned to her. "Janice, talk to Margi. I don't want to stay here tonight," she pleaded. "I want to sleep in my own bed."

Janice threw her hands in the air. Pecking a kiss on Emma's forehead, she shook her head. "Uh-uh, I'm not getting involved in any of this. Margi's bigger than me."

"Shiish, as if that mattered," wheezed Margi.

Julie embraced Janice. Clinging to her for a moment, she muttered, "Thanks so very, very much for what you did. You're truly the bravest person I've ever known."

"Yeah, and I want to thank you too." Everyone glanced toward the door. The voice belonged to the wounded police officer being pushed in a wheelchair by an orderly. He had raven hair with gray streaks feathering back at the temples. His square chin was freshly shaven, but a hint of blue indicated that he was a man who was plagued by a heavy beard. He wore the shirt and pants that matched his winter uniform, and his shoes were spit-shined.

"Well, come in," exclaimed Emma. "You look like you're doing just fine."

"Thanks to this lovely lady," he said pointing at Janice, "we are all doing fine." He clapped his hands. Others followed suit.

Janice peered down at the floor. "It was nothing…really," she sputtered.

"I wanted to see with my own eyes that all of you made it," said the cop. "Sorry all of you got caught in the crossfire. But that Janice LaRosa…ain't she somethin' else?"

"That guy was going for a gun…" Janice shivered, "and you were out of commission…something had to be done—and fast. I didn't give a thought to anything except making damn sure nobody else got hurt."

"What a creep," fumed Margi. "He just kept coming right straight at cha."

Janice twitched. "I got so mad…I kicked him as hard as I could, right where it hurts."

"But you didn't get hurt, did you dear?" Emma asked, eyeing her daughter-in-law for bruises.

"Not a scratch," Janice grinned.

"On the outside," said Margi. "But inside you're still a wreck, I can tell."

Janice shuddered as slow motion pictures of everyone lying on the frozen ground filled her mind. "When reality set in, I lost it. Adam held onto me—tight, until I stopped shaking. And Elliot, he kept whimpering, 'You okay, Mom? You okay?'"

"Poor little fella," Emma sympathized. "Tell him to come and see his Nana tomorrow—at home. Right Margi?"

"Yeah, Ma. Tomorrow," her daughter conceded. "But only if you behave yourself tonight."

Emma frowned and turned to the police officer, "What happened to that dreadful man?"

"He's being detained in the prison ward here in the hospital. Pretty banged up I'd say, but not as bad as you. Obviously he's got the harder head," the cop concluded. Nervous levity filled the room. "He was arraigned a little while ago from his hospital bed."

"Serves him right," spouted Margi.

"Well…I gotta go," said Julie as she went to kiss Emma's hand. "Mom's probably wondering where I am. I'll try to stop in again later."

"Tell her that Janice and I'll be there in a while," said Margi as she hugged Julie.

"Me, too," added the cop.

❧   ❧   ❧

Elizabeth had been moved into a semi private room and was napping peacefully in the bed next to the window when Julie pushed open the door. The other bed was empty. Julie studied her mother's face, bathed in sunbeams, looking so peaceful. The tubes and machines were gone. Only one intravenous line remained attached to the back of her hand. It pleased Julie to see Mom in more friendly surroundings. She set the flowered overnight bag in the corner. As she pulled up a chair, Elizabeth awoke. "Julie..." Her voice was hoarse and dry.

"You're looking so much better," Julie said then kissed her mother's forehead. "Here, how about some water?" The girl toyed with her mother's bangs and watched the water level rise and fall in the straw.

Elizabeth coughed then groggily jested, "I feel like a truck mowed me down."

"You might've fared better if a truck *had* mowed you down," said the surgeon. Nonchalantly he strolled into the room and took her hand. Taking her pulse, he winked. "That bullet certainly wreaked havoc on your insides." He lifted the bedclothes and inspected the incision. Pressing lightly here and there, he replaced the sheet and warming blanket. "Looks good, young lady. I'm going to have the nurses get you up in a few hours. I want you to start moving around, but you're staying put for a few more days." He turned to leave, but then turned back. "Now, remember, no more playing chicken with bullets."

Her face brightened as Elizabeth gave a weak shrug.

A short time later, Margi and Janice showed up. The four women got right into analyzing every minute detail of the ordeal, this way and that, trying to make sense of the horror they had experienced. After everyone left, Julie said to Elizabeth, "Nice to have others to talk to about things."

"Yeah," said Elizabeth, thinking how they had both lacked family and friends for too many years. "Emma and her family have really adopted us."

When Ken walked in, Julie's heart flip-flopped. Surprised and relieved, she looked at the clock. It had gotten late.

"Look's like you two have settled in," he said, noticing the flowers in vases scattered about the room.

"That bouquet of yellow roses over there on the sill is the one you sent me. Thank you very much," said Elizabeth. "They're quite fragrant."

"Don't mention it. These rooms need brightening," he said. "Did you get some rest, Julie?"

"No, but I'll sleep like a log tonight," Julie replied.

Ken's eyebrows fluttered, "Wish I could."

"You have trouble sleeping?" Elizabeth asked.

"Getting my wife and daughter out of my mind isn't easy."

Elizabeth saw the hinges of his jaws tighten and muscles flex down the side of his face. "How long has it been?" she quietly asked.

He cleared his throat. "Four years." He took a deep breath. "It's been rough. But at least things worked out right for you and your daughter."

Making eye contact, Julie instantly sensed his sincerity. Without being asked he had reached out to her when she needed him most. Too bad she had not been there for him. How awful to lose one's mate—no one left to turn to in the darkness, no one who understands, no one to love.

Later as they left the hospital, Julie and Ken stepped out into brisk night air. "It's snowing," she said as they pulled their collars up to their faces. It was long after rush hour and few cars were on the street.

"Two to four inches of the white stuff in the next twelve hours," said Ken as he took her arm. She looked up at him. Even in the wintry night, his face was handsome. She leaned against his shoulder, feeling safe, as if she had known him all her life. Their conversation floated like the puffy flakes that cavorted around the street lamps, sparkling with a casualness usually known to only those who had been together for years. They were friends. They were lovers without the benefit of physical intimacy. They made love with words.

CHAPTER 12

The next morning, Julie peeked into Emma's hospital room. It was empty and the bed had been stripped and left unmade. "Oh. Em's gone home," Julie muttered and took off for her mother's room. When she got there, Emma was there, sitting in a wheelchair, all dressed up with the coat that she wore to church on Sundays laying across her lap. All the clothes she had worn the day of the robbery had been pitched into hospital trash bins. Margi was teetering off the bed, her legs swinging back and forth while Elizabeth, freshly bathed and wearing the mint green robe that Julie had purchased yesterday, basked in the sunlight near the window in a reclining chair. Her hair had been shampooed, dried, and neatly combed, in contrast to the past two days. Julie grinned. "You look great, Mom. I knew mint was your color."

Guilt rippled through Elizabeth. It had been cruel to hide that flowered overnight bag. Even more for Julie to find it the way she had. After Emma and Margi leave, Elizabeth thought, I'll have to talk to Julie about it. Shaking off the guilt, Elizabeth stammered, "They let me take a shower. Getting all that crud off made me feel like a new woman. The candy stripers here are real gems. One of them did up my hair like a pro." She picked up the mirror from the bed stand and gazed intently into it.

"Looks great, Mom," said Julie.

"Hey, speaking about looks," Margi barked, "take a gander at you, kid."

Julie scanned all the faces scrutinizing her new haircut. "Like it?" Seeing nodding approvals, Julie flounced her honey-blond hair and said, "I called your hairdresser, Margi, this morning. She had a cancellation so she took me right away."

"Nice change, kid" said Margi while sucking something out of a side tooth.

"A bob flatters your face," said Elizabeth as she handed the mirror to Julie.

Julie took it and held it at arms length, scrutinizing herself. "She cut off five inches."

"Your hair looks a lot thicker," said Emma.

"She did a great job, huh?" Julie asked. A haircut might seem trivial, but she figured it was as good a place as any to start making changes in her life. Hopefully, better days were on the horizon, she thought as she handed the mirror back to Elizabeth.

Margi twisted up her face while stuffing her hair under her bandanna. "I gotta see her next week—*again*. This mop of mine grows too darned fast."

Julie giggled as she leaned down to kiss Emma. "The bruises on your face have faded quite a bit already."

"I am a fast healer," boasted the old woman. "Especially when I'm itching to escape a place like this." She winked at Margi and added with a hint of sarcasm, "I appreciate sleeping in my own bed, thank you very much." Emma wanted things to get back to normal as soon as possible, but also was eager to get back to the room where Seth had promised he would always be. It seemed that the only goodness out of all of these past few days was that she now knew for certain that he was still with her. She had to believe his words about how important she was to the people in her life. And most of all he was not gone from her forever. Indeed, they would be together again.

"We wanted to celebrate Ma's homecoming but at her insistence put it off," Margi said and turned to Elizabeth. "But when you get outta here, there's gonna be an awesome bash—lots of people, food, wine, the whole enchilada."

Julie laughed. "You got it all planned out, don't cha?"

"Yeah and don't think that you're gettin' out of it easy, kid. You're helpin' me get Ma's house ready for the invasion."

Without warning, glass shattered. Happy chatter abruptly ceased. As apprehensive eyes shot in the direction of the noise, Emma gasped, "Good Lord…"

Horror had taken over Elizabeth. Her face was devoid of color. Hyperventilating, her lips moved without sound. Her hand slowly elevated as if controlled by an invisible puppeteer. A trembling finger straightened, pointed, as she uttered, "No…it can't be…"

"Mom…what's wro…" cried Julie. Her eyes followed her mother's bore. There in the doorway stood an apparition—the shadowy figure that appeared during dark sleepless nights or during lonesome childhood hours at the park watching other children with their dads or during dreams of a far-off wedding day without a father to give her away. Her heart thundered. The man who had been nothing more than an aging photograph now stood in the doorway like a life-size mannequin set there by some heartless jokester.

"It can't be," Elizabeth moaned, her head wavering side to side. Surely she had lost her mind. She was just wishing him there. Her guts turned inside out, denying the sight. This was just a dream. Oh, God, there had been so many dreams. Her eyes scoured every inch of the slightly graying, clean-cut man. A tan topcoat was slung over his right arm, and the pale yellow oxford shirt was opened at the neck the way he always wore them. The golden brown v-neck sweater drew out the amber brindled in his uncertain brown eyes, the eyes she had drowned in that first moment of their meeting. Creases across the lap of his brown pants hinted at hours of sitting. How could this be a dream? For there he was, right in front of her eyes, awkward, unsure, just like that day so long ago on the shores of the Charles. "Yes…yes." Elizabeth struggled to her feet.

"Mom, no," cried Julie. She tried to stop her mother, but it was no use. She found herself being nudged aside as if she wasn't even there.

"Peter," Elizabeth screeched. "It's you! It's really you!" And as she hobbled towards him as fast as her injured body would allow, she beheld that silly little grin of his plastered on his face and his arms stretched wide. His overcoat rumpled to the floor as he captured her in his arms. And she felt his breath. And once again heard the voice that had echoed so distantly all these years. "Bethie. My own sweet Bethie." Hungrily Elizabeth and Peter consumed each other's lips. They clung to one another, never ever wanting this moment that they had craved for so many desolate years to end. His breath warmed her ear as his voice swept through her, "I have never stopped loving you, Bethie."

"I love you so, so much," she whimpered. "More now than ever."

"Oh, my sweet morning eyes. You have no idea how much I have missed you, how much I have needed you."

Closing her eyes, Elizabeth soaked up the incredible reality of his body pressing against hers and inhaled his essence as if he was the first rose of spring along an ocean path. Although thinner now, he still felt like he did that summer so long ago, sensuous, wonderful, and oh, so real. She stared into his eyes that wordlessly pledged that he would never again leave her.

"Mom?"

"Julie?" Elizabeth turned. Why, look at Julie…she's standing there so all alone, bewildered, like a child lost in the wood, awaiting rescue. Elizabeth backed away from Peter. Her fingers entwined his and she gave a tug. "Come, I want you to meet Julie…your daughter."

Peter froze, gawking at the nineteen-year-old in disbelief. His brow arched as his incredulous eyes shot back to Elizabeth. Seeing silent affirmation, he felt her hand tug his once again. "Come," she said.

Hesitantly, Peter reached for his daughter's hand. "I...I didn't know..." He raised her hand to his lips. Tears streamed down their cheeks. "I am so overjoyed to meet you," he whispered.

As the stranger's arms enveloped Julie, words failed her. Over his shoulder, she stared at her mother who looked upon father and daughter with silent adoration. Julie smiled and beckoned until her mother stepped up to them and encircled her arms around them.

From her wheelchair, Emma watched the three embrace. So this was what Seth meant. Yes, she needed to be here for this moment...to bear witness to these three people finding their way back to each other after so many years. Within her soul, Seth stirred. Her eyes filled with sentimental tears as her hand squeezed Margi's. "This long overdue reunion is indeed a miracle."

"How did you find me, Peter?" Elizabeth asked. "Here, of all places?" She didn't give him a chance to answer. "Where have you been? What happened to you?"

"Sshh, Bethie," Peter chuckled while placing his finger upon her lips. "One question at a time. First of all, I was going through the newspaper yesterday morning and came across an article about a bank robbery. I couldn't believe it when I spotted your name. I went nuts. It said you had been shot and in serious condition. I had to see you. I was so worried. I called every hospital in the area until I found you. But once I did, I freaked. What if you had forgotten about me and moved on? Married. Kids. I almost didn't come. But I just couldn't get you out of my mind. I had to find out if there was still a chance for us. So I jumped on the next plane."

"And I'm so glad you did," murmured Elizabeth. She looked up at him. She swallowed hard. "I waited for you, you know, in the same apartment...until just a couple of months ago."

"I'm so sorry. So much time went by that..." he paused. Pain riddled his face. "I was missing in action for four and a half years. They found me in a village somewhere in Cambodia. I...I didn't know who I was and...I didn't have a clue about how I had even gotten there." His voice was thick and labored. "I was sick, real sick, malaria and other things. I didn't come out of it for a long time. The doctors at the VA Hospital in Virginia were surprised when I did. Vietnam is still a blank to me...all blank. Tortured...and brainwashed—that's what the doctors say. But I can't remember one blessed thing." His head drooped and wavered side-to-side.

Elizabeth lifted his chin. He turned away. "Listen to me," she said. "You did nothing wrong."

"Yes, I did, Bethie...I didn't come back...I didn't come back to you." His hand jounced. "I didn't come back to us.

Snagging his hand, Elizabeth drew Peter into her arms. "You're here now," she whispered.

"No," he moaned and struggled to turn away. She held tight. He looked into her eyes, his eyes filled with grief. "I didn't have guts enough. When my mind cleared, so much time had passed and...I didn't think you wanted a...uhm...a sick cripple hanging on to you." He raised his right arm that he had been hiding behind his back. A prosthetic hand.

Holding back her shock, Elizabeth said, "Nothing matters but you."

"I don't know what happened to my hand," he groaned. "When I came to my senses, it wasn't there."

She gently shook him by the arms, saying, "We can face anything now that you're here. Right, Julie?"

"Mom never gave up on you," Julie nodded. "So don't give up on her...or me."

"Come on, Margi," said Emma. "Let's give this family some privacy. They have a lot of catching up to do."

Margi wheeled her mother towards the reunited family and whispered in Julie's ear. "Call me later, kid."

Julie gave a little giggle. This was the first time she had ever heard Margi speak in less than a howl. "Thanks Margi, you too Em, for being here…for me and Mom…" she said. A crooked smile grew on her lips. Her eyes rolled as she winced, "Again."

Squeezing the girl's hand, Emma murmured. "Remember your vow about making your life better? As you see, time has a way of making good things happen. Just give it a chance." She kissed Julie and Elizabeth goodbye and then clutched Peter's hand with both of hers. "You made the right decision to come back," Emma said. "Elizabeth and Julie needed you through all these years. Not one bit of that has changed. So now is the time to throw away any of that self-doubt and fear rumbling around in that head of yours. You are home now."

CHAPTER 13

Stubbornly, the New England winter gave way to a mild, rainy spring. Crocuses popped up through thawing ground, boldly unfolding purple and white petals that animated grimy pillows of receding snow. Within the ensuing mud, lemony daffodils spiked then unfurled and seemed to provide some semblance of a habitually absent sun. And within the rolling mist of eventide, songs of amorous redbreasts courting mates echoed among leafing trees.

The homecoming celebration for Emma and Elizabeth had taken the back seat to Elizabeth and Peter's desire to marry in the shortest time possible. It seemed to Julie that they were afraid to let go of one another. They never stopped holding hands, even at the breakfast table while sipping coffee. Strange how much Mom had changed. For no good reason she would smile, skip through the house, or sing silly songs of 60s vintage in loud, falsetto productions.

Julie remembered the day when upon answering the telephone a woman with a sharp voice asked, "Elizabeth Spencer, please." It was only days after the wedding invitations had been mailed.

"May I say who's calling?" Julie had asked. Hearing the pointed reply, "Joan Blackman," she handed the phone to her mother and said, "It's for you, Mom. A Joan Blackman."

Well, instantly the color had drained from Mom's face and she had stood there, staring at the phone as if she had just witnessed the rebirth of a genuine dinosaur. Julie became frightened. "Mom?"

Slowly Elizabeth had put the receiver to her ear. "How are you...Mother," she said in a monotone voice.

Julie nearly croaked. Joan Blackman? Her grandmother? Seems she lived in Arizona and had received her invitation and intended to fly in to attend the wedding with her second husband and Elizabeth's brother, his wife, and fourteen-year-old son. Not only had the tight-wad called, which was unarguably a once-in-lifetime thing according to Mom, but also was actually going to spring for the trip? Several times during the wedding festivities, Julie had felt like demanding of the thin-lipped woman of medium height and thinning white hair the reason why she had not even attempted to be more involved in Mom's life. And what about her granddaughter? But Grandmother had such an ingrained appearance of volcanic wrath that Julie let the urge pass. Some other place, some other time.

Peter's sister, who was several years older than he, and her husband had motored in from Richmond. Their children were grown and though one was married and lived in Georgia and the other was going to college in northern California they all came. Peter's mother was fighting the effects of Alzheimer's disease and remained confined to a nursing home in Virginia. His father had died of a heart attack shortly after Peter had returned from Vietnam and before his only son emerged from mental haze.

Over fifty people attended the simple civil service at Julio's Ristorante. As awful as that robbery had been, Elizabeth insisted they should wed there. After all, if that day had not happened, Peter wouldn't have come back to her. Wearing an unpretentious yellow dress, she carried a single white rose cradled in baby's breath and tied with a satin knot. Peter sported a brown suit with a pale yellow oxford shirt. The colors brought out his eyes. His tie matched the brighter yellow of Elizabeth's ankle-length dress as did the rose, baby's breath, and ribbon pinned to his lapel. As the Justice of the Peace spoke, Peter squeezed Elizabeth's hand. Julie could read her mother's mind as she stared into Peter's eyes. Like Julie, Elizabeth felt as though all this was a dream—one that she had dreamed time and time again for so many obscure years. *Please Lord, don't let me wake,* she prayed. And even at the moment when his lips formed that silly little grin of his, then parted to whisper like the tide lying at its ebb, "I do," she still could not believe all this was real. Her eyes closed, letting his voice filter into every nook and cranny of her mind. "I love you, Bethie."

How romantic, Julie had thought. Dressed in a mint green dress, she scanned the assemblage. There was Ken, tall and confident, wearing a gray three-piece suit and smiling...yes, smiling...smiling at her...only her. And it seemed as if his cocoa eyes had never left hers, enveloping her in a sense of inner security that no coat of armor could ever give. She caught Emma's gaze that was marveling at the bridal party. As her weathered hands slowly rotated a glass of ginger ale on a table in front of her, the sunshine that streamed in through the front window fell upon her as if she was an angel sent to bless this reuniting family. Emma winked and Julie flushed with joy. Turning to admire Elizabeth and the handsome Peter, who was everything she had ever longed for in a father, Julie could not help but notice how vivacious, peaceful, and so incredibly happy Mom looked. Dreams of belonging to a family had finally come true for all three of them.

A month later, as windswept rain pounded at the windows, Julie drifted off to sleep. Contented with the changes in her life, she looked forward to a leisurely start the next morning. She finally had the day off from work. She wondered how Mom and Peter were doing. They were sailing somewhere off the South Shore. During their honeymoon in the Caribbean Islands, they had chartered a crewed fifty-foot sailboat. Peter had great concerns about captaining the boat all by himself because of his prosthetic hand, but he was pleasantly mistaken. Once he had learned the newly engineered machinery and regained his confidence, the ex MIA ran off the hired captain and took over the helm for the rest of the adventure. Since their return, Peter and Elizabeth could be found sailing out of Boston Harbor every weekend, weather permitting. Overjoyed to be together again, their happiness spilled over into everything, including Julie's life. Now Julie was a part of a real family and at last her life had changed for the better.

Once again, her parent's wedding and the headiness of the wine and music washed over her. She was in Ken's arms. She smelled him. She felt his ardor. And they danced. It was all so real. Oh, if only it were happening again at this moment. She never would let him go.

Julie rolled on her side. Her hand reached out, wishing to find him lying beside her. She had feelings—like she was ready to take another chance. But this time, if any relationship were to happen, it must happen naturally. Hormones were not going to drive her the way they did with…Finishing that thought seemed sacrilegious. But what would it be like to…to make love to…a man who actually loved her? A gentle man?

The jingle of the beige princess phone on the nightstand shattered the stillness. She rolled over to her other side. Her hand searched out the persistent bugger. "Who the heck is calling at this time of the night?" The receiver clunked against her head as her voice cracked, "Hullo?"

"Julie! It's me! Margi!"

"Margi?" Julie ran her tongue over her parched lips. "Uhhhm…what time is it?"

"Lemme look. 6:45. Ya gotta turn on the TV right now! Someone knocked off Jim Martin!"

Julie's brain was mush. "What the heck are you talking about?"

"It's true," Margi insisted. "That bastard pummeled some poor wench to a pulp. And she knifed him," she shrieked. There was a pause and then came a low hoarse rumble, "Imagine that? Man, he sure got his, huh?"

Pummeled…to a pulp? Knifed? Jim Martin? Suddenly her mind banished the night and Julie bolted upright. That hideous monster from the past had reared his ugly head and seemed to be leering her right in the face. Within her, rage rekindled. Burning with forgotten schemes of unholy revenge, she demanded, "You sure it was Jim? Who killed him? How come?"

"I have no clue," returned Margi. "I caught the end of the newscast as I turned on the TV. I'm waitin' to hear the whole thing at 7."

"Call you back." Julie slammed the receiver down. Someone killed Jim Martin seemed to echo throughout the empty apartment. "Wow. Vengeance is mine, sayeth the Lord." Grabbing her robe off the bottom of the bed, she shoved her arms into it and hurried off to the living room. She cinched the belt so tight that it hurt her ribs, but the pain of that was nothing compared to the memory of that freak mounted on her back, lambasting every inch of her. Recent thoughts of new found peace vanished, replaced by anger and hostility as she groped around for the ever-missing remote. "Where is that damned thing?" she grunted. Her hand pried apart the seat cushions of the sofa. "Ugh. Forget about it," she puffed and defiantly turned the television manually.

A stoic anchorman with a plastic smile was just beginning the 7:00 A.M. report. "Topping news stories at this hour…another tragic case of domestic violence shakes this city. Last evening, Jim Martin was stabbed to death by live-in girlfriend, Leslie Sands. Police sources report that the incident occurred shortly after 9 P.M. on 743 Western Avenue following an argument in which Martin allegedly beat, sexually assaulted, and attempted to strangle his live-in girlfriend. Neighbors summoned police, reporting a woman screaming.

This morning, Sands is hospitalized in serious condition. More on this tragic story as details become known."

Julie sat there stunned. Tremors shook her body and her brain vomited, *My God. That freak did the same thing to somebody else?* She held back the bitterness as she dialed the phone. "Hi." Then words failed her.

"So how 'bout that?" Margi snapped. "That slime-ball actually shacked up in that ol' rat-trap all these months!"

"It's all my fault," Julie lamented.

"What?" Margi shot back.

"I should've reported that coward to the police back in November."

"O-o-oh no you don't. Don't even go there, girl. You handled it the best way you could. Besides, the cops probably would have only looked the other way. And what if you did press charges? Some fancy lawyer would've gotten the worm off."

"But that woman could've been dead right now instead of Jim," Julie argued.

"Yeah. And he might have wasted you, too," spat Margi.

The thought mortified Julie. Her shoulders stiffened. Her eyes closed against the pressure mounting in her head.

"Hey," Margi fumed, "at least this time, the neighbors got off their fat butts and called in the cops."

"I gotta tell the police that it's not that poor girl's fault. I can't see her going through one more minute of hell because of that son-of-a-bitch."

"I'm goin' with ya," Margi spouted.

A weak smile lifted Julie's lips. "Guess I'd rather not go it alone."

"Pick you up in an hour." The line went dead.

As Julie peeled off her nightgown and slid into jeans, shirt, and shoes, the reality of recounting the whole ugly ordeal swept over her. What would she say? How should she say it? No words were powerful enough to describe what Jim had done to her and how she detested him for it. Julie froze. But he had raped that poor girl. Raped. Her jaw clenched. She had never given a name to what he had done. Ghastly vignettes rattled her. Struggling to maintain logic, she could see his black dilated eyes—not a lick of blue was left. His fists, clenched, came at her…again…and again. Her brain exploded white from blinding pain. "Stop," Julie shrieked. Her hands squeezed her head. "You're not doing this to me again!"

At the police station Detective Ben Chase peered over wire rimmed reading glasses perched on his nose. Thick lenses distorted his cheekbones. His expression temperate as Julie and Margi walked into his office. Introducing herself and Margi, Julie said, "Leslie Sands is a victim. Jim Martin preyed on girls like her," Julie hesitated then said, "and like me."

Chase's eyes grew critical. His swivel chair screeched as he tipped back and laced his fingers behind his neck. A few moments elapsed. Chase got to his feet and went to the door to close it. The details of physical and mental cruelty that Julie had endured were not going to be part of stationhouse gossip. He turned and studied both women. Chase was tall but the desk job he held for several years had replaced muscle with fluff, which he had neither time nor the inclination to rectify. Slowly he returned to his desk and sat down. It had been months since Jim Martin had manhandled this Julie Spencer. Sitting before him now, it was quite apparent that her memory was not the least bit clouded. Pungent feelings resounded in her voice and mannerisms. Chase never felt inclined to interrupt to clarify points, as often was the case with other victims or witnesses. Halfway through, his stone-face, which cops come to master after years of seeing just about everything, softened. He shook his head and pulled off his glasses. Dropping them on the desk, he spun his chair sideways. Once again Chase was on his feet. His hand ran through his graying auburn hair, leaving it askew as he clasped his hands behind his brown tweed jacket and stepped over to the window. He stared out until Julie spoke no more. Silence. He studied the hordes of sparrows flitting noisily among the bushes in the parking lot below. Sure was nice to see spring come. Drawing in a chest full of office air, he turned and leaned against the sill. His arms folded across his chest. His ankles crossed. Pondering this development, he looked down at the rust-colored knitted tie that his mother had given him for Christmas. It covered a stain of unknown origin on his white shirt. Chewing the corner of his mouth, he glanced at Julie Spencer from time to time. Her trembling fingers picked at her fingernails. Suddenly her companion, this Margaret LaRosa woman, clasped Ms. Spencer's hands and squeezed reassuringly. Chase weighed his words. Clearing the phlegm in his throat, he swallowed. Though soft-spoken, his intensity was clearly evident when he said, "Well, Ms. Spencer, from the beginning it looked to me as if Sands was justified in defending herself." Spindly gray eyebrows arched, moving up and down while accentuating particular aspects. "What you just told me corroborates evidence already collected in the case."

"Of course, that poor girl was justified," Margi cut off his words. Her body warped sideways in her chair and her palms were as expressive as her face. "Whaddaya think, for crying out loud?"

Chase had trouble hiding his amusement. After all this was serious. He returned to his desk and sat down. Picking up his glasses, he used them to point at the paperwork in front of him. "With Miss Spencer's sworn statement added to all this plus the support of the LaRosa family, it's likely that Leslie Sands will not be charged with any crime."

"Big whoop. No jury in their right minds will convict her," Margi spouted like a person affirming a long-held presumption. She leaned forward, looking Chase square in the eye. "How is that poor wench?"

Julie cringed, dreading the answer. Shame crushed her. If only she had had guts enough to stand up to Jim the way Leslie Sands did…or at least to come forward to the police with what he had done last

November. So what if nothing ever came of it? Perhaps it would have at least put Jim on notice. He might have thought twice before flying off the handle the next time.

The detective frowned. "Tough shape." He picked up a pencil and tapped the eraser end on the desk. "Doctors are concerned that Ms. Sands might have internal injuries…and that she might not walk again."

Julie reeled. She felt like vomiting. "I have to go talk to her," she said in a half-requesting, half-informing manner.

Giving an approving nod, Chase tossed the pencil on the desk. "Ms. Sands needs all the friends she can get just about now."

Margi stood up. Her hands braced against the desk, her eyes probed Chase's. "Where'd they take her?"

Perching his glasses on the tip of his nose, he looked down at the paperwork before him, avoiding Margi's bore. "St. Anne's Regional." he said.

Margi shot Julie a look. "Come on, kid."

Julie got to her feet and with some hesitancy turned to go. She took several steps then stopped and turned back to Chase. Julie swallowed hard. "One more thing." Detective Chase looked up. "I'm curious," she said. "How did Leslie Sands and Jim Martin meet?"

The detective peered over his glasses. "Like you…a pick-up."

Pick-up, pick-up… The words skewered Julie. *Slut, dunce, trash*—that's how she translated them—that's what she was. *Like a million others*—that's what Jim had said.

"Shiish," Margi fumed as she opened the door to leave. "Seems that's the only way that jerk operated."

"You got it," Chase said flatly.

❦   ❦   ❦

The sight of Leslie Sands sickened Julie. Margi stopped short. "Geez," she wheezed. "She's only half our size!"

"Yeah," Julie winced. "He must've tossed her around like a rag doll." She wanted to run, hide, but she just couldn't. She had run once before, but this time she was determined to face the terror.

The two women stepped into the room and gazed upon Leslie, lying there, motionless, shrouded in depraved, deathlike darkness. A sling supported her broken arm. Gauze enwrapped her right ear. Her nose, broken and swelled, had become the most prominent feature on her small oval face. Her fractured right cheekbone was golf ball size. And somewhere within the blackened distention were eyes, but the color was not discernable. A necklace of purple fingerprints encircled her milky neck. Fighting to contain the fury that strained release from her gut, Julie mumbled, "Hi. My name is Julie Spencer."

Leslie tissued away saliva that drizzled out her swollen cracked lips. Her eyes squinting at the two visitors, she sputtered, "Whaddaya want?"

"We heard what happened to you on the news," Julie said. Her voice felt shaky, retarded "My friend here Margi and I went down to the police station and talked to the detective who's working on your case. He said that it's all right for us to come and see you." The words kept coming, surprising Julie. All the way here, she had been afraid that she would not be able to find words at all, especially any of the right ones. What could she say that might comfort the girl who had taken a worse journey to hell and back than Julie had—especially when Julie had failed to stop it from ever happening again? "I just want you to know that if you need someone to talk to, you can call me…anytime. And I'll be here for you. You see, Jim beat me up too, almost as bad as you. I feel like I'm responsible that it's happened again. I am so, so sorry. I should've done something a long time ago to stop him."

Panic-stricken eyes glazed over. No longer did Leslie blot away the drizzle of saliva as she whimpered, "I had no choice. He was sitting on top of me, hitting…hitting me with those enormous fists…first one…then the other…. on and on…He wouldn't stop." Tears gushed from her eyes and she began to writhe. The cast of her broken arm flailed and repeatedly dropped onto the bed. Perspiration beaded on her forehead and froth lathered unchecked on her mouth and down her chin.

Choking back her own terrorizing memories, Julie yanked a tissue out of the box on the bed stand and made a vain attempt at blotting up the moisture flooding Leslie's face. She heard Margi weeping in the corner. With all the compassion Julie could muster, she took hold of Leslie's hand and squeezed. Leslie's body convulsed. "He...he forced himself.... I thought he was done...he shoved me away...And I crawled away. But then...oh no! He hollered...aurgh! He wasn't done."

Julie turned her head, unable to take any more of this. She looked to Margi for strength, but she was swaying back and forth in the corner.

"He called me a useless, frigid bitch," Leslie belched. Her eyes flashed wide, shocked, like a deer caught in headlights. "He said he did this to other ignorant whores. 'We're all alike,' he said. I tried to get away..." she whined. "He...he grabbed my arm and twisted it up...behind my neck. It couldn't go any farther...but...but that made him even more furious...so he...he twisted it. I heard it...arghugh...crack." Her face had turned crimson-blue as spasms wracked her body.

"Margi," Julie shouted. "Go get somebody. Quick!"

Margi stopped swaying. Her terrorized eyes stared at Julie.

"Go, Margi," Julie hollered.

Margi teetered.

"Now," Julie roared.

And Margi bolted out of the room.

Leslie panted and her voice sounded like fingernails grating across a chalkboard. "He seethed, lathering like Satan. Horrible black eyes. He pounded into me...on and on...he got off me...and... and...right there right next to me." Her finger pointed as her eyes bulged with revulsion. "He jerked o…" Her head shook denying the sight. She gagged and turned away, hiding her humiliation. Suddenly, she looked straight at Julie. Her brows came together as pupils became searing daggers that sliced through swollen sockets. "Ha…there's a knife…ah-ha…" Her voice slowed and became ominously low and raspy. "I grabbed it…" Her teeth grated together, maliciously portending vengeance. Her hand arced over her head, brandishing the invisible knife. Down it came, again…and again, goring the fiend as though he was right there. "With everything I had…I stuck him…hard…right in the gut…hard…hard as I could…and I screamed…'Don't you ever, ever, *ever!*…touch me *again!*'" Bloodcurdling gasps filled the room. She stiffened and was silent but her eyes pierced Julie's in a desperate search for redemption. Suddenly she grabbed the corner of her pillow. Unbridled anguish belched into it.

Nurses rushed into the room. Shoved aside, Julie fled to the wall and hid her face against it. One nurse held Leslie down. Another grabbed hold of an arm. A third injected a needle into a vein and squeezed out the contents. They tried to calm the thrashing patient while the sedative took affect. Margi's arm sheltered Julie. Moments passed. Julie looked back. Leslie's eyes were becoming dull and her body was beginning to relax. Backing away, one nurse covered up Leslie then straightened the bedclothes. Sporadically Leslie twitched. A second nurse wiped perspiration off Leslie's face and arms while the third jotted down notes on the chart tethered to the foot of the bed. One by one the nurses left the room. The last one lingered, plucking dark strands off the girl's bruised face and pushing them off to the side. She waited for Leslie to doze off completely. Not once did she look at Julie or Margi. At length, she muttered, "You two should go. Leslie needs to rest."

Margi quietly retreated as Julie nodded, though the nurse did not see. She dug out a notepad from her pocketbook and jotted down her name and address with a message for Leslie to call when she awoke, no matter what the time. Putting the note on the bed tray, Julie then patted Leslie's shoulder. The nurse looked up. Her eyes were troubled and distantly angry.

As Julie left, she ran head on into Margi who was staring down a fidgety brunette with fatigue lines drooping her eyes.

"She's asleep," Margi was saying dismally. "You know her?"

When the brunette shook her head uneasily, Julie cast her a side-long glance. That woman had seen Leslie's tirade. It seemed as though she was struggling to get something out in the open. Either she didn't have the guts to or she didn't know how. Julie knew how that felt. The brunette's eyes rolled, stopping at Julie's. She stammered, "Uhm...I went to high school with Jim Martin." As her confession trickled from her lips, her head dropped avoiding Julie's gaze. "After a football game, he...well, I was walking home, and he was following me. I knew him from my English class so I waited up for him. We were walking along and he began to tell me a creepy story about an old deserted house that we were about to pass. I didn't believe a word of it and told him as much. He insisted he could prove it. So when we got in front of the old house, he tricked me into going around back. Then...he pushed me into the bushes. He, uhm, well he tried to, uhm, hold me down as he...tore at my pants."

"For cryin' out loud," Margi spat. The butt of her hand banged the side of her head. "How many of yous guys did this idiot take down?"

The brunette gawked at Margi then gave a muted shrug. "But I was a real fighter...and I struggled very hard. That surprised him, I think. But he had a knife..."

Margi gasped and Julie's hand covered her horror.

"I can still feel how sharp it was...and cold." The brunette shivered. "It dug into my throat. His voice was so menacing. 'Shut up or I'll cut ya.' He had my hands pinned over my head but by then I wasn't thinking straight and managed to yank my arms loose. I think he figured that I was just going lay there, but I surprised him. I gave him a swift kick right where it hurts and got away. I never told anybody, not even my mother. She would've said I asked for it. Still, the whole thing has gnawed at me all these years. And when I heard what he did to that poor girl, something told me to come over here."

Margi got in the brunette's face. "You should go to the cops, ya know."

Knowing that she was expected to do the right thing, the brunette gave a tentative nod. "I s'pose," she mumbled.

Julie nodded reassuringly. "That's the best thing to do. If all of us tell our story to Detective Chase, this whole thing will go a lot easier on Leslie Sands."

The woman looked dubious. "Guess I better go now."

"We'll go with you," said Julie. "Okay Margi?"

"Shur thing." Margi gave a decisive nod. "But after this mess blows over, do yourselves a favor, kids. Put that maniac completely out of your heads. Every minute of thought you waste on him, he brutalizes you more."

Julie found it somewhat amusing that such sage advice was coming from Margi. She rolled her head in a vain attempt to ease the stress knot in the side of her neck. Following Margi to her car, Julie was empty. They got in and Margi turned over the engine. While they waited for the fidgety brunette to pull up, a vintage 442 Olds convertible with the top secure against the elements passed. The base from within it vibrated Margi's car. Julie could feel her friend's eyes and avoided them, fearing questions for which she knew no answers. When the brunette pulled up next to them, Margi turned the key and the idling engine griped. "Shoot," Margi winced as she put the car in drive and edged out of the parking spot. Leading the way to the police station, Margi was the one who ultimately broke the silence. "I've been fortunate." A small tremor jounced one shoulder as she took in a chest full of air. Her lips pursed and a soft whistle came out as she exhaled. "I never had to put up with violence of any sort. It's kinda hard to understand how such things come about."

Julie shuddered. "Nothing like that ever happened to me before I met…" Once again she felt that the mere mention of his name might make him reappear. "I didn't ask for it. It just happened."

"Why can't everybody just love each other?" Margi huffed.

"That's all any of us really want," Julie sighed and gazed at the pedestrians on the sidewalk scooting about their business. "What makes a guy like that, handsome, well built, good job, be such a monster?"

Margi shrugged. "Wish I could tell ya, kid."

"Something must have gone terribly wrong in his life to make him that way." Her voice was laced with more anger than sympathy.

"Bullpucky," Margi belched. "That's a piss-poor excuse if I ever heard one."

"Margi?"

Her face still flushed with anger, Margi squinted at Julie. "Yeah?"

"After we're done with this…" Julie hesitated.

"Yeah?" Margi's face instantly lost its red cast.

"Let's stop and see your Mom, okay?"

The side of Margi's face scrunched then the corner of her lip lifted. "Shur thing, kid. I told Ma we were off to the cops and then the hospital. She's proud of ya, ya know that don'cha?"

"How come?"

"For layin' it all on the line for Leslie."

Julie felt like puking. She could have helped Leslie a hell of a lot more if only she had opened her big mouth last November.

When Julie saw Emma's face at the door, dreadful memories of that night when she met the old woman erupted. Her head was throbbing. Every fiber in her body was thoroughly spent. Once again, Julie found herself in her old friend's arms, hearing that gentle voice whispering, "It's all right dear. Everything is going to be all right."

CHAPTER 14

$\mathcal{J}$ ulie picked up the phone. "Hello." She heard only silence. Her voice sharpened when she repeated, "Hello?" She waited and was about to hang up when she detected a barely audible sound. Julie's insides flipped. Had she heard the name Leslie Sands? Julie pressed the receiver against her ear and taking shallow breaths, strained to hear. But there was only silence. "Leslie? Is that you?"

A throat cleared. "Yah."

Julie could not find her tongue.

There was a small sigh, then, "Thank you…for coming by today…and your friend too."

Julie winced. "Wish I could've done more."

"Sorry about what happened. I…" Leslie muttered.

"Hey, it's okay," interrupted Julie. "You needed to get it off your chest, that's all."

Leslie cleared her throat again. "It meant a lot." She paused. "Glad you left your phone number."

Julie glanced at the clock. "You slept all this time?" It was almost eight at night. She had begun to think that Leslie was not going to call. Who could blame her for not wanting to talk about such an ordeal? Yet how impossible something like that was to forget. Then Julie remembered Detective Chase mentioning something about internal injuries. From what she had seen, she knew that was entirely possible. Several times she had felt like calling the hospital just for an update on Leslie's condition. Oh God, what if that poor girl was paralyzed? How was Julie ever going to live with that? She was responsible. She should have put a stop to Jim long ago. If she had not heard from Leslie when she did, Julie would have more than likely called before the night was through.

"The nurse woke me up when my parents called," Leslie sputtered then came the sounds of a tissue blotting up saliva.

"That medication they gave you was strong stuff," said Julie.

Leslie sighed. "Mmm, yeah."

Julie was at a loss for words.

"Mom and I had a long talk and my Dad and Grandma want me to come home. It's been a long time since we talked like that."

"Where's home?" Julie asked. If no other good comes of this at least it had brought Leslie and her family together. It had done the same for Julie and Elizabeth and had also produced many new friends along the way. But most of all it brought about new hope that Julie could achieve a better life, if she only would put her nose to the grindstone and not take the first thing that comes along. Hopefully, Leslie had someone like Emma in her life to give her a boost.

"Pennsylvania," Leslie said. "I got bored with the small town life. Boston seemed like the place to be even though I had never been here. I thought I could get a good job and be independent and all that great stuff. Pretty dumb, huh?"

"Your parents must've freaked," said Julie.

"Oh yeah," Leslie groaned. "They blew their tops. But I was bound and determined. They hardly spoke to me at all whenever I called."

Julie took a deep breath. "Lots of things go wrong when you don't know anybody."

"Yeah, everything they warned me about came true." Leslie's voice trailed off.

"How long have you lived here?" Julie asked.

Leslie heaved a sigh. "Going on a year. It's been real tough. A decent job is hard to come by. My savings dried up so I finally took a job at the donut shop near the boarding house where I lived."

"Let me guess," interrupted Julie. "You met Jim on the way home from work."

Surprise laced Leslie's voice, "Well, partly that way. He and his crew came into the shop for donuts and coffee all the time. And when they told me they were surveying near there, I went out of my way to find…" Leslie paused. "I knew better than that, but I was so sick of all the loneliness. And Ji…uhm…he seemed harmless enough…uhm…clean cut, quiet, and all."

Tremors wracked Julie. This sounded all too familiar. It seemed that Jim had a habit of using this disinterested act to capture his prey—like a vigilant snake lying in wait for hapless dupes to come begging for a taste of his venom. Once caught, there was no escaping the savagery. "I was on my own, too. So you moved in with him?"

"About two weeks after we met," said Leslie. "I knew that it was too soon, but I wanted out of that dreadful boarding house real bad. All kinds of bizarre people hung out there."

"Humph," Julie grunted. "I'll take bizarre people over him any day."

There was silence as Leslie let that thought sink in. Then she said, "Anyway, one night I simply stayed. He didn't tell me to leave, but he didn't tell me to stay either. Weird how he hardly ever talked. And when he did all he said was a word or two at most."

Julie cringed. "Yeah, a real couch potato."

Leslie gave a loud shudder, saying, "I never knew what he was thinking. I got all these creepy crawly feelings. Something wasn't right with that guy, but I thought it was my imagination."

"Hey, I don't ignore intuition any more," Julie said. "That apartment was mine, you know."

"Is that right?"

"Yeah. He just moved himself in one night like he owned the place."

"Just like me," Leslie moaned.

"Guess he had it in his mind to keep all my stuff when I ran off." Julie huffed. "But he was wrong. Some friends of mine went over there while he was at work and got every last thing. There wasn't much, but at least it was mine. I threw a lot of the stuff away…like the coffee table. One leg was broken. And the bedspread. He had a nasty habit of…uhm…well, let's not go there. But he ended up on it afterward, passed out."

"He did that in front of me, too," Leslie admitted. "I was there only days before he started to get rough. I figured it was because he really didn't want me there. But I had already moved out of that boarding house and by the time I went back, they were all full up. I couldn't afford anything else, so I was stuck."

Julie felt gooseflesh spike. "Bet you told him nobody was looking out for you, didn't you?"

"Yeah. How'd you know?" Leslie asked.

"And he didn't have a phone."

Leslie said slowly, "Yeah."

"He knew you had no one. And with no telephone he could get away with anything. He did as he pleased without anybody butting in. Even those people upstairs."

"What a coward," Leslie spat. "You know, he never had friends over and acted as if he really hated his folks. Wish I knew why. But I tried to be nice to him so he wouldn't get mad at me, but I got sick of the silent treatment and sleazy hand-jobs. He got real mad when I didn't come across when he wanted. Oh, God," she gasped. "The beatings got worse and worse…until this. I can still see him…"

Julie shivered. "Try not to think of it. But you will relive those things for quite a while. Think of better things so you don't have time to think about the bad stuff. That's what I did. Unfortunately, what happened to you has brought it all back to me."

"Gee, I'm sorry," said Leslie.

"No, I'm sorry," countered Julie. "I should have reported him last November, then this would not have happened to you."

"Don't be so sure of that."

"Huh?"

"Whackos like that don't know when to quit. And as long as there's stupid females like me out there, things like this are bound to happen."

Julie found herself nodding. She scratched her head and asked, "So what's your plans?

"Dad and Mom are thinking about flying here tomorrow," said Leslie. "I know they're gonna push for me to go back with them. But I don't think I can…"

"How come?" Julie asked.

"Detective Chase stopped by a while ago," replied Leslie. "When I told him that my parents were coming to take me back to Pennsylvania, he said I had to stay put until after all this mess gets cleared up. He says the red tape might take several weeks, but he has no doubt that I did it out of self-defense. I gotta call my parents back and tell them not to come 'cause they don't have a lot of money and can't afford to stay in a hotel waiting around for me to get cleared of any charges."

"What about your injuries?" Julie asked dreading the answer.

"At first Doctor Gilchrist thought my spleen was damaged from the way Jim picked me up and threw me against the kitchen table. Doctor Gilchrist was here when Detective Chase came in. After the doctor checked me out, he said he thought everything's healing okay…and uhm, he suspects the paralysis in my legs may be only temporary—like in my head, you know? He offered to help Detective Chase prove that I did it in self-defense. He said it was either Jim or me that night. Anyway, all the x-rays look normal and there's no sign of internal bleeding. He wants me to start physical therapy after I get out of here tomorrow—that's if nothing else comes to light. My arm needs six to eight weeks to mend. And boy, does it throb."

"Call the nurse," Julie suggested. "She'll give you something for the pain."

"I can't," Leslie said. "I don't have insurance and the thought of Mom and Dad paying for my foul-up drives me nuts."

"Where are you staying when you get out?" Julie asked.

"Who knows?" Leslie muttered. "And I don't have any of my things either. Detective Chase says everything in the apartment is evidence. Even my wallet with my license and pictures—all of it. The clothes I was wearing when the paramedics brought me here were torn to shreds and soaked with blood. The police took them for evidence, but there's no way I could wear them anyway. And I can't go around in this hospital gown I'm wearing."

"I'll bring you some things in the morning," Julie offered. "What size shoes do you wear?"

"I can't put you out like that," Leslie protested. "You've been too kind already."

"Don't worry about it. I've been there, remember?" Julie insisted. "Besides, I work there at the hospital so it's really no bother. I'll arrange for a place for you to stay so don't go worrying about that."

"I don't know what to say," said Leslie.

"Don't say anything," said Julie. "Someday someone might need you."

❧   ❧   ❧

Julie dialed Emma's number. With ol' mother hen's attention Leslie would not stand a chance at remaining down in the dumps. Yup. That girl was going to bounce back in no time. When the old woman answered, Julie said, "I got a favor to ask of you, Em."

"Is something wrong, dear?" Emma asked.

Julie glanced at the clock. The hour was late. She probably scared Emma. "Everything's okay," reassured the young woman, "but uhm,

Leslie's in a bit of a pickle. She's getting out of the hospital tomorrow. She's got nowhere to go, Em. Sound familiar?"

Emma tsked. "Well, I'm glad you called, dear. Bring her right over here. A bit of company should do me good."

"Her parents want to bring her back to Pennsylvania, but there's a glitch. She can't leave until things get cleared up," said Julie. "I'm worried, Em. All this might take a lot longer than any of us think."

"That don't matter a particle," interrupted Emma.

"Gee, thanks Em." Julie hesitated, swallowing hard. "One more thing…she's gonna be in a wheelchair for a while."

Emma was silent. A moment later she said, "Now, Julie, I don't want you worrying. We will get along just fine. Time has a way of working out those things. Meanwhile, I'll take good care of the dear child."

Julie felt a little better. "That's how come I called you, Em. Leslie needs some of your TLC, just like I did."

After hanging up the phone, Emma got to her feet and with great satisfaction rubbed her lower back. Every time she turned around someone called upon her for help—this time some poor child in a wheelchair. She glanced skyward. "You were right, Seth." It seemed as though Emma had found her niche, easing the loneliness that her husband had left behind.

The next morning, Julie rummaged through her closet and packed up a pair of stretch pants, a sleeveless shirt, and some under-wear—all loose fitting, easy to put on. She scrounged around for the cable-knit button-down sweater that she had almost thrown away because she had snagged one of the sleeves. Upon locating it, she held it up. The snag was on the same side as Leslie's broken arm. It would be no great loss to unstitch the seam so it would fit over the cast. Julie was almost out the door when she remembered shoes. How could she have forgotten shoes? Or forget the sight of Emma bending over, rummaging though Margi's bedroom closet, determined to find a pair of size seven shoes? A lump formed in her throat.

Julie's feet were bigger than Leslie's. So on the way to the hospital, she stopped and bought a pair of slip-ons. At the hospital, a nurse helped Julie with getting Leslie dressed. Even though the clothes were somewhat large, Leslie still struggled to put them on and it was hard for Julie to hear Leslie wince with pain. Pretending not to hear, Julie jabbered on and on. "I'm bringing you to my friend Emma's. I didn't like the idea of you being all by yourself at my house without anyone to talk to while I'm at work. Oh. I ran into Detective Chase on the way in here, so he knows where he can find you. Don't forget to call your parents from Emma's and tell them where you are." Unexpectedly, Julie saw the cigarette burns on Leslie's back. In a flash the feel of Jim's cigarette searing her own flesh came rushing back. Julie trembled. Flexing her spine, she held back angry tears and forced her mind to focus elsewhere. "Emma is Margi's mother. She helped me after that freak beat me up. I know you'll just love her to pieces."

Emma was watching for the two young ladies in the front window and when Julie's car pulled up in front of the house, came out to greet them. In her usual warm manner, she hugged Julie and after the battered girl was secure in her wheelchair and Julie made introductions, Emma hugged Leslie as if they had known each other for ages. Leslie was obviously taken aback.

With a little giggle, Julie started to push the wheelchair towards the back door. "Now, Leslie," she teased. "You must listen closely to me now. Keep your guard up for Emma's tricks. She likes to see people eat. And eat. And eat. Those old pounds will creep up on you before you know it. Believe me, I speak from experience."

Leslie caught the old woman's wink as she puffed, "For heaven sakes Julie, don't say such things."

Caught off guard, Leslie flushed. But ensuing banter began to light up her battered face.

At the back door, Emma helped Julie to turn the wheelchair backwards, saying "Come on, now. Let's get you inside."

"Ma! Whaddaya doin' there?" Margi's voice thundered from the street. "Hold your horses, you guys. I'm comin'." She breezed up to them, wearing cutoff jeans and a T-shirt. The signature bandanna was madras. In no way did it add to the getup. Dumping the bag of groceries that she was carrying into Emma's arms, Margi took over the project and maneuvered the wheelchair into the house. "Listen, deary," she blustered in Leslie's face. "Ma's gonna try ta convert ya into a little home-bound cutesy, cooking, cleaning, humming, and all that nonsense, so ya bettah keep a wary eye out."

Emma closed the back door. Her eyes twinkled as she wagged her finger. "Now Margi, don't you start on me too."

CHAPTER 15

$\mathcal{A}$ week later, Julie reentered Emma's living room with her arms full of paper towels and a refill of glass cleaner. "Margi, are you talking to yourself again?" she jabbed.

"Bonehead," Margi shot back with withering scorn. "You shoul-dah given me a head's up that you was duckin' out." Getting down off the stool in front of the bow window, she stretched backwards and sideways with her hands on her hips. "What's wrong with talk-ing to yourself anyways?" she grunted. "I powwow with myself every chance I get."

"I catch myself at it quite a lot lately," said Emma as she settled behind the baby grand and lifted off the cover. "But that's because I am old and can get away with it." Her fingers glided over the keys and filled the air with rich, flowing chords.

"Don't say that Ma," Margi barked. Julie giggled as she spritzed glass cleaner on the window seat. Suddenly she found herself eyeball to eyeball with Margi. "Whaddaya laughin' at, kid?"

Julie feigned submission. "Sorry," she said and proceeded to scour out the stains that a number of potted plants had left.

"Yeah," Margi huffed, "you look it."

The music suddenly stopped as Emma jammed her hands into her hips. "Well, just who else do I have to talk to? There's times the silence in this place drives me crazy. Hearing a voice, even if it's my own, stirs things up."

"You have me," said Leslie in a small voice. Wheeling herself into the living room, she was careful not to spill a mug of tea that was wedged between her legs.

Emma patted the bench and Leslie brought her chair up next to it. "Yes dear, I know. But when your folks come to get you, I will be alone again, just like after Julie left."

Julie shot a guilty frown at Margi who shrugged it off. As they started to replace the potted plants onto the window seat, music filled the room again.

"Being alone isn't exactly inspirational," said Elizabeth. She came into the living room with a cup of black coffee. She cautiously lowered herself into one of the overstuffed, high back wing chairs. It seemed that some days, the wound she had suffered during that bank robbery nagged her to no end. Yet she wasn't about to complain. It did bring Peter back.

Wagging her index finger at Elizabeth, Margi proclaimed, "That's 'cuz ya don't yap it up wit' yourself, girl. When you don't talk to yourself, you're actually worryin' and then you start ripping yourself apart 'cuz you don't have the slightest clue about how to fix what's worryin' ya, and then you get down in the dumps 'cuz you're good for nothin', tah ta dah ta dah…It's one big viscous circle, I tell ya."

"Yeah, but thinking is part of logic and reasoning," said Leslie. Both hands cupped the mug in front of her. Blinking through the rising heat, she took a sip of tea.

"Pshaw," sputtered Margi. "Logic takes all the fun out of stuff."

Julie chuckled as she rearranged the Priscillas. "Funny thing, when you lie to yourself, especially if you do it out loud, you always get caught. Your own ears will tattle on you every time." She looked at her mother who had a curious look on her face. Julie flushed. "That was a long time ago, Mom…I was just a kid then."

Elizabeth raised her chin as if to say, oh…

"Big whoop. I'm proud to tell ya that I tell myself the darnedest things," bragged Margi.

"Like what, dear?" Emma asked.

"Oh, wouldn't you like to know, Ma," Margi chortled.

"When I become flustered about something, I can cuss and nobody hears it," said Emma.

Elizabeth raised her eyebrows. "Come on, Em, cuss? Not you."

"I get it off my chest—that's all that matters. And I get a big kick out of hearing such dangerous words coming out of my own mouth."

"And it helps my Alzheimer's," said Margi.

"Margi," Emma sputtered as her hands trounced upon the piano keys. "You don't have Alzheimer's!"

Julie spat out laugher. She loved this bantering.

"Whatever," croaked Margi but if I don't keep telling myself what I'm up to, I'll be smack dab in the middle of whatever it is and stop dead in my tracks, 'cuz my mind blanks out what I was up to."

Elizabeth rolled her eyes and put down her empty cup. "Don't you hate that? The other day I wanted to mail a letter, so I goes to the kitchen for a stamp and got in there…well, Peter looks at me. I look at him. He slouches, his arms spread out to his sides and says, 'What?' I just stood there. Pfft. Gone. I turned around and went all the way back to the dining room where I found the letter on the table."

"So you picked up the letter and went all the way back to the kitchen for a lousy stamp with that letter clutched in you grubby little paws, right?" Margi postured.

"Yeah," Elizabeth sheepishly admitted.

"My case in point," Margi boasted with a wave of a hand as her thumb and finger came together in an open-palm jounce. "Ya gotta keep tellin' yourself what you're up to." She rubbed her hands together and turned to Julie. "Well kid, looks like our job is done here. We are women, hear us roar!"

Julie gave Margi a high five. "Next week, we're on to Mom's."

"Come on you guys," Elizabeth protested, "I don't want you fussing."

"It's all decided," Margi blew her off. "Julie and I are doin' your windows, now that's that!"

Julie nodded decisively while gathering up the towels and cleaner.

"But Julie," Elizabeth whined, "your father and I are planning on getting a bigger place."

"Well then, I won't have to do the windows after you move out," said Julie.

"But you're going with us," insisted Elizabeth.

Julie shook her head. "I know what you're thinking, Mom, and you don't have to worry. No guy's ever moving in with me again."

"That's not the point," countered Elizabeth as she struggled to her feet.

"Listen, Mom. You and Dad keep the cat, okay?"

"I'm not keeping the cat," Elizabeth said emphatically.

Normally it was useless to argue with her mother, but this time Julie's mind was made up, so quickly she changed the subject. "All I know is that when I'm looking for lost car keys, if my voice bounces off the walls, the vibrations always seem to make my keys magically appear."

"No dear, you are wrong," Emma butted in. She lowered the cover over the piano keys and then started to push Leslie's wheelchair into the kitchen. She signaled for everyone to follow. "Your voice scared the devil out of the little people, so they decided they better bring your keys back."

"What little people?" Julie asked.

"Oh, for heaven's sakes, kid," Margi barked. She stood there with her legs spread wide, her hands jammed into her hips, and her head teetering side to side. "The little people who live under the stairs!"

With scrunched eyebrows, Julie glanced at the wall under the stairs. Laughter filled the room. Julie shook her head. Her forefinger rotated around her earlobe. "You guys are all nuts!"

"What is the difference, singing to yourself or talking to yourself?" Emma asked as she let Leslie wheel herself across the kitchen. At the stove, Emma stirred a pot of simmering tomato sauce. She held out a wooden spoon for Margi who was right there to sample.

"At least singing involves someone else's words," said Elizabeth sinking onto a kitchen chair.

"There for a while, I was talking to myself all the time," said Leslie in a matter-of-fact voice. When everybody glanced her way, she shrugged. "Well, only a couple of times, and that was when nobody else was around. I had visions of throwing rotten tomatoes at Jim's grave.

"That's much too civilized for the likes of that boboe," Margi spouted.

"That's one of the mildest ideas I came up with," said Leslie.

"Too bad he got cremated," grumbled Margi as she cut a piece of apple pie and slid it onto a plate. "That put the kibosh to things, huh?"

"Now, Margi, don't eat that," Emma whined. "You know lunch is ready."

Waving off her mother, Margi silently offered to cut a piece for Julie. She shrugged when Julie shook her head and tramped to the refrigerator for a slice of American cheese.

Julie picked at her fingernails. "I dreamed up ways of getting revenge. Wish I had guts enough to follow through." She saw Leslie shift in her wheelchair. Guilt continually gnawed at Julie.

Emma went to the refrigerator and took out a salad. Handing it to Julie, Emma said, "I resented Margaret Bascuino after Seth passed on. You should have heard me hollering like a jealous schoolgirl up at that star that she finally had him to herself."

Margi's eyes popped out of her head. With a mouth full of pie and cheese, her voice came out muffled and singsong, "Ma."

Emma scanned her guests. Not one of them had any inkling about what the heck she was talking about. "My Margi was named after Margaret Bascuino."

"You never told me that, Margi," said Julie. She and Elizabeth had started to set the table. "How come?"

"Dad had a thing for this girl when he was twelve-years-old and she came down with the flu and croaked," said Margi. She flailed her mouth with a paper towel as she got up and took her empty plate to the sink. When she dropped it in, porcelain clacked on porcelain.

"Now, Margi, it certainly was more than that," chastised Emma.

"Well, I'm not the same little cutesy-poo that Margaret Bascuino was," Margi railed. Her chest stuck out and her behind wriggled.

"We never expected you to be," countered Emma. "You know very well that you were the apple of your Papa's eye and the name was only to honor her memory."

Margi made a face. Her head jiggled as her lips twittered without sound.

"How can you live in the shadow of someone who was loved so much?" Julie asked. Her voice sounded puny as her fingers toyed with a teaspoon.

"You don't," said Emma. She knew that Julie was referring to Ken's deceased wife and child. "You honor what she meant to him and make him happy just by being yourself. I had no right to be jealous. Seth loved me in a different way than he did Margaret Bascuino."

"But Ken is still so sad about Regina and Katrina," said Julie.

"It's been months since Seth left, but I still can't believe he's not here anymore. I don't think I ever will. When I think of him being gone, every last fiber within me empties out any strength I might have left in me. I try to put my mind on other things and to get on with it, but then the whole thing comes crashing down on me, all the way to my heart." She took a deep breath and straightened her apron. "But then, I wouldn't trade the life I have lived for anything."

CHAPTER 16

On the last Saturday in June, multi-colored kites, diverse in size and shape, soared above the meandering Charles in the crystalline sky. The whole world so it seemed was taking advantage of this magnificent sun-filled day after the harsh winter and rainy spring. On the Cambridge side of the river, Ken and Julie roller-bladed in, out, and around pedestrians and lampposts. She had resisted his suggestion to learn the fine art of survival while wearing footgear bearing only single rows of wheels, but boyish charms plus a near tantrum on his part ultimately decided the issue. Her fears of running amuck into the river or mowing down some unsuspecting being, whether human, animal, or plant, proved to be totally unfounded. Julie adapted instantly to the new experience and actually became quite good at it. Ken was tremendously impressed. There she was bounding off the sidewalk where a break-dancer twirled on his back to the blare of a boom box, and then up she jumped, landing back on the sidewalk a little ways beyond. She taunted Ken with her newly acquired abilities. Blading across innumerable bumps and cracks in the antiquated Longfellow Bridge, she sailed along, her hips swaying beneath her cut-off denims. It seemed as if she had been on skates all her life. Ken found it hard to keep up as they barreled down the Esplanade. Thank goodness Julie slowed down near the Hatch Shell to take a gander at the assemblage of groupies rocking to 60s music sponsored by a local radio station. Giggling with delight, she performed a thirty-second rendition of the twist after which she raced on ahead. Needing respite, Ken spotted a vendor selling snacks from a cart shaded by a hundred-year oak. "Hey, Julie," he hollered. "How 'bout a chili dog?"

Julie stopped on a dime. Eat? Her tongue moistened her bottom lip. Spinning around, she clasped her hands and squealed, "Sounds good to me!"

"Well then, get your little tushie back here." Never doubting for one moment that Julie's stomach would bring about quick submission, Ken watched her speed back. She was going too fast and hit the grass running. Just before she lost control, he caught her in his arms. They both came pretty close to crashing into the umbrella-covered concession stand. With a twinkle in his eye, Ken gazed into her flustered face then shouted over his shoulder to the mustached vendor, "Make sure to double wrap m'lady's chili dog. The little woman here tends to slobber all over herself."

"K-e-n," Julie sang out a flimsy protest. Yanking her arm from his grasp, she poked him in the ribs. With great flourish she readjusted her clothing.

The vendor took a shine to the playful couple and joined in the revelry. "Well, man," he blustered, "tah be honest wit'cha, looks ta me like ya got more of a problem than yah woman—what, wit' dem white shorts an' laht green shirt yer sportin'. And forgid about dat whi'e belly pack. Man…yous don't stands a snowball's chance in Hades."

Julie shook her finger at Ken and chided, "So there, troublemaker. Worry about yourself, why don'cha." She grabbed his face between her hands and gently shook. She planted a kiss on his cheek and giggled at his surprise. It seemed everywhere they went an uproar ensued. Julie had never laughed so much in her entire life as in the last few, absolutely wonderful months since she met Ken. And yet how easily they talked about their troubles. And if they had differing opinions, they talked them out without flying off the handle like…well, you know who.

Her heart overflowed with admiration and fondness for this gentle man. All her life, she had existed on the outside of life, looking in, but now, she was on the inside. Now she was truly living. Julie noticed Ken scooping up an apple-red rubber ball that had bounced in his direction. He tossed it to a bashful blue-eyed tot with curly blond hair. He then wistfully ran his hand through his chestnut-colored hair. This was one of those rare times that Julie saw him let down his good-humored facade, for he lived with the ever-present loss of his wife and daughter. It had devastated him and he had set about rebuilding his life, letting nobody close to him…not until Julie. Masking pain and loneliness, it seemed that now Ken fully appreciated every moment that life had to offer.

Julie would never forget the time that Ken had taken her to his exquisite home in Cohasset. She was aghast as he drove up to the wrought iron front gate and beheld the brick manse. She had no idea that Ken was so well off. From atop a broad precipice etched by tides and time, the hundred-year-old manse overlooked the open Atlantic Ocean and Minot's Light. Wheeling above, seagulls and terns screeched while below on the bleached sand sandpipers chased receding waves and dodged incoming surf in a never-ending search of food. Sparrows chirped from within the foundation shrubbery. Ken and Regina had restored the home, completing the work just before her death. A gray, longhaired cat greeted Julie and Ken at the front door. It weaved in and out of their legs, rubbing and purring loudly. As Ken slid the key into the lock sadness filled his voice when he said, "That's Ralph. He gets terribly lonesome being here alone so much." Reaching down, he scooped up the cat and rubbed its head back and forth across his chin. He handed Ralph to Julie, saying. "Ol' Ralph and Katrina used to play together for hours on end." He opened the door and stepped aside, gesturing for Julie to enter. "She dressed him up in doll's clothes and made him sleep in her doll carriage all covered up with pink and yellow baby blankets. Ralph never openly objected but you could not help but notice his tail twitch underneath the blankets."

Ken led the way, showing Julie the first floor furnished with antique furniture and ancient-looking nautical prints, but at the stairs leading up to the master bedroom and his child's room, he put his mouth against her ear and whispered, "You go ahead up. I just can't."

Julie backed away. "No. Uhm, no. It's okay. Really. I don't need to go up there."

Ken took her arm and forced her to look into her eyes. "I want you to."

"But I…" As their eyes met, something inside prevented Julie from finishing her thought. Battling the sensation, her skin spiked. Why did she have to go up there all by herself? What was up there? Her head wavered side to side while she searched his face for answers. Ken put his hands on her shoulders and without words expressed his need for her to go up there and witness for herself the things that pained him so. Giving a slight nod, Julie backed away and hesitantly took one stair at a time. Ralph zoomed past her, but half-way up he stopped. His urgent meowing made Julie feel as if he was leading her, as if somehow she could save the cat and his master from an ongoing nightmare.

At the top of the stairs, Julie peeked into the master bedroom. The bed was made. Sunlight streamed in through an expansive skylight that over time had faded the burgundy comforter. On the antique bureau was a photograph of a bride, tall, elegant, and incredibly beautiful. She was holding a cascading bouquet of white lilies and stephanotis. Flawless make-up brought out the color of her blue eyes. Golden tresses rippled down one shoulder and arm. A single pearl droplet from the silver chain about her neck hovered above the subtle curves of her breasts that filled out a low-cut bodice of beaded ivory satin. A flowing train meandered about the floor. Pangs of jealousy shot through Julie and she spun around and fled down the hall. She ended up at the doorway to Katrina's room. Running her hand along the doorframe, Julie was apprehensive about looking in. She swallowed hard. She wanted to run, but then thought of Ken and felt a tug inside. She had to do this…for him. She took a deep breath and looked inside the little girl's bedroom. Everything was the same as Katrina had left it. The white canopy bed was carefully made up. Stuffed animals were assembled on it with a candy-colored clown centered in their midst, an invitation to fanciful amusement. A thickness built in Julie's throat. Her eyes scanned the two white bureaus that stood before sky blue walls adorned with arched rainbows of red, yellow, and green stretching from corner to corner. Julie spotted a picture on one of the bureaus and crossed the room. She picked it up. It was the dusty portrait of a blue-eye cherub with freckles across the ridge of her nose and a mass of golden ringlets swirling about her head. With the arm of her sweater, Julie swiped away the dust. She took delight in the pudgy little arms that lay across the hand-smocked flowered dress. All at once the realization smacked Julie in the face. This poor child was no longer of this world. Tears brimmed in her eyes. "God, how awful this must be for Ken."

She set the picture back on the bureau and stepped over to a pink playhouse that remained abandoned in the center of the room. She rubbed the back of her neck and then as if someone had just called to her, she turned around. In the corner of the room was a wee lavender doll carriage. And it seemed at that very moment that the ghost of the blue-eyed cherub hovered above it. A tiny finger pressed against her lips admonishing Ralph to be still, for it was naptime for all good little kitties. Reality struck when Julie caught sight of the lonely gray cat rubbing against the carriage wheels, sorely missing his young mistress. Choking back heartache, Julie glanced at the doorway, half-expecting to see Katrina come skipping into the room. For Ken's happiness Julie wished it were so. She would even be willing to give him up to make it so…if only to take away the desolation that now she too possessed.

"Julie?" She heard Ken call. "Julie, over here." A loud, shrill whistle shook her back to the present. She glanced around discovering that she was standing in front of the hot dog stand.

"You comin' or what?" Ken hollered from a grassy knoll at water's edge.

She took a deep, trembling breath then skated across the walkway. Hobbling across the grass, she hunkered down next to Ken and took off her fanny pack. She kissed Ken on the cheek and the color rose on his face. He avoided her eyes as he handed her a chilidog and cherry coke. "I'm famished," he said.

Swooshing away a bee that insisted on sharing her meal, Julie sighed, "Yeah. Me, too."

Ken devoured his chilidog in a heartbeat. Sucking down the last of his drink, he mused, "Those dogs didn't stand a chance, did they?"

Julie nodded while chewing the last delicious morsel. After swallowing she puffed, "I was hungrier than I thought." She glanced sideways at the food vendor. "But I think I'm going to have to go over there and apologize to that guy."

Casting her a strange look, Ken spied her looking down at her blouse. "And rightfully so." She looked up to see him pointing a goopy finger at the stream of ruddy gravy besmirching her yellow blouse. His eyes caught hers and he began to roar with laughter. Julie reexamined the stain, then looked up at Ken again. He pretended to pull himself together and said, "Here, let me see that." His hand came at her, groping at the spot.

"You stay away from me," Julie squealed and rolled away.

Once again Ken exploded into hysterical laughter. That, of course, drew the attention of passersby. Stone faces melted into toothy grins and as they continued on their way, their heads shook.

Julie stretched out on her stomach. Drinking up the fresh warmth of the day, she picked at blades of grass and tossed them into the sun-drenched river. A sculling team rowed past, barely making a sound or leaving a trace of being there. Even the crew chief was silent. In contrast voices of day-sailors from the sailing school just beyond Julie and Ken echoed across the shimmering azure water as they practiced tacks and jibes. It reminded Julie of her mother and father who were on another sailing adventure, this time to Plymouth. Those two had readapted to sailing as if they had never been away from it.

Ken lay back on one elbow. Plucking a coarse blade of grass, he put it to his lips and blew. The loud vibrating whistle drew startled attention, but that did not faze Ken in the least. When the blade disintegrated, he selected another and chewed on it while watching the mischievous breeze tussle Julie's honey blond tresses. He loved the smell of her—honeysuckle. How different she was from Regina who detested sweet perfumes. So prim and proper, Regina would never have let the wind blow her hair like Julie did. Nor would she have ever leaned back with her eyes closed the way Julie was doing and listen to the sounds of the afternoon. Julie exuded romance. Every word Ken had to say, she ate up, no matter how insignificant. Not at all like Regina who always had some sort of goal dominating her mind. And it was awesome how much Julie loved that little clam shack down on Scituate harbor. It had always been Ken's favorite, but he had to drag Regina there kicking and screaming. Finger-food was definitely not her forte. He loved how Julie would sit with her legs tucked under her on the sandy blanket as they ate cartons of clams on the beach. How she could eat so much was beyond him. She talked all the time, but that was fine with Ken. He loved to hear her voice, her life, her complicated simplicity. There were times when Ken sensed that Julie could actually hear the beating of his heart and yet she was nowhere near. Her eyes gleamed in the sunlight and lit the darkness of his lonely nights.

Ken grabbed at a wayward wisp of Julie's hair. Twirling it playfully around his fingers until the palm of his hand was against her head, he gently drew her to him and murmured, "Know how much I love you?" She smiled and when she kissed him tenderly, he savored the taste of her moist lips. He was sure that she could hear the beating of his heart. "Marry me, Julie," he murmured.

Julie drew back. Her eyes grew wide.

"I want you in my days and in my nights," he said. "I want you in my life...forever."

For a second there Julie could not catch her breath. Her heart raced as she searched his hungry eyes.

"Look, I realize we haven't known each other very long," Ken rationalized. He released her hair and placed his hand on his chest. "But in my heart I know you're good for me...and I'm good for you. Whenever I'm with you, I'm happy. When I'm not, something's missing. It's you, Julie. I need you." He reached into the side pocket of his white fanny pack and took out a pale blue velvet pouch with edges accentuated by delicate white lace. Her jaw dropped. He picked up her hand and gently placed the pouch into it.

Words escaped Julie. Her breath came in soft, quick gasps as she gaped at the pouch and then at Ken. His smile was urgent.

"Go ahead," he said. "Open it."

Skittishly Julie lifted the flap and peered in. "A ring. Oh my God," she squealed. Her thumb and forefinger fished it out. "It's the most beautiful ring I have ever seen."

Watching Julie finger the sparkling diamond and the gold that surrounded it, Ken said, "Emma helped me to pick it out. She says it reminds her of a star perched upon an ocean wave at midnight."

"I love it almost as much as I love you...wait a minute...when did you and Em get together to shop for this? Huh? Are you two holding out on me?"

"Listen." Ken winked. "That fine lady and I have our own little secrets, you know. Things you are never gonna know about." He remembered how after they had picked out the ring, Emma had asked him to stop by the grocery store to pick up "just a few odds and ends." Well, as it turned out, he ended up with a trunk full of bags containing a myriad of eggplants, tomatoes, and just about one of everything in the store.

"Ooho…wait till I see her," Julie jabbed. "Em's going to have to account for her whereabouts."

"Marry me, Julie," Ken entreated. "I love you more than anything in the whole world."

His voice swept her along like a leaf caught on an Indian summer breeze and she was content for the sensation to go on forever. "Yes," she murmured. Her arms stretched out to him and as his arms tightened around her, her full weight fell against him and they toppled backward onto the lush grass. "Yes, yes," she squeaked. "I will. Of course, I will!"

Ken lay there flabbergasted with Julie sprawled on top of him. As they gazed into each other's eyes, they became silent and somehow alone in this busy world. Ken nudged Julie off him and took the ring from her hand. As he placed it on the third finger of her left hand, tears of happiness welled in her chocolate eyes. Smiling at her childish innocence, he fought back his own happy tears. Moments passed while their eyes soaked up the miracle of each other. And then they started to laugh again like a couple of school kids. When they came to their senses, Julie rubbed her forehead gently against his chin. "When?" she asked.

"Let's not wait too long," he pleaded.

She peered at him thoughtfully. Insecurity as well as an overpowering loneliness was clearly evident in his face.

"But it's up to you," he quickly added.

"Oh, gosh. Let me think," she said. As she sat upright, the world became a dizzying carousel. "A big church wedding takes lots of time and serious money…"

"I'll pay," interrupted Ken. "Whatever you want, it's yours."

Julie shook her head. "I'm not really into that kind of thing." Noticing a monarch butterfly perched on a black-eyed Susan at water's edge, she watched its wings fan open then close. The sparkle of the water beyond drew her eye away and she began to marvel at the extraordinary nature of water. With every changing season, it took on new form and yet it always found a way to glisten. It always glistened. At this particular moment in time, it reflected the early summer light as the wind tickled its surface. Fall mornings brought out the intricate patterns of spider webs, glistening with frosty dew. As the season passed, ice crystals sparkled like diamonds while dancing around streetlights throughout long winter nights. She remembered as a child the windowpanes in her bedroom becoming etched with icy translucence on Christmas Eve. "Christmas," Julie blurted out.

Ken's brows lifted. "Christmas?"

"Yeah," Julie bubbled. "The most enchanting night of the whole year." She clasped her hands in front of her heart. "Oh, yes. Christmas Eve. With lots of red poinsettias. And boughs of fragrant evergreen." Savoring the thought, she murmured, "And dreamy ivory satin. Oh, how exquisite…And of course we must get married in the Chapel at St. Anne's Hospital." She gazed at Ken. "'Cause that's where our relationship began. How about that? The Chapel's big enough. What do you think about that idea?"

"Love it," Ken exclaimed. "But for one other reason."

"What's that?" Julie asked.

His arms draped about her shoulders. Gazing upon his beloved, his heart spilled over with this second chance at happiness. "You will be my Christmas gift from God."

CHAPTER 17

*I*ce crystals waltzed around the iridescence of streetlamps to the melody of cathedral bells that called the faithful to Christmas Eve services. Storefronts were dark, movie theater marquees went unlit, and traffic signals cycled through red, yellow, and green on streets devoid of traffic—except for one white limousine and a pearl Cadillac. Their headlights illuminated snowflakes that refracted into glistening diamonds. Gliding to a stop in front of the entrance to the Chapel at St. Anne's Regional Hospital, the limousine driver let the engine idle as he hopped out and opened the back door. Peter Blair emerged and turned back holding out his hand. "Out you go, my sweet Bethie."

Adam pulled his Caddie up behind the limousine and switched off the engine and got out. Sprinting around the front of the car, he stopped to straighten his tuxedo before opening the passenger side door. Emma took his hand, smiling up at her oldest son, and as they stood face to face with their hands still locked, Adam kissed her and said, "Wish Papa could be here to see how lovely you look."

"Thank you, Adam," Emma said softly. The tightness she had felt after Seth's passing had given way to an inner strength. She looked up into the night, knowing that he would always be right by her side.

Adam linked his mother's arm with Elizabeth's and for a moment he and Peter stood together, watching the two women climb the two stairs to the Chapel. As female chatter echoed throughout the crisp night air, Peter said, "Quite a sight, huh?"

"Sure is," said Adam. As the two women reached the polished teak door decorated with an evergreen wreath garnished with brass bells and a red bow, the picture he had kept all these years flashed into his mind. It had led Adam to a better understanding not only about the man in the picture but also his mother. What a life she had led, one of grace, dignity, love, but most of all honor. He should be so lucky.

Peter peeked into the white limousine and said, "Ready, Pumkin?"

Julie took a deep breath while clutching a gold chain and crucifix around her neck. Emma had worn it the day of her marriage to Seth. Julie had been hesitant to take it when her old friend offered it, but then Emma had insisted saying, "For good luck, dear." Julie peered up through her own frosty exhalation fleeing from the warmth of the limo. Oh, how wonderful it would be to have that many years of happiness with Ken as Emma had with Seth. She gazed up at the sliver of the moon that was playing peek-a-boo from behind a transparent cloud. So many, many stars sharpened the depth of the midnight sky. Over there was Margaret Bascuino's star. Emma had pointed it out one night while showing Julie Seth's star. Julie wondered if someone in her life would ever name a star for her. A solitary snowflake landed upon her upper lip. The tip of her tongue sought it out. In the blink of an eye, the tiny crystal melted into a miniature pool of moisture. Oh, how swiftly it disappeared. She wished the snowflake had lingered just a little longer. How silly though it was to complain. A bride could not ask for a more splendid evening. She felt the warmth of her father's hand as it enfolded hers. With her other hand Julie tightened the ivory cape that Emma had crocheted just for this occasion. She thought about her undergarments. She held back a giggle. Even they coordinated with her outfit. Peter's arm entwined hers and as she got out of the limousine, her ivory satin gown stiffened in the cold air. Places where it touched her silky flesh bubbled into gooseflesh. Strolling up to the Chapel steps, Julie hesitated. Her father glanced her way, silently questioning. She shivered up at him, "I love you, Daddy."

The gentle radiance of the winter night blending with Chapel light set his face aglow. "Love you too, Pumkin. Wish I could put my arms around you, but that would mess up your get-up. Sure missed a lot, I did, not seeing you grow into the beautiful bride you are at this moment."

Julie squeezed his arm. "I'm just so grateful you're here now."

Peter grinned. With a twinkle in his eye, he said, "Better get going or all those people in there will come charging out here to haul us in."

Just then Adam opened the cumbersome wooden door. "Here they come now," Julie chuckled.

Climbing the Chapel steps, they entered a small anteroom. Peter helped Julie to remove her cape whereupon Elizabeth made sure Julie looked perfect. Then the bridal party lined up to await their signal to begin.

At the front of the chapel, the side door slit open and Ken peeked out. "Wow," he mouthed. "Will you look at this! This is unbelievable." Scads of friends and family had clustered beneath the etched globes suspended from the high-pitched ceiling. Ken had expected that many who had been invited would beg off, what with this being Christmas and all. So what if they didn't come? This setting would have been perfect even if not one single person showed up. His eyes scanned the ivory candles mounted in elevated brass candelabras. Their flickering flames fanned aurora borealis across the polished teak walls. Poinsettias, white, pink, and red, accentuated the evergreen boughs that perfumed the air. Ivory and red velvet bows garnished the ends of pews. "Superb," he breathed.

Just then Ken spotted Samuel escorting Emma down the aisle. Her youngest son had brought his family home from Connecticut for the holidays and this wedding. He settled her at the organ where softly she began to play. Ken smiled. That old woman was a gold mine of strength and understanding. He remembered the day he had spoken to her about his feelings for Julie. When he told her that forgetting about what had happened to Regina and Katrina was virtually impossible, Emma had helped him put his grief into perspective. Encouraging him to accept the losses in his life, she had said, "Such things are beyond our understanding, dear. Your wife and child will never die in your heart. And that's the way it ought to be. But you have oh so many years ahead of you. If Julie makes you happy, if you love each other, don't deny yourself of her."

Julie was never jealous nor resentful of what he and Regina had together nor what Regina and little cherub Katrina still meant to him. She continually urged Ken to remember and talk openly about Regina and Katrina and each time he recounted lost days, Julie listened with great compassion. This night, Ken sensed Regina and Katrina's presence. Yes, he had their blessing. Closing the door, Ken leaned his forehead against the doorjamb. He felt a glow within his being. How blessed he was for this second chance at happiness. God had not forgotten him.

His brother Jake's incessant teasing began to get to Ken. Trying to ignore Jake and rising nervousness within, Ken tugged at the gold fob chain attached to an antique timepiece in his tuxedo pocket. Emma had given it to him, saying that it had belonged to Seth. She hoped that this time happiness would last for him as long as it had for her and Seth. Ken glanced at the time, though it did not register in his brain.

Once again, the bridegroom peeked out the door. The pews were jammed. Several coworkers were standing at the rear of the Chapel. He noticed his mother and father, sitting in the second pew. Next to them were Regina's parents. Julie had insisted that they must be invited, since they were still a part of his life and always would be. They were so grateful for that, since Ken had all but disappeared after the loss of their only daughter and grandchild. The tragedy had left vast emptiness in their lives.

Adam, Janice, and Elliot were making their way to the pew behind Ken's parents. "Sure Shot" Janice beamed, for just today, an ultra sound had revealed she was carrying twins, more than likely a boy and a girl. Emma was ecstatic with the news. Looking back in the generations of LaRosas, there were no twins. These would be the first. Seth would be extremely pleased.

A wheelchair folded in the isle caught Ken's eye. Next to it, sitting in the pew, were Leslie Sands and her parents. He gasped. "Oh, no! Leslie's waving at me!" He felt his face flush. Caught in the act of peeking, Ken sheepishly grinned while his fingers wriggled a fleeting response.

The Sands family had driven in from Pennsylvania and was staying with Emma. How nice it was that they had kept in contact with Emma and Julie. Leslie had started college in September. Funny thing. After everything that Leslie had been through, she decided to major in psychology.

The music stopped. Ken shot a look at Emma. Her hands were folded upon her lap. Restrained coughs and shuffles echoed throughout the Chapel. Ken gnawed on his bottom lip. Any moment now. Emma glanced over her shoulder, time and time again so it seemed to Ken. The world had come to a standstill. Finally, the doors at the rear of the Chapel opened and Emma spun back to the organ. Once again, her weathered fingers glided across the keyboard as guests shifted their weight and craned their necks for a glimpse of the bride. But their wait was to go on a little longer as Elizabeth started down the isle and the doors closed behind her. The Mother of the Bride was also Maid-of-honor. It was indeed a great honor, since she had never experienced either. Her brown eyes twinkled in the flickering candlelight while a vibrant smile replaced the muted expression that she had carried throughout the many years without Peter. Dressed in red velvet trimmed with ivory lace, she carried a simple bouquet of red tea roses and baby's breath. As she approached the altar, Ken and his Best Man stepped in from the side door. The music paused. Muffled anticipation echoed throughout the hall. The chaplain, wearing white liturgical vestments with a gold cross and chain adorning the yolk, glided in from the vestry.

At long last the doors at the rear of the Chapel swung open. There stood Julie on the arm of her father. The dazzling sight of his bride took the groom's breath away. Ken knew at once that Julie was the only woman for him and always would be.

Poised and elegant, Julie wore a tea length gown of antique satin and in her hands was an opulent cascade of long-stemmed ivory and red roses laced with baby's breath. Scanning the friendly faces lining the aisle, she could not help but think about how much things had changed since those impoverished days with Jim Martin. Ice chilled her veins. How dare she think about that maniac…at a time like this? *Wait a minute, Jim's here! There he is…standing in my way halfway down the aisle! What's he doing here? He's glaring at me. He's going to grab me! Hurt me!* Julie felt a tug on her arm. She cast a wary sideways glare. A man. His hair was the color of hers. He had a silly little grin on his face as his amber-brindled brown eyes studied her. She was about to turn and flee for her life, when he leaned his head against her forehead and whispered, "You sure about this, Pumpkin?" Julie peered into his eyes and as the Rhapsody on a theme of Paganini by Rachmaninoff filled the Chapel, that silly little grin of his broke through her defenses. Her lips parted. The man was her father, her long-absent father. He was actually here for her, like in the dreams she had so many times as a child. Her tongue ran along the inner edge of her bottom lip. *Don't Julie. Don't let a bad memory spoil this day. Don't.* "Daddy?" Her voice was childlike.

"Yes, Pumkin?"

Her heart raced. "Daddy, I…I just want to tell you one more time…" A tear trickled down her cheek. "I love you, Daddy, so very, very much."

His face flushed with pride. "I know this is against the rules, but…" He lifted the side of her veil and kissed her cheek. "I love you, too, my sweet, my very own daughter."

As her father gently brushed the tear from her cheek, the sound of oos and aaahhhs overpowered the music. Glancing about the Chapel at all the adoring faces, Julie blushed. She spotted Ken. He was waiting for her. This gentle, loving man was waiting only for her. Within her, determination renewed itself.

"Come on, Pumkin," Peter said while smoothing her veil into place as best he could. "Let's do this thing, whaddaya say?"

Julie squeaked and father and daughter began to float down the aisle. "This is my favorite song, you know," she whispered.

"Emma sure can play," Peter whispered back.

Julie peered at her father. That priceless silly little grin that her mother had fallen in love with so many years ago never once left his face. She tingled all over thrilled that he had come back into her life and was here for her at this moment. "This night is absolutely perfect."

"Uh-huh," Peter whispered while patting her twitching arm. "You are the most beautiful daughter a man could ever wish for."

Suddenly they noticed Margi who had been fidgeting from having to keep her yap shut but now was throwing the bride and her father a flurry of kisses. She and Julie had become just about inseparable since that November day at Emma's house. Back in January, they had seen each other at their ultimate worst and absolute best as their mothers' lives were held in a balance. A bond of friendship like none other had been forever forged. Julie shifted her bouquet, revealing a fishhook with a green plaid ribbon caught on its barb. Margi yipped, "Way to go, kid," and gave a boisterous thumbs-up.

It felt like a dream when Ken reached out for her hand. His smile was the broadest, most unburdened that Julie had ever seen on him. His eyes were clear, bright, and full of hope. She sensed that at that very moment they could see into each other's soul. Love swelled within her so much that she felt as though she was going to burst. And when he murmured, "I adore you, Julie," tears flooded her eyes.

Ken and Julie stumbled over their vows then spoke together. "I was a lonely wreckage, my life a storm, buffeted by events beyond my control. The Lord looked down upon my dark existence and sent a guardian angel to take my hand and lead me to you. Now, His Light and promise of the future shines in your eyes. I will love you until I die. You are my soul mate. Walk with me, forever, into eternity."

Emma leaned out from the piano. The fragrance of roses filled her lungs. How proud she was of Julie, a girl of great inner strength and determination. The young bride had found the happiness she richly deserved. And needless to say Ken was quite a handsome man. Look at him all guzzied up in that tuxedo. Why, he was almost as magnificent as her own dear Seth. Ken had lived through some pretty tough times and possessed an appreciation for life that many other people his age could not even fathom. Emma knew instinctively that Ken and Julie would have a long and happy life together. When they kissed, she felt Seth's heavenly breath warm her ear, *They are almost in love as much as we.*

Emma nodded while sending silent reply. *Yes, my Angel Seth, God has truly painted a rainbow over this devoted couple, just as he did for you and me.*

The couple turned to face the assemblage while the chaplain announced, "Ladies and gentlemen, it is my great pleasure to introduce to you for the first time Mr. and Mrs. Ken Waters."

An explosion of cheering and applause erupted and the jubilant couple fled down the aisle. In the vestibule a reception line formed. Later as Ken and Julie exited the Chapel, she held him back. Her palm arced across the wintry scene crowded with friends and family. "Isn't everything perfect?"

Ken soaked up the site. Snowflakes flounced like confetti in the light of a timid crescent moon playing peek-a-boo from behind a translucent cloud. Such things had existed all his life, but he had never noticed them before this night. Ken squeezed her hand and said "Yes, my sweet. Absolutely perfect. Just the way you said it would be."

Filling her lungs with brisk air, Julie withheld it while listening to a group of carolers vocalizing to the beat of distant Cathedral bells. Her breath exploded into a frozen cloud when she said, "Those carolers and bells and their music honor us this awesome night."

Ken nodded and gave a tug on her arm. As they hurried down the snowy steps, friends surrounded them, tossing birdseed. The driver of the idling limousine held the door open and tipping his cap as they slid into the back seat, he inquired in a highly proper intonation, "Dinner and dancing at Julio's Ristorante, Mr. and Mrs. Waters?"

Julie giggled and Ken pronounced stoutly, "If you please, my good man."

Julie giggled some more.

While the crowd rushed to vehicles, Elizabeth lingered with Peter on the landing in front of the Chapel door. The limousine sped off, scattering the dusty snow into carousels of glitter that gradually stopped rotating and hung in the wintry air. Her arms encircling his waist, she snuggled against him and sighed, "I still can't believe that you are standing here next to me, watching all this."

"Julie and Ken's life together is just beginning," Peter said as he kissed the top of her head. "Too bad ours didn't begin at their age with such a nice celebration. Lots of friends and family and all."

Elizabeth gazed up into his eyes. Her fingertips caressed his cheek. "But as our dear Emma says, 'we are a family, now. That's all that matters.'"

Peter lifted her chin and kissed her. "I'll never let you go again, Bethie."

"I thank God everyday for sending you back to me," she murmured.

Yet Elizabeth continued to torment herself for neglecting Julie during those lonely years without Peter. How terrible to have a mother so lost in sorrow like that. But the Man Upstairs had watched over Julie and brought her to be a beautiful, sensitive, and loving woman. And thank you Lord for that incredible woman, Emma LaRosa, who had not only rescued and befriended Julie, but also had reunited mother and daughter—and for that matter reunited an entire family. Every member of this reunited family were now living, not merely existing. Elizabeth laced her fingers around Peter's. Her heart had healed then was blessed with a miracle that filled her with more love than one lifetime could ever hope to hold. Peter kissed her. His lips soft, moist, real. "Come on," he said. "We got a party to go to."

And she murmured, "Then we gotta get home and feed the cat."

Epilogue

Weathered fingertips drifted across the paint-laden door, gently caressing. Nudged open, the hinges gave way with a low metallic lament. Just like the old woman, they required long overdue attention. She hesitated, gazing into the bedroom. Throughout the years without beloved Seth, Emma LaRosa had kept this place unchanged, despite the urgings of others. Whenever she wished she came here to slip off into the past, to meet him on her own terms and in her own way without any interruption of updated doodads.

Emma closed her eyes as if that might take away the oppressive silence—silence that had echoed from every remote corner of her being since that day so long ago when Seth had drifted off into eternity. A chill ran through her. Her eyes opened. Beyond the window-pane, rust-colored leaves took flight on the late season blast. *Another summer has come and gone*, drifted into her thoughts. And Emma responded, "Time has a way of slipping away…"

The years had lingered like pastels of orchid, pink, and gold that blush the aqua sky after the daystar deserts the horizon. Without wishing it so, the colors of life had begun to fade, soon to be overcome by night. The sun had set in Emma's life many years before when Seth had passed away. What remained was a portrait, half-finished, of the life that he and Emma had begun. She alone had been left to finish it so that future generations might gaze upon it to recall fond memories or to marvel at the cornerstones of their lives. On the palette of life that Seth had left behind, Emma had blended together friends and family, making his loss tolerable and the coming darkness welcomed. *For every lovely thing, something must be taken away,* warmed her thoughts. In her heart there was peace. A new dawn was coming.

So it was that Emma came, weary and drawn, to this chamber, empty and so barren. And it seemed as though the essence of roses was drifting up from the garden below the window, holding her spellbound while the summer breeze tickled white Priscillas and marshmallow clouds danced across a brilliant moon, casting innocent shadows upon the pastel wallpaper. But there was no garden below the closed window. No roses issued up their essence. Only black macadam existed where summer's bloom once thrived. Inside the panes, curtains drooped, yellowed and tattered with age. The gray of the oncoming winter shed no light upon the walls where designs had become as indistinct as her bridal glow of long ago.

Emma settled her bones upon the double bed that sagged on one side. To her aged fingertips, threadbare chenille felt new, tufts thick and soft. Her ashen eyes, once starry ebony, falsely perceived lemony-yellow, the color of tangy gelato. The bedroom breathed around her as though it was that July night so long ago when its timeless haven had welcomed her and Seth and had shielded them from an intrusive world. The nuptials were over then. All the cacophonous guests had withdrawn. And Emma had glanced toward the bedroom door. She waited expectantly.

The old woman glanced at the door. She heaved a sigh. Her eyes scanned the room. Her head tilted. There was the mahogany dresser. It stood as a constant reminder of young, innocent love, a love that had grown through the years and in spite of unforgiving time and unwanted separation, carried on. Dust. Emma tsked. She should have dusted. There's no excuse. And she should have arranged some white daisies and red tea roses in the jade vase. *Where is that vase?* Her brows came together. For the life of her she couldn't remember.

One of the children broke it. Emma rolled her eyes ever so slightly and muttered," "Ah yes, one of the children broke it."

Still, the reflection of flowers in the etched mirror had always pleased Emma. They highlighted the reddish-brown wood grain. But now, what was the sense of putting flowers there? Only she would see them. How sad that the ecru doilies she had crocheted by her own hands so long ago now droop colorless in the dust. Sugar-starch used to stiffen the edges into high rolling waves, but arthritic fingers prevented Emma these days from making new ones and holding a hot iron to set the starch. Her vacant eyes gazed at her deformed hands. Thickness built in her chest. Had she made a good wife? As far as housekeeping and child rearing were concerned, she was quite confident that she had. But the things that went on behind bedroom doors? "Oh my." She rubbed her palms against her cheeks where color rarely tinged. Her hands were cold against her sallow skin. "Aarch, you are much too old to think of such things, old woman."

Doddering to her feet, Emma plodded to the dresser where the ravage of time caused the top drawer to slide out faster than she expected. Nearly knocked off her feet, she steadied herself then selected a faded flannel nightgown. To this day Emma still recalled how sad she had felt about removing her luxurious wedding attire and how the boudoir chair had taken on the appearance of a satin munchkin as she had draped each piece over it. The gown had been preserved in a cedar chest at the foot of the bed, but the chair was long gone. She thought of the veil, bespeckled with rhinestones that had glittered as it had trailed her down the aisle. Her wedding day had been filled with music, wine, and gaiety. Oh, if only she could once again dance with her handsome groom, so tall, his midnight eyes sparkling at her with adoration. Warmth sheeted through her as if those eyes were looking at her now.

Light-hearted moments became lost as the leaves upon the wind outside the window. The old woman removed her clothing. She slipped the nightgown over her head and taking a step back, checked herself in the mirror. *Look what time has wrought. Poor Em.* Chestnut tresses had mutated into silver strings that refused to hold a set or take a perm. Wrinkles lined her pallid face so bad that she looked like a charcoal sketch of some old crone that menaced within nightmares. Her five-foot frame had shrunk, becoming bent and pearlike. Flannel hung without form or purpose. As her knotted fingers struggled with the last stubborn button, a slight draft sent shivers throughout her body that no hot bath could overcome. Wait! Did the door close just then? Emma turned. "Who is there?"

No answer came from beyond the open door. Neither did she see Seth standing there. Though, as if he was there, the same awkward silence sheeted over her that she had felt on their wedding day when their innermost thoughts had connected. As he had stepped towards her, she had backed away. The old woman chuckled inside and it made her cough. Breath was becoming shallow. She coughed again. How his sable eyes had soothed away her anxiety. Her palms automatically lifted, opening wide, expecting his lips, expecting to feel the warmth of his freshly shaven cheek. Oh, if only to feel his strength…if only he would draw her close…if only to hear his velvet voice once again whisper. Oh how her arms ached so for him. Why was it that her eyes kept searching the pillow next to hers for his tranquil face when she knew full well that she would never again see him adrift in a lover's deep repose? Or see his raven hair tussled on the pillow? Why did her ears not pick up his low, even breathing?

I have waited a lifetime for you, my sweet Emma, and now that you are here in my life, I will love and cherish you for all of God's lifetime. You have always found me here, my love. I have never left you.

In dream-like flux, Emma crawled into bed and covered herself with blankets that failed to warm her weary body. Within the shadows of her mind, a song issued forth. Roses perfumed the air as the weight of life began to lift and within her soul Seth called to Emma.

Come back to me—With all your heart.
Don't let fear—Keep us apart.

Long have I waited for your coming home to me
And living deeply our new life.

Alabaster luminescence surrounded Emma as blessed serenity enraptured her being. Weightlessly her spirit arose and floated upwards upon a sea of drifting clouds. Gazing down at the timeworn bed, she witnessed a withered form lying there. Sensing a presence behind her, she peered over her shoulder. Her heart leapt. *Seth!* Anticipation arose within her as his arms beckoned. *It is time, Emma,* his velvety voice persuaded. *Leave now this room that you have shared with me throughout the tender years and throughout all our solitary years.*

No fear existed as willingly she followed him, closer...ever closer to the open window. He paused at the sill, his eyes gazing into her soul. *I have never left you, Emma.* His love, long withheld, lived like never before, enveloping her in touchless embrace, absorbing her into his very essence. One in spirit, words of love, so long unspoken, flowed ceaselessly, uninterrupted. Intimate bliss soared, reborn within eternal togetherness. Their spirit levitated and floated away as the night sky gave way to the break of day.

Two white-crowned sparrows lit on the narrow, cracked sill. One peered at the other, his wings twitched.

Time to go, called a Voice from Beyond.

One bird turned looking back through the windowpane. Fleeting moments passed. Glancing at her companion, she peered into his eyes that beckoned her toward an ordained destination. *Come! Come! Let me cherish you, my sweet Emma, for all of God's lifetime!*

Her wings stretched. Wide. Wider. Tentatively they fluttered. Abruptly her wings extended fully and she spiraled upward. He took flight after her. The two untrammeled birds encircled one another, higher, ever higher, spiraling upwards...up... away...beyond all earthly bounds.

And as with all God's lovers, Emma and Seth were together.

And they were gone.

About the Author

K Spirito has always been a history buff. She loves to browse though microfilm of old newspapers, especially at the Boston Public Library. Noting stories of human interest, both significant and otherwise, she weaves them into works of historical fiction.

K holds a Bachelor of Science Degree from Franklin Pierce College in New Hampshire and an Associate in Arts for Interpreting for the Deaf from L. A. Pierce College in California. In the '60s she built power supplies for the Lunar Excursion Module that now sits on the moon. In the '80s she transcribed <u>Five Little Firemen</u> by Margaret Wise Brown and Edith Thacher Hurd into Braille for the L. A. Public Library. She was a licensed Cosmetologist and owned a hair salon.

She and her husband of thirty-six years managed to get four children through high school; two went on to college. They are now blessed with one granddaughter and four grandsons. K's goals are to continue her education and become the best storyteller she can be.

If you enjoyed reading **Time Has A Way**, you must read K Spirito's first novel **father sandro's Money**, published by Writer's Showcase, presented by Writer's Digest, an imprint of iUniverse.com, Inc.

It is the story about a nefarious priest who meets his end at the hands of Maria Avita LaRosa. She uncovers his misbegotten money and uses it to flee Italy. Finding her husband Joseph in East Boston, injured and out of work, she nurses him back to health. He goes back to work, and they live happily ever after, right? Not in this historical epic. World War I, the Mafia, and the Great Molasses Flood manipulate destiny. One son befriends Bartolomeo Vanzetti. Another must stop the assassination of FDR. Still another is hexed by a childhood memory that keeps him suspended in time. Christian living and prayer will pull the family through anything—that's what Joseph believes. But Maria Avita has learned that God helps those who help themselves. She goes along with his convictions, though when push comes to shove, she's the one who does the shoving. More often than not, **father sandro's Money** figures into the mix, conjuring up surprises and conflicts that continue to the very last word. **father sandro's Money** is the first book in the series of the LaRosa family and friends.

K's second novel, **Yesterday Tommy Gray Drowned**, is also published by Writer's Showcase, presented by Writer's Digest, an imprint of iUniverse.com, Inc. Chronologically, **Yesterday Tommy Gray Drowned**, follows **Time Has A Way**. Although all three novels stand-alone they compliment each other through recurring characters and familiar references.

In Yesterday, Tommy Gray Drowned, 'Lizbeth returns to her hometown in Massachusetts. She comes face to face with hideous truths—truths that refuse to stay hidden in the murky depths of Echo Lake any longer.

Tommy Gray never should have drowned on that splendid April day in 1959. For all of his ten short years, the kid had lived on the shores of Echo Lake and bragged that he was the best swimmer around.

Thirty years later, Elizabeth Blair's husband goes back to Vietnam where he was a prisoner of war in the late 60s. Not knowing if Peter is coming back this time or not, 'Lizbeth searches for strength to carry on without him. Out of her loneliness arises the memory of

Tommy Gray, her fourth-grade classmate. She feels he too had deserted her.

Other projects are in the works as well, so expect to be reading creative works by K Spirito for years to come. **Find out more! Log on to kspirito.com**

0-595-21244-1